Lessons on Love

A Logical Man's
Guide to Dangerous Women Novel

CATHY MAXWELL

AVONBOOKS

An Imprint of HarperCollinsPublishers

Excerpt from *His Secret Mistress* copyright © 2020 by Catherine Maxwell, Inc.

HIS LESSONS ON LOVE. Copyright © 2022 by Catherine Maxwell, Inc. All rights reserved. Printed in the United States of America. No part of this book may be used or reproduced in any manner whatsoever without written permission except in the case of brief quotations embodied in critical articles and reviews. For information, address HarperCollins Publishers, 195 Broadway, New York, NY 10007.

First Avon Books mass market printing: January 2022

Print Edition ISBN: 978-0-06-289735-0
Digital Edition ISBN: 978-0-06-289687-2

Cover design by Amy Halperin
Cover art by Patrick Kang
Cover images © Getty Images; © Shutterstock; © PeriodImages.com

Avon, Avon & logo, and Avon Books & logo are registered trademarks of HarperCollins Publishers in the United States of America and other countries.

HarperCollins is a registered trademark of HarperCollins Publishers in the United States of America and other countries.

FIRST EDITION

Printed in Lithuania

22 23 24 25 26 SB 10 9 8 7 6 5 4 3 2 1

MIX
Paper from
responsible sources
FSC® C021394

For Samantha and Joe,
Molly, Nathalie, Astrid, LJ (another Joe),
and Zavier (Zman!)
With much love

His
Lessons
on Love

The Logical Men's Society

The Logical Men's Society started as a jest, as many things do.

Over a pint or two in The Garland, where men gathered in Maidenshop, it was noted that a sane man wouldn't choose to marry. It went against all logic . . . and so the "Society" was formed.

Oh, men had to marry. It was expected and life was full of expectations. A man gave up his membership in the Logical Men's Society when that happened and he could only return once he was widowed. But in the years before he tied the parson's knot, the Society offered good fellowship that was highly valued and never forgotten.

So it went for several generations. The irony of the name of their village, Maidens-hop, was not lost on any of its members. The Logical Men's Society provided a place of masculine goodwill and contentment . . . until the women began to win. First, they took over The Garland, turning it into a tea garden, and the men shuddered to think what could happen next.

Could this be the end of the Logical Men's Society? Had they met their match?

Chapter One

A mistress who has fallen in love with you is a
tiresome creature.

—*Book of Mars*

London
July 1815

$\mathcal{T}$he shouting woke him.

Lawrence Grant Talmadge Eddington, the Right Honorable Earl of Marsden who would never go by any other name except Mars, raised his head from his pillow. It took effort.

He'd done it again. Over-imbibed.

And he had really made an effort of late to be more circumspect. He'd actually agreed with his close friends Balfour and Thurlowe when they had taken it upon themselves to express their concerns. He *had* been drinking too much. And when he was in London, well, he did like the dreamy state of the pipe. His solution to that was to stay away from Town and the lack hadn't bothered him.

However, drinking . . . ?

His friends had taken themselves and their wives off to London for business and he'd been alone. In a bout of self-pity—he was honest enough to know exactly what it was—he'd uncorked a claret, followed by some Port, and finished off with whisky.

His forehead ached as if it had been used as an anvil.

He pulled the pillow over his ears, trying to shut out all noise. Besides, the sun wasn't *that* high in the sky. It probably wasn't even noon and too early for him to wake—

Struck by a new concern, Mars pushed the pillow off his head and squinted around his bedroom. Why hadn't his valet, Nelson, drawn his curtains last night?

Then he remembered. *He'd* opened them. Whisky and anger had fueled anguished memories of his father's death, and Mars's paltry attempts at vengeance.

For well over a decade now, the murderer, Lord Dervil, had never been held accountable. It had a been a duel, they said. An affair of honor. Death happened. They claimed his father had understood the consequences. After all, he had been the one to challenge Dervil.

Except, Mars had witnessed the shooting. There had been no honor on that field.

And when the drink hit him like it did last night, he was haunted by visions of his father crumpling to the ground, gasping for his last breath. He recalled the smell of blood mingling with black powder and how helpless it had made him feel as he'd watched the light fade from his father's eyes. These memories always set Mars off.

He had been particularly full of himself last night. He groaned as he remembered throwing open the window and howling at the moon like a madman. In fact, he'd even stood on the window ledge, he now remembered, wearing nothing more than what his Maker had given him. He'd braced himself against the frame, high above the pavers in front of the house, and had let go with a sound that would have made any lone wolf proud. He could have sworn he'd heard howls back.

It had probably been the hunting pack. They were easy to rouse. Especially in the middle of the night. He'd done it more than once.

Of course, the gesture was futile, derisible even. Dervil still thrived and Mars was powerless beyond stopping his nemesis from buying up Maidenshop or blocking a lucrative investment here and there in London. He had not as yet made Dervil pay for what he'd done.

But someday . . .

In the meantime, he was truly and completely convinced his friends were correct and he should mend his ways. He'd forgotten how truly debilitating the day after a drunken rampage was.

Mars collapsed on the bed. *God*. He had definitely given the servants something good to gossip over, even though they were loyal. They kept his secrets. He hoped.

And no, the howling had not been one of his wisest ideas. He could have fallen out the window, especially in the state he'd been in.

But now he was awake, driven by a new need, one to relieve himself. All that whisky had created a powerful urge and his teeth felt woolly. Mars hated having a sour mouth.

He rolled out of bed with a groan. It hurt everything in his body to move. He seemed to have pulled a muscle in his hip when he'd done all that scrambling around the windows.

Windows?

Yes, windows. From the hazy recesses of his memory, he realized he'd howled from more than one window.

Such was the danger of being left to his own devices. If his friends had not been out of town, he would have been over at their houses being outwardly bored by their married lives, and inwardly jealous at how content they were. Who knew a wife could make a man happy . . . ?

With a groan, he reached for his breeches, which were lying on the floor. Keeping his head as still and steady as possible, he pulled them up his long legs, not bothering with the buttons, and stiffly made his way to the privacy screen. There had been a time when he'd bounded out of bed with energy in anticipation for the day even after an evening of drinking. That seemed decades ago. At seven and twenty, he shouldn't be feeling so low. Even his back was sore, and he was too aware that his complaints were those of a creaky old man whose only enjoyment was the blessed relief of emptying his bladder and a nap.

Yes, a nap. Just the thought of it made him almost giddy. Later today he'd have a nap— that was, if the commotion in the house ceased. The shouting was still going on. It always amazed him that as massive as Belvoir was, sound carried as if he lived in a cottage.

He set to cleaning his teeth, the tooth powder thick in his mouth until he rinsed it out. He popped in a mint lozenge that Gemma, Thurlowe's talented wife, had concocted. Mars was beginning to believe himself as obsessed with her pastilles as he could be to opium, if given the chance . . . and the latter was the true reason he had dodged the happy couples' entreaties to join them. Being around so much marital bliss would have broken his resolve not to indulge in the pipe.

And standing there in front of the mirror over his washstand, looking at his face sporting a growth of whiskers he wouldn't let Nelson shave because his head had hurt too much, his wheat-colored hair in sleep-tossed disarray, and his eyes red-rimmed and tired, he knew he *must* change.

Mars just didn't understand how matters had come to this. Life was passing him by. And the men he most respected and admired, his closest confidants, now focused on their wives.

They claimed they were in love with them. *Love.*

Mars was a pragmatic man. Love turned

one into a fool. If his father had not been so "in love" with his wife, Eleanor, he wouldn't have challenged Dervil—who also claimed he'd loved her.

For his part, Mars couldn't stand the sight of his mother. He had refused to talk to Eleanor since the duel. Because of her, he had a low opinion of the fairer sex. He slept with them, had kept more than his share, but he never trusted them. Not one.

Except, standing behind the privacy screen of his well-appointed bedroom on an estate claimed to be one of the finest in the country, Mars realized a hard truth. He was lonely.

And he hated it. He detested feeling the way he did.

The terrible racket that had first woken him now sounded as if it was making its way up the stairs. Mars didn't worry. He had servants to worry for him. His butler Gibson would handle the matter.

What *he* needed to do was end his maudlin musings. God, he bored himself.

Mars leaned over the washbasin and poured what water remained in the pitcher over his head. The splash of cold helped. He straightened, letting his hair fly back, droplets of water splashing the screen behind him. He needed to start the morning right with tea and Port, a remedy Nelson always prepared when Mars was a bit under the weather. Then he would regain his equilibrium.

In fact, he was surprised his valet hadn't already made an appearance. Nelson was usually right in the room the second he heard Mars stir. And Mars had done more than stir. He'd splashed water, he'd polished his teeth—

"Stay back. Don't you dare touch me," a woman's voice commanded from the hallway. Apparently the commotion had reached this floor.

Gibson answered, "You *mustn't* disturb the earl."

She laughed at that statement, a short, bitter sound. "I can and *I will*."

Her bitterness was familiar.

Curious, Mars dried his face and hands on a fresh linen towel and buttoned his breeches as he came out from behind the screen—just as something, like a fist or a body, hit his bedroom door. The handle twisted. The woman shouted, *"Don't touch me."*

Yes, he did know that voice.

Before he could puzzle it all out, the door flew open and Deb Millner, his last mistress, all but fell into the room. She righted herself after a few steps. Deb had always had good balance, even with her arms carrying a bundle of what looked to be blankets. She pushed back her fashionable chapeau, a plume-covered cocked hat that Mars had probably paid a small fortune for, and growled at his manservants to *"Stay back"* with the fierceness of an Amazon.

She needn't have gone to the trouble. At the sight of their master standing in nothing save his breeches, the servants froze in almost a comical tableau. His valet was amongst them. No wonder Nelson hadn't appeared with tea and Port.

"My lord, we shall remove her," Gibson announced, sounding as if he was mortified an intruder had reached the inner sanctum, so to speak. He would have sent the servants forward save for Mars stopping him.

"Don't bother. She is fine."

"Are you certain, my lord?" the butler pressed.

"I am." *And he was.* He wasn't thrilled to see Deb, however she certainly was an antidote to boredom.

Gibson's expression said he didn't think it a wise idea, except he was too well trained to argue. After exchanging glances with Nelson, they and the footman all backed out into the hall.

"And close the door," Deb ordered.

Gibson's brows shot up in outrage. "My lord, is this safe—"

"Close it," Mars said. They had no choice save do as he ordered.

Deb gave a triumphant crow before letting her brown eyes settle on Mars. Her lip curled in derision. He found that interesting. When they had parted, she'd been all emotion and heaving bosom. *I love you. I won't let you leave . . .* and other drama.

Now she acted as if the sight of him curdled her stomach.

Deb was a tall brunette who was all legs, exactly the sort of woman Mars favored and, in truth, his first qualification for any mistress he kept. Her magnificent figure was dressed for travel. She had dashing tastes and Mars had always enjoyed seeing what she would get herself up in. She didn't disappoint today. She was wearing a plum-colored striped dress with dark blue trim and a very low bodice under a military-styled jacket. Deb had always enjoyed displaying her assets. She even let her bundle slip a notch to give him a look because she knew he was looking. To not look would have disappointed her.

She moved toward him with the swagger of a pirate. "Lawd, Mars, you are barely decent."

He was not insulted. Women were spiteful creatures. "First, these are my private chambers. Second, you have seen more of me than this."

"Unfortunately."

"Don't be unpleasant, Deb. Say what you've come to say. I have an uninteresting day ahead of me."

The fire went out of her. She pinned him with a sincere-looking gaze. "I loved you so much."

"No," he corrected, "you loved my money. You always had trouble telling the difference." When they'd parted—a year and some months ago—he'd given her a town house, a coach and pair, and two thousand in funds. He was a generous protector.

Her expression changed as if she was seeing him for the first time, and was disappointed. "You were always honest with me, Mars. I will grant you that. What is it you always say? That you are incapable of lying?"

Mars nodded. That was true.

Her chin lifted. "I have a new protector."

"Good."

"He finds me enchanting."

"I'm certain he is right."

"You don't rule my life any longer, Mars."

"I never pretended to, Deb."

"But you broke my heart."

There was the manipulation. Women wielded it like a long, thin blade, cutting away at what they didn't like.

Back when they'd parted, she'd camped on his doorstep, tried to barge into his club, and had tearfully followed him all over the city, flooding his life with love notes and, later, threats. Once, she broke into his London house and he'd found her in his bed. He'd had to physically carry her out of the room with her trying to kiss him and wrap her arms around him. Gibson had not been concerned without reason.

She didn't appear in danger of throwing a scene today. In fact, her manner was one of superiority, and he could let her have her final say if it meant she'd leave him alone.

"My new gentleman worships me," she informed him.

He nodded.

"And I am not your concern any longer, Mars." She began moving toward the bed. He moved away from it. "I can take care of myself. As for *this*, it's yours and *your* responsibility. You will be able to care for it better than I." She dropped her bundle of blankets into the middle of his bed.

A sound escaped from the bundle. Or was it his imagination?

"What is this?" he asked.

"Something you left with me," she replied moving to the door. "I'm returning it. After all, a mistress shouldn't have encumbrances. Her name is Menadora."

"Her? Menadora?" The bundle began to move.

"Yes, it means 'gift of the moon.' Menadora is the name of a saint who was martyred along with her sisters Metrodora and Nymphodora. I adore the lyricism of it."

"What the devil are you talking about?" He was still caught on the word *her*.

"She is probably hungry, although I nursed her before I brought her in. I warn you, she eats all the time. Worse, she pisses as much as you do. The two of you should rub along well." She opened the door, shooting him a disdainful look. "I also wish to say, I don't think you should brag about your inability to lie, Mars. I believe you make the claim to hide that you are simply incapable of love."

"That is a nasty barb." He could love. He just hadn't—yet.

Her expression said she thought he was fooling himself. "Goodbye, my lord."

At that moment, a worried sound escaped from the bundle. The covers moved and a decidedly feminine head popped out. A *baby*. She was on her belly. She pushed herself up and looked around with large, searching eyes—and then focused on him.

Mars knew nothing of children. He stayed away from them. He even kept a respectable distance from Balfour's baby and he'd been present when she'd been born.

This baby had hair as dark as Deb's. Except, instead of the mother's curls, her hair stood up like a hedgehog's spines that pointed wherever they wanted.

She swiveled her head to look at the door where Gibson, Nelson, and the footmen peered in with what could only be described as fascinated horror—a look that was probably mirrored on Mars's face.

And then the baby appeared to grasp that she had been left. Abandoned. *With him.*

A lip puckered and then she gave out a cry so loud and so heart-wrenching it could have summoned the troops for miles around, and she didn't stop. Not even for breath.

The wailing sparked Mars into action. He went charging from the room, barefooted and half-naked. He shouldered aside Gibson and the others. Reaching the top of the stairs, he saw Deb almost at the foot of them. *"You can't leave,"* he demanded. "You can't just walk off."

Glancing up at him, she coolly answered, "Yes, I can."

"But that is a *baby. Your* baby."

"No, *your* baby, my lord—"

"It couldn't be. I take precautions. I'm always careful." He'd never wanted to pepper the countryside with bastards.

"Not all the time, you didn't. And to be perfectly honest, because I, too, am incapable of lying, I'm done staying up through the night with her, having her pull on my breasts like they are udders, and then spit up on my clothes. I can't stand the smell of it. I'm *not* a good mother. I don't want to be one. So, now it is your turn. Truth is, it will be easier for you—you have plenty of money, so hire someone to take care of Menadora. Or . . ." she paused self-righteously ". . . toss her aside the way you did me. She is no longer my concern."

On that note, she sailed out the open front door to a waiting coach, a coach he had paid for. Meanwhile, that child with the ridiculous name was growing increasingly vocal. Her cries rang through the house.

And Deb didn't care. Her step didn't falter.

Mars did the only reasonable thing a man in his position could do—he ran down the stairs and out the door, thinking to stop his ex-mistress. She couldn't leave a child with *him*.

Unfortunately, he was too late.

With impressive speed, Deb boarded her coach and, with a snap of the whip, her driver sent the horses racing down the drive.

Mars stood for a long moment in its wake as if he could will her back. The coach rounded a curve and disappeared from his view. "Damn her to hell," he muttered. And then added, "That baby isn't mine." It couldn't be. He and both of his parents had blond hair. Besides, *he took precautions*.

But had he always?

He could recall a time or two when he hadn't been as disciplined as a wise man should be. Times when his vices had the better of him.

Dear God.

Mars turned toward the door to see that all his servants from the haughty Gibson to even the scullery lad stood on the step watching him with wide-eyed, concerned looks.

Nelson weaseled his way through the crowd with Mars's dressing robe. "My lord," he entreated, holding the garment up as if to preserve his master's dignity—but a more pressing concern had claimed his lord's attention.

From where Mars stood, he could still clearly hear a squalling baby.

"Who is with the child?" he demanded.

His servants, all male, all long in his family service, looked at each other as if they had expected the man standing to the left or right to be watching Menadora. Even the usually efficient Gibson.

Then he remembered Deb's warnings. "Does anyone know about babies?"

Evans, one of the footmen, said, "My sister's had one."

The others were silent.

Could this day be worse? He really needed his tea and Port.

Swearing under his breath, Mars charged forward, bare feet flying over pavers. The servants parted as if he was Moses and they the Red Sea. He took the front stairs two at a time.

As he moved, a thousand thoughts ran through his head. Deb wouldn't be the first mistress to lie. They were never reliable and she was obviously worse than others. She did like to gamble—so, what if she'd gambled she could latch on to him with a claim of a child?

What if she was at the end of the drive, waiting for him to call her back? It would work. He might be a rake and a bit of a rascal but he wasn't completely irresponsible and Deb knew it.

He entered his bedroom. The crying baby was right where she'd been left, except she had rolled over and kicked off her blankets. She was obviously very angry at being left alone. Highly insulted even. Oh, yes, this was Deb's child.

But was she *his*? Because he could tell. Eddingtons always knew their children, and that could be the hitch in Deb's plans.

Nelson and Gibson had followed him up the stairs. He looked to his two most trusted servants. "What do I do to make her stop?"

"Pick her up, my lord?" Gibson suggested as if uncertain.

Yes, that was good advice. Mars approached the bed. He reached for the child and lifted her, his hands under her arms. Her weight surprised him. She was heavier than he had anticipated. She looked at him with an expression of outrage and possibly even hurt feelings, her mouth in the deepest frown he'd ever witnessed—but, blessedly, she stopped crying.

The two of them took each other's measure.

Her long dress was a light green with lacy sleeves. Her feet in wee leather shoes dangled in the air. Her skin was hot and slightly sweaty from the exertion of her temper. The dark, spiky wisps of her hair were now plastered around her head. She reminded him of nothing more than a miniature Caesar in a gown.

She didn't appear impressed with him either.

Her brow furrowed in an expression as critical as that of any self-important dandy or discerning mother in Almack's.

"Menadora," he said, tasting the sounds.

Brown watery eyes considered him solemnly and it was as if he could read her mind and he nodded. "You believe it is a ridiculous name as well. Cheer up. She could have named you Nymphodora."

Her whimper let him know this situation was as difficult for her as it was for him, and he understood. Uncaring mothers were the worst. They had at least that in common.

He walked into his dressing room. There was a full-length looking glass in the corner. Menadora's head turned as she noticed the reflection of the glass. She was a bright and alert little thing. Holding her against his chest, he stood so that he could see both of them in the glass.

Shock held him still.

There was a painting in the downstairs hall of himself at about this age and she could easily be an exact copy for him in spite of her dark hair and brown eyes. Except she was more intent and focused than he could ever have been. She seemed to study their reflection and form her own conclusions, one he sensed wasn't flattering.

Dread coupled with an inexplicable excitement. This was not what he wanted. Oh, no. Not him. And yet, he *had* to know.

Mars pulled off her shoe, then tugged on

the stocking. He found five perfect toes. He reached for the other foot and did the same, and his breath caught.

The left foot was not perfect. There were five toes but they were not aligned. The toe before the little one looked a bit deformed and appeared to be growing out of the toe beside it— just like his father's had, and his grandfather's, and all the Eddingtons before him.

Just like Mars's own.

It was proof that one was a true Eddington.

This *was* his baby.

His daughter.

To his surprise, a sense of wonder filled him.

He'd *created* her. She was a new soul in this world, in his life. This little being with a silly name. He had *family*.

Deep within, something shifted, opening him in a way he'd never thought possible. It was the two of them together in the face of a world that was unrelenting when it came to the weak. She *needed* him. *He* was her protector, her parent, her guardian.

And he didn't know what to do with her.

He knew one thing, he wasn't going to call her Menadora. "Dora," he said, testing the name. He liked it.

There was also no doubt the cloth covering her tiny bum needed to be changed. Mars could smell it. It was also damp against his chest. She had wet herself through her dress.

He looked to the doorway where Gibson and Nelson watched him with confused alarm. "Did Deb leave a bag? Or supplies?"

"No, my lord," Gibson answered. "She left nothing."

Mars held Dora away a bit. He wasn't good with foul smells. He also didn't have the slightest inkling of a child's needs and wants.

Then, as if reading his mind and realizing she was in trouble, Dora opened her lungs—and this time, she wouldn't stop, no matter what he tried.

Chapter Two

Men are beasts. I know. I am one of them.

—*Book of Mars*

Just as she feared she could not take another step forward, Clarissa Taylor arrived in Maidenshop.

Her journey had been exhausting. She had worn these clothes for three days straight as she'd struggled to find her way home from London by the Post, a farmer's cart, and her own two aching feet.

She dropped her valise, overwhelmed by the familiar sight of St. Martyr's stone walls and the neat and tidy cottages of the village. She wore a gray cambric frock that was very serviceable, good sturdy shoes, and an olive-toned sarcenet pelisse that one of the women in this village had given her as a castoff. Her straw cottage hat had also been a gift. The village matrons had given it to her along with their good wishes before she'd left for the position as a gentlewoman's companion that was supposed to change her life.

There were some people busy and about at this hour of the day but they hadn't noticed her. Not yet.

And even though she recognized them, after all, she had grown up here . . . she felt a stranger. She viewed them as if there was a pane of glass separating them from her.

In many ways there was, except the divider was called Life. When she'd left Maidenshop, it had been mid-spring and all was hopeful and perfect in the world.

Now the garden flowers were peaking and would too soon be overtaken by autumn and then winter—just as London had overtaken her.

If she'd had any pride, she would not be here, except, the village was very dear to her, even if she was returning in disgrace. She had nothing to her name, not even a farthing. It had taken all that she owned to bring her back *home*.

The side door to the church opened. Mrs. Summerall, the minister's wife, came out of the building. She glanced Clarissa's way and stopped, a foot poised in the air. She stared as if uncertain she believed her eyes.

Then she took a step forward and then several more, picking her way through the gravestones surrounding the church. "Miss Taylor?"

Clarissa's throat tightened. She couldn't speak. And so, she did the only thing she could do. She burst into tears.

Mrs. Summerall rushed to her and wrapped her thin, long arms around Clarissa. "Dear, dear, dear," she repeated. "Please, it is all right. Whatever it is, it is all right." Finally, she said, "Let's go see Mrs. Warbler."

Clarissa nodded.

Elizabeth Warbler was the widow who lived in the center of the village. She was one of the doyennes of the Matrons of Maidenshop and had been a good friend to Clarissa over the years since her adoptive parents, the Reverend Taylor and his wife, had passed away. She'd always been able to help Clarissa make sense of the insensible. And if all else failed, there would be sherry. Mrs. Warbler was known for her sherry bottle.

"Here now, Landon," Mrs. Summerall called to a boy who had just come out of his cottage. "Please carry Miss Taylor's valise for us."

"Miss Taylor?" the lad repeated. He stared at Clarissa as if she was an oddity. "Good to see you, Miss Taylor. How was London?"

Clarissa's answer was a hiccupping sob.

"The valise, Landon," Mrs. Summerall said, sounding a bit desperate. She linked an arm with Clarissa's and the two of them walked down the road to Mrs. Warbler's two-story stone home. It was located across the road from The Garland, a tea garden and specialty shop owned by the woman who had stolen the future that Clarissa was supposed to have.

No, that wasn't true. Gemma hadn't truly connived her way into Ned Thurlowe's heart. It had not been intentional.

And Ned *would* have married Clarissa if she had insisted. He was an honorable man. He'd made a promise and he would have honored it. She was the one who had cried off.

In fact, once Clarissa realized she was clinging to Ned as her only hope, she had been rather excited to go out in the world. With Mrs. Warbler's help, she had accepted a position as companion to the wealthy Mrs. Emsdale.

But that had all been back in the spring.

Clarissa took a moment at the foot of Mrs. Warbler's step to swipe at her eyes with her dirty gloves. "She'll be disappointed in me."

"Nonsense. Elizabeth will be as happy to see you as I. Isn't that right, Landon?"

"Everyone will be happy to see you, Miss Taylor," the boy said dutifully, although his side glances indicated he was ready to discharge his duties.

Though she feared Mrs. Summerall was only being polite, her kind words caused Clarissa to release the breath she'd been holding.

It turned out Mrs. Summerall had been right.

Mrs. Warbler swept Clarissa into the house. She was silver haired, energetic, and, in the past, had worn purple in memory of her husband, the colonel, but that had changed over the summer as well. Today, she wore a dress in a lovely shade of rose. Matching ribbons decorated her lace cap and her hands sported ivory lace fingerless mittens.

"Clarissa," she said as if delighted. "I'm happy to see you. Do you need a moment to yourself?

Jane," she called to her maid, "prepare a basin of warm water for our guest." To Clarissa, she directed, "Now, you take as long as you like to freshen up. Jane! We shall need cheese and some of the bread you baked this morning. Clarissa appears as if she hasn't eaten in days."

"I haven't," Clarissa admitted.

"Is there chicken left from last night?" Mrs. Warbler asked Jane.

"Yes, ma'am."

"Excellent. We will prepare quite a late breakfast for you, Clarissa. Now, you run up the stairs and see to your needs. You know where to go. Dierdre, please join us," Mrs. Warbler said to Mrs. Summerall. "I shall grab the sherry bottle."

And that is exactly what she did.

When Clarissa returned feeling much better for warm water and a lovely-scented soap, she found the table was set and her friends waited for her. Mrs. Warbler poured a too-generous glass of sherry for Clarissa. The bread was still warm.

"Eat, eat. We don't stand on ceremony here. You know that," Mrs. Warbler said.

The food tasted delicious, even the cold chicken. However, once her appetite was not the first thing on her mind, Clarissa knew she had to be honest.

"I was sacked," she announced bluntly, wanting them to understand they should not be so happy to see her. She had shamed them.

Mrs. Warbler pressed the sherry glass into

Clarissa's hand, wrapping her fingers around it. "Emerald Emsdale is known for the abrupt departures of her employees. You are not the first. You will not be the last. Drink."

"Why didn't you tell me?" Clarissa asked.

"And jinx you? No, I wouldn't do that. Besides, you didn't have any references. You had to start somewhere. And now, not another word until you have finished that sherry."

Clarissa would have preferred a cup of tea. Still, she did as ordered and gave the sherry a sip. It tasted good. Before she knew it, she'd drained the glass.

Mrs. Warbler refilled it.

Clarissa drained the second glass as well.

"Elizabeth," Mrs. Summerall said, "perhaps a good cup of tea is in order."

"Except sherry has edifying properties," Mrs. Warbler countered, sipping her own third drink. She did adore her sherry.

"Perhaps," Mrs. Summerall answered. "Except you do want to hear her story, don't you?"

"Jane, brew tea." Mrs. Warbler twisted in her chair to face Clarissa. "Now, what happened? Because I know you, my dear. There is no way you didn't try your best."

"I did and yet it was never good enough."

"I warned you she was a sour one. Emerald has always nitpicked and complained. Even in school. I don't believe she is happy unless she is unhappy."

"You did warn me and I *believed* I could please her." There was some validity to Clarissa's belief. She'd always been able to ingratiate herself to even the most difficult of people. She had a skill for it.

Twenty-four years ago, Clarissa had been abandoned as a newborn on St. Martyr's step. Old Reverend Taylor and his wife had adopted her, and they had been more than kind. However, they had also reminded her that she'd been one of the lucky ones. She could have been sent to a foundling home. Instead, she'd spent the bulk of her life serving the needs of the parish as a minister's daughter. That meant being sweet and thoughtful, anticipating the needs of others at all times, and carefully blending in wherever she was. When the Taylors had died, the matrons had found a place for her with Squire Nelson and his family. They had also arranged for a husband. Clarissa was no fool. She knew they had badgered Mr. Thurlowe into making an offer. Unfortunately, all their efforts had been for naught.

Still, what better training could one ask for a hired companion?

"Were you ever successful at pleasing her?" Mrs. Summerall asked.

"Oh, yes," Clarissa said, smiling gratefully to Jane as the maid delivered a cup of strongly brewed tea. While the sherry had been restorative, it had also made her head spin a little. Jane had also thoughtfully brought another plate of bread. "Mrs. Emsdale claimed she had never had a companion who was so attentive."

Clarissa had taken pride in that compliment, even though working for the old woman had meant almost stupefying boredom in between the rudest comments. A more cantankerous, difficult person one could hope never to meet. Mrs. Emsdale could be up a good part of the night and expect Clarissa to read to her or to play cards. During the day, Mrs. Emsdale spent her hours tatting lace and issuing numerous silly orders such as *Move that vase to the left, Clarissa. No, you went too far. Move it back. I didn't mean all the way back. To the left*, and so on and so forth until Clarissa could have politely screamed.

But she didn't share this with Mrs. Warbler and Mrs. Summerall lest they think poorly of her. Instead, she waited for the question she knew they were going to ask . . . and Mrs. Warbler did not disappoint her.

"So, why did she let you go?"

Clarissa took another sip of tea, and then said, "Mrs. Emsdale has a grandson she is very fond of—"

"Warner," Mrs. Warbler injected, sitting back and crossing her arms.

"Warner?" Mrs. Summerall echoed.

"A little toad of a man. She sent him to the duchess last year, hoping she could convince Her Grace to encourage Winderton to recommend him for a position in government." She referred to Lucy, the Dowager Duchess of Winderton, another of the Matrons of Maidenshop. The Winderton they spoke of was the current duke. "Her Grace said the lad is stupid."

"Oh, he is," Clarissa assured them. "And mean. Except, she dotes on him."

"What did he do?" Mrs. Warbler asked as if she already knew.

Clarissa felt heat rise to her cheeks. "I never encouraged him."

Mrs. Warbler placed a reassuring hand on Clarissa's arm. "None of us believes you would."

"He was very forward in his intentions," Clarissa said. "However, never in front of his grandmother. I mean, the other servants saw, but they said nothing, even when he made me very uncomfortable."

"Of course he was rude," Mrs. Warbler said. "What can one expect of someone named Warner?"

Clarissa relaxed slightly, encouraged that her friends seemed ready to believe her. The rest of the story came pouring out. "I refused his advances. Repeatedly. Then, the other night, I went to my bed and he was in it. Without clothes." She wished she could erase the image from her mind.

"The *outrage*," Mrs. Summerall said stoutly.

"Impudent," Mrs. Warbler pronounced, her lips curling in disgust. "A very unattractive feature in a man."

"It was *all* unattractive," Clarissa admitted.

Mrs. Summerall leaned forward. "What happened?" Even Jane lingered by the table for the rest of the story.

"I ordered him to leave," Clarissa answered. "Instead, he jumped off the bed and attacked me."

Mrs. Summerall grabbed her heart in alarm.

Jane gasped. Mrs. Warbler's brows came together as she asked, "What did you do?"

"I ran. I opened the door and went out in the hall. He followed me. He tried to grab my arm and drag me back in. I pushed him and rushed to the door at the end of the hall, the one that separated the servants' quarters from the family's rooms. I opened it and saw he was going to follow. The door opens to the inside. I slammed it shut as hard as I could—" She broke off, almost overwhelmed by the memory. "He grabbed the door to stop me." She looked to the other women, begging for their understanding.

"*And?*" This came from Jane.

"I slammed his fingers in the door. I'm actually strong. Or he's very weak. Anyway, I may have broken some. I used all my strength."

There was a second of quiet as the women digested her words and then a glad cheer went up.

"You shut that scoundrel's hand in the door? And he was stark naked?" Mrs. Warbler said, incredulous. "What a shame it wasn't his willie." She burst out in laughter, as did Jane and Mrs. Summerall.

"You don't understand," Clarissa said. "He was *hurt*. He shrieked in a way I've never heard a man cry out before. He woke the other servants. *And* Mrs. Emsdale, whom I had just managed to escape after she'd nodded off in her bed. He started dancing around and holding his fingers. It was a frightful scene."

"I have no doubt of that," Mrs. Warbler assured her, barely able to control her laughter.

"Oh, dear," Mrs. Summerall said, her hand over her mouth, her eyes happy slits of mirth. "As my husband says, the Lord works in mysterious ways."

"I think he received what was coming to him," Jane chimed in.

"And then I was sacked," Clarissa finished, not seeing any humor in the situation at all.

"How could she fire you over her grandson's rotten behavior?" Mrs. Summerall demanded. "You didn't hurt him intentionally."

"She should have," Mrs. Warbler murmured.

"I was just trying to escape," Clarissa explained. "However, Mrs. Emsdale didn't believe me when I told her he had attacked me." She'd said several rude things about Clarissa's person, as if her grandson would have never stooped so low as to pay attention to her. "She told me whatever happened, I had brought it on myself. Except, I never encouraged him. *Never.*"

"And we believe you," Mrs. Warbler answered.

Such a simple statement and yet it went straight to Clarissa's heart. *They believed her.* "Mrs. Emsdale doesn't. Her grandson claimed I tried to seduce him, that it was his manly weakness that had led him to me."

"His weakness?" Mrs. Warbler suggested. "Oh, please tell me he was dancing around in the hall completely naked."

"Not even socks," Clarissa said, and the women broke out again into laughter.

She failed to see the humor. "You are the only ones who have listened to me. Mrs. Emsdale made me sound like some Delilah and all the servants nodded their heads."

"Because she pays their wages," Jane said.

"She turned me out without references, right there in the middle of the night." Clarissa had never been so frightened in her life as when she'd found herself wandering London in the dark. "And speaking of wages, she didn't pay me. She said I was too grave a disappointment. I should have at least received the quarter wages she'd promised—"

"Miserly woman," Mrs. Warbler muttered.

"But what bothers me the most is what people in the village will think," Clarissa finished. "I failed. I wanted to prove I could take care of myself like Kate and Gemma could." Kate was Kate Balfour, a well-known actress before she married Mr. Balfour. Ned's wife, Gemma, had been a sought-after healer and had made a success of The Garland. Both women had triumphed at their endeavors before they'd married. They had made it look easy.

"I can't take care of myself," Clarissa said. "I wasn't going to return to Maidenshop until I proved I could. Yet, I couldn't *not* come home either. I had nowhere else to go."

Mrs. Summerall placed an empathetic hand over Clarissa's. "I'm glad you returned to us.

I also think you were very brave to fight off your attacker."

"I wasn't very afraid of Warner," Clarissa confessed. "He looked rather silly and I did feel bad that I had hurt him."

"*I* don't," Mrs. Warbler said. "Believe me, child, he had every intention of forcing himself on you."

"Just as he probably had to a maid who had been dismissed right before I joined the household. The whispers were that she had loose morals and had been in the 'family way.' I feel terrible that I believed what they told me about her. Now I know differently. I shouldn't believe rumors."

"Not all rumors, but don't worry," Mrs. Warbler said. "We will find something for you. We matrons will put our heads together. We'll figure it out. Until then, you will stay with Jane and me."

"I don't wish to be a burden," Clarissa said. "I'll do whatever you ask of me. Certainly I can be of service."

"Not to worry," Mrs. Warbler pressed. "All will be good. Now, finish your sherry—"

Abruptly, their huddle of womanhood was interrupted by the slam of the front door. "Hello!" a gruff male voice called a second before heavy footsteps sounded on the wood floor. And then, a hatless Earl of Marsden appeared in the doorway.

It was almost as if he had materialized out of nowhere. One moment they were alone in the room and in the next, there was a shout and then this huge, bold man intruded into their cozy group.

Clarissa did not like or admire the earl. The feeling was mutual.

She'd known him all her life and a more self-centered, lazy, rude fellow she'd never met. Well—until she'd met Mr. Warner Emsdale . . . but the earl had had years to improve her assessment of him, and had failed.

He was tall with broad shoulders and long, long legs. The sort of man who took up all the air in a room. She acknowledged that he was handsome, although she found his jaw too stubborn. Right now, he appeared as if he'd had a bad night. He'd not shaved and his untamed hair was hopelessly windblown. When he was younger, she remembered him as being the white blond of a Viking. Now his hair was the color of winter grain.

The earl had first annoyed her when she was six. She had accidentally fallen into a puddle. The white cotton of her favorite dress had quickly soaked up the muddy water, ruining it forever. She'd been panicked because how was she going to explain that to Mrs. Taylor—and then she'd heard him laughing. Clarissa could perfectly recall the amusement on his face.

Nor did it stop there. Over the years, he had continued to snipe at her. No matter what she was doing, there he was.

Even on the worst night of her life, when she'd realized that the man she had been promised to for years was in love with another, when her only security for the future had crumbled around her, Marsden had been completely un-sympathetic. He'd actually taken her to task as if he was the headmaster of the School of Life and lectured her as if she was a dunderhead while ignoring the fact that *he'd* been well into his cups. Which was not surprising. The only thing the man did well was drink.

On top of those complaints lurked some-thing else. Something she couldn't name. It wasn't exactly fear . . . more of an awareness. Marsden was a dark shadow in her life, always lurking when she wasn't at her best.

So, of course, he would show up *now*.

She braced herself, knowing that once he learned what happened in London, he would have some cutting comment to make.

Except, he wasn't interested in her. Instead, he stood awkwardly in front of the table hold-ing a bundle of blankets as if he didn't know what to do with himself. "I knocked. I let myself in when no one answered." He was dressed for riding and even sans hat appeared the very model of a country horseman. Buff leather breeches hugged strong thighs, his boots dusty from his ride. He wore a jacket of the finest bottle green worsted. Clarissa could be jealous of the quality of that material.

Mrs. Warbler rose. Like all the matrons, she had a secret soft spot for the earl. They always forgave his antics, even in the face of his obvi-ous disdain for them. They didn't know him the way Clarissa did.

"It is fine, my lord," Mrs. Warbler said. "Is there a way I can be of service?"

"I pray so." He hadn't even looked in Clarissa's direction. "I don't know what to do with her."

"Her?" Mrs. Warbler echoed.

At that moment, a wee foot with a tiny shoe popped out of the top of one of the blankets.

"Oh, God," Marsden said with genuine alarm. He righted what he was carrying and a goblin's head with a halo of straight black hair and an expression of outrage popped up out of the bundle.

A baby?

Clarissa knew she wasn't the only one shocked.

The child scrunched her eyes, looking slightly confused.

Clarissa rose to her feet. "*My lord.*" She didn't mean the title as a sign of respect but as a true, horror-filled cry to a higher deity. "Were you holding that baby upside down?"

"I fear so," he admitted, appearing almost as shocked by the child in his arms as the other women were. "I mean, momentarily . . . apparently."

The child's face crumpled. "Oh, no, here it comes. She never stops," he muttered, a beat before the baby screamed her outrage. And Clarissa understood. The child protested his callous treatment of her—oh, yes, Clarissa could commiserate too well.

She reached for the baby. She was the only one to move. The other women were too stunned.

To her surprise, he held on. "She's mine," he said.

"Do you know what you are doing?" Clarissa asked.

"No."

"Well, then, let me have her."

He did, practically shoving the child into her arms.

Chapter Three

Women do have their place in society . . .
although I'm not quite certain where.

—*Book of Mars*

The moment Mars handed his infant daughter off to Miss Taylor, he wanted to collapse with relief.

Dora was safe. She was here with *women*. *They* would know what to do. He could relax.

Of course, he would rather Miss Taylor not be here. He didn't have the patience, especially right now, for her self-righteous huffing and puffing. Oh, she was easy on the eyes with her golden hair and well-endowed figure, even in such a dowdy dress. In fact, in spite of her being no taller than a sprite, Mars thought her possibly one of the loveliest women in several parishes around—but then she would open her mouth and it was always to criticize him.

Wasn't she supposed to be off being a companion to some old, rich hen in London? Isn't that what he'd heard?

Well, apparently she had returned and was sipping tea at Mrs. Warbler's table along with Reverend Summerall's wife. Damn his luck.

The worst insult was that Dora immediately stopped her soul-rattling cries. Instead, she looked at Miss Taylor as if the spinster was her hero.

Mars consoled himself, and his still pounding head, by reaching for the only bottle on a table covered with teacups. He had missed his strong tea and Port this morning and he still dearly needed it. "Please tell me this is Port?"

"Sherry," Mrs. Warbler answered.

"She is soaking wet," Miss Taylor declared as if this was news to Mars.

"Yes," he agreed, hefting the sherry. "She is. She needs a dry whatever she has to have."

"A clout," Mrs. Summerall said as if trying to be helpful. "A rag will do of course but a clout is designed for a baby's bottom and has ties to hold it in place."

"Oh," Mars responded, wondering why anyone would think he knew about such a thing. He really didn't even want to know now.

"Do you *have* a dry clout?" Miss Taylor asked in that arched voice of hers.

"If I did, she wouldn't be wet." He sniffed the top of the bottle and shuddered. Sherry was such a vile drink.

"With all due respect, my lord," Mrs. Warbler said, "is this a social call?" He understood her suspicion. There wasn't a soul in the village who didn't know that he avoided the Matrons of Maidenshop. They were barely on cordial terms. He'd not minced words when denouncing their power and manipulations, and yet here he was.

"Sherry will have to do," he muttered to himself just as Dora restored his faith in her and broke down into tears—again. He turned to the maid, "I need a cup of *very* strong and hot tea."

The maid glanced at Mrs. Warbler who, thankfully, nodded her assent. Mars didn't know what he would have done if his request had been denied. Probably tipped the bottle right in front of them, and that would have outraged their feminine sensibilities.

Then he remembered he owed his hostess an answer. "This isn't a social call but a desperate plea for help." Yes, he could be that honest. To Miss Taylor he said, "Is that enough explanation for you?"

She shot him a look that said clearly, *What is wrong with you?* followed by a glance in the direction of the other women as if to say, *Isn't he a disappointment?*

He was.

Although, to find the answers, he'd braved putting himself into the center of their little coven. That must count for something. It also made his daughter's crying easier to take now that he wasn't the sole one in control. He hated feeling inept.

"Did you even bring a sucking bottle?" Miss Taylor wondered.

"A sucking bottle?" he repeated blankly. "*Yes*, that is what she needs. She's hungry. She must be. But what to feed her?"

"Where is her mother?" Mrs. Summerall asked.

"Gone." He wasn't going to tell them that Deb had foisted the baby on him before she went off to accept another man's protection. Or even make the excuse that he truly was a responsible lover who always took precautions with his partners because obviously, he had not been completely successful.

No, he'd keep all of that to himself. Poor Dora didn't need any more counts against her than being abandoned. He'd seen what Miss Taylor had endured over the years. *His* daughter would be treated better.

With a beleaguered sound, Miss Taylor shifted the baby into the crook of her arm as if she'd practiced the move. Then she did something he would never have thought of doing— she bent one knuckle and offered it to Dora. His child latched on to it as if desperate and began sucking. "When did she last eat?"

Mars didn't understand why Miss Taylor thought he'd have a clue about Dora's eating schedule. Although something tickled the back of his still drink-hazy brain that he should know. However, before he could frame an answer, the maid returned to the room holding a cup and saucer and a fresh pot of tea. He could have cried at the sight. She placed the dishes on the table in front of him and poured the steaming brew into a cup. He uncorked the sherry and topped the cup off. "Bless you," he whispered to the maid and the world. "Bless you, bless you." He sat in the nearest chair, ready to take a sip.

"Well, I'm so pleased that we have met *your* needs, my lord," Miss Taylor snapped.

"You don't sound pleased." He took a swallow of tea. The sherry wasn't half-bad and his body wanted to groan with the pleasure. "And I wish I could answer your questions, except I don't know the answers. Dora has been in my care for all of—what? An hour? Maybe a bit more? Wait. She was fed shortly before being given to me."

There, that was what he'd been trying to remember. Deb had told him she'd fed Dora before delivering her to him.

There was a beat of laden silence.

And then Miss Taylor said, "*Who* in their right mind gave *you* a baby?"

He had asked himself that question several times on the ride from Belvoir to Maidenshop with a sobbing child tucked against his chest. It was just not one he wanted to hear from *her*. Still, he did have an answer.

"God," he said with great finality. "God gave me a baby." He drained the cup of tea, not even minding if it burned his mouth a bit.

"She's *yours*?" Mrs. Warbler asked. "With the dark hair?"

"She is. Do you think I would be doing all of this if she weren't?" He answered Mrs. Warbler but he spoke directly to Miss Taylor, daring her to make a sharp comment . . . except, for the first time in their acquaintance, she appeared speechless.

It was a pity he couldn't enjoy the moment because Mrs. Warbler filled the void. "*Well.*" There was a wealth of the unspoken in that single word.

"Yes, *well*," the minister's wife echoed.

Mars winced. "You are right. I'm as perplexed as you are." He stared into the empty teacup wishing that sherry could magically change to Port.

He'd known the risk coming here for help. The gossip would run wild. And yet what choice did he have? The people whom he would normally have turned to in such an emergency—the Balfours and the Thurlowes— were not available.

"Are you certain this child is yours, Lord Marsden?" Mrs. Warbler asked as if approaching a delicate topic, one he had anticipated.

"*Yes*," he said. He'd not have anyone doubt the parentage of his daughter, although he was not going to tell them about his family birth trait. Toes were a personal subject.

Again silence.

Then Miss Taylor found her voice. "Mrs. Summerall, do we have clouts and a sucking bottle in the charity box?"

"Charity?" Mars repeated. "I don't need charity."

"Are you going to conjure clouts out of the air, my lord?" Miss Taylor asked. "Do you have that sort of power? Or the time to race to Fullbourne?" She referenced the larger village up the road some ways.

"I will pay the charity box for the items," he said stiffly.

"As you should," she replied without sympathy. "And you must send someone to Fullbourne, even Cambridge, to purchase what you can't find in Maidenshop."

Mrs. Summerall came to life, rising from the table hesitantly as if she was wary of Mars's mood. At least someone had some respect for him. "We should have what you need, my lord. Mrs. Burnham keeps the box. She is right across the road. I will go straightaway."

"Thank you," Miss Taylor said before he could reply. "The quicker the better. The baby will be chapped if we don't put something dry on her."

"I'll see about some ointment as well," the minister's wife offered. "Gemma donated some." She rushed out the door.

Like Wellington on a battlefield, Miss Taylor focused on the next concern. "Mrs. Warbler, is there anyone in the village who is nursing?"

Mars could have slapped himself in the forehead. Who else could feed a baby other than another nursing mother? Why hadn't he thought of that?

"No one save for Mrs. Balfour and they are out of town," the older woman answered.

"Right then," Miss Taylor answered. "Please send Jane to Lester Ewan for goat's milk."

"Ah, yes, of course," Mrs. Warbler answered. She rose from the table.

"Goat's milk?" Mars questioned.

"Babies have very sensitive stomachs," Miss Taylor answered. "Goat's milk seems to agree with them if mother's milk is not available."

He didn't believe he had any goats at Belvoir. He would purchase a herd of them. "How do you know all this?" he had to ask as Mrs. Warbler left the room. After all, Miss Taylor was a single woman.

"I was the minister's daughter," she answered as if he was a dullard. "I ran the charity box for years and often visited the orphan's home in Fullbourne."

"Ah, yes," he murmured, and discovered he'd been left alone with Miss Taylor. He wished he had somewhere to run off to, but since he didn't he helped himself to more sherry. He wanted to guzzle the bottle. His mind still struggled to understand the day's turn of events. He could almost believe he was caught in some dream that was all too real.

Miss Taylor watched his actions and then shook her head, looking down her petite nose at him, which took genuine talent since, at six foot four, he was a foot taller than her—and yet she made him feel small.

A length of silence stretched between them, punctuated by Dora's sucking noses and whimpers of dissatisfaction. The sound of them tugged at his heart, and conscience.

Miss Taylor began pacing, jiggling the baby. "Poor thing," she whispered to Dora. "Poor, poor, *poor* thing. What is her name?"

He'd been lulled by the cooing and caught off guard by the question directed to him. "What? Yes, um, Menadora."

She tested the word. "Men-a-dora? What strange name is that?"

Mars shrugged. "One her mother liked." What had Deb said? "It is some dead saint's name. One of three virgin sisters put to death . . . I think. Be thankful Deb didn't choose one of the other two's names."

Miss Taylor's eyes widened in disbelief.

"I didn't name her," he protested. "And I've never given her mother credit for good sense. Still, there you have it. I've been thinking of her as Dora."

She reacted as if even that name was an assault on her ears. However, when she continued her pacing, she murmured, "Poor, poor Dora. Poor, poor Dora."

"She's not poor," he had to insist.

"She doesn't have a mother who wants her."

"She has me. I'm here. You may mock me all you like, however, I am trying to help."

Before she could answer, Mrs. Summerall called out from the front hall that she had returned. She entered the room a beat later with Mrs. Burnham on her heels.

Dear God, more women. Mars rose from the table. The minister's wife held several cloth clouts. "I brought a dress as well."

"Good idea," Miss Taylor said.

"Only one dress?" Mars asked.

"We must save items for the poor," Mrs.

Summerall explained, making Mars feel churlish. He made a mental note to purchase his daughter a dozen clouts and a dozen dresses.

Mrs. Burnham was the blacksmith's wife. She was usually full of good humor and had always been a bit sweet on Mars. She went straight to Dora. "Oh, what a little darling. Hello, my lord. I have a bottle." She waved the sort of bottle with a leather teat one would use for suckling lambs. It was smaller than Mars's palm, a flattish shaped thing that rested on its side. The teat was an odd, conical shape with straps tying it around the lip of the bottle. "And Gemma's special ointment."

"Thank you, Mrs. Burnham—" he started, ready to be full of humility, except Miss Taylor talked over him.

"Wonderful, Mrs. Burnham. Let me change this child."

She took a clout from Mrs. Summerall and walked toward another room. Mars followed.

Miss Taylor stopped and gave him a puzzled look. "Where are you going?"

"I'm going with you."

"I can manage without you, my lord."

"She is my child." He also assumed that he needed to know what changing a clout was about, whether he planned to do it or not. Nothing had made him feel more incompetent than having his daughter dumped upon him and his not having a clue. Her cries had been pitiful. They'd also stretched his nerves thin. From now on, he wished to be more competent.

Miss Taylor shrugged and said, "Then bring one of her blankets. Preferably a dry one."

She spoke as if she believed he had hay for brains.

He turned back to the table just as Mrs. Burnham whispered to Mrs. Summerall, "Where's the mother?"

"I'm not certain. However, he insists she is his," the minister's wife replied.

"With all that black hair? Those eyes are brown as well. Never saw an Eddington with brown eyes—"

Comment broke off as he reached the table and picked up the blankets that had been on the floor beside a chair. Anxious to leave the room so the matrons could gossip in peace, he charged after Miss Taylor and found himself in Mrs. Warbler's kitchen.

Miss Taylor had found a rag and dampened it with her free hand in a bucket of fresh water. "Let's make you comfortable," she said to Dora while she transferred the rag to her hand holding Dora and reached out to Mars for the blanket.

Dutifully, he handed the driest to her.

"Oh, dear, this is a bit damp, too." She spoke to Dora but he knew the words were criticism of himself.

Again, with an efficiency he could only admire, she doubled the blanket with one hand and placed it on the center table. Laying Dora on it, Miss Taylor lifted the wet skirts. "We will put you in dry clothes but first, let's change your clout." She undid the strings holding the cloth contraption in place. "You poor thing."

Dora watched with solemn eyes interspersed with soft cries of protest. She tried to roll when Miss Taylor started tying on the dry clout. Mars put a hand out so that she wouldn't go too far.

"Her rolling is a good sign," Miss Taylor said.

"Of what?"

"She's strong and very healthy. Do you know how old she is?"

He frowned his answer and, at last, Miss Taylor understood. "Ah, yes, you have no idea."

"This is not something I'm proud of," he grumbled.

"No, I suppose not." Her answer could have meant a dozen things, and none of them complimentary. He let it go.

"It would be nice to bathe her," Miss Taylor said. "That can be done later."

Bathe? He wondered how one gave a baby a bath.

He looked down at his daughter, who appeared exhausted, and he realized this was hard on her as well. "Things will become better," he promised her.

She whimpered her response that was far more forgiving than what he deserved.

Miss Taylor changed Dora's dress. She wasn't cooperative. Dora chose that moment to pitch a right royal fit. Just as Mars was thinking, *Oh yes, this baby takes after Deb*, Miss Taylor said in that false sweet tone of hers, "Why, she acts exactly like you, my lord."

She flipped the dress over Dora's head and then placed the baby on her shoulder while drawing the lacings in the back of the dress. Dora turned to root on Miss Taylor's neck and then put her hand in her mouth and chewed on it.

Miss Taylor started for the door to return to the dining room but found him in the way. He stepped to the side, just as she did. He was still in the way. He returned to his left; she her right. Blocked again—and he felt superfluous.

What he wanted was to hold his daughter. The right way this time. A comforting way. And with Miss Taylor's confidence.

A sound came from the front door of the house. "We have the milk," Mrs. Warbler called out. Jane walked into the kitchen with a pail. Mrs. Warbler followed with the sucking bottle in her hand.

"Just in time," Miss Taylor said and carried *his* baby into the other room, this time easily bypassing Mars.

Meanwhile, Mrs. Warbler and the maid filled the bottle with milk. They hurried past Mars for the dining room where Miss Taylor sat, cradling Dora in her arm. The baby latched on to the teat like any hungry lamb and the women made soft sounds of approval.

Miss Taylor informed them the baby's name was Dora. Again the women murmured their thoughts.

From his position in the doorway, Mars felt very much out of place—and yet fascinated by his daughter.

His daughter.

Only that morning, he had lamented the lack of anything meaningful in his life and now here *she* was. And Miss Taylor had praised her strength? Her health?

Maybe he *had* done something right in his life.

Miss Taylor pulled the bottle from Dora's mouth. Dora had closed her eyes as she ate. She didn't bother to open them but her mouth tried to follow the nipple, sucking at air. Miss Taylor put the baby to her shoulder and patted her back. Almost immediately, Dora gave a belch that would have made an ostler proud. The ladies laughed and Dora earned the bottle back. This time, the baby placed her hand over Miss Taylor's as if to say she was going to hold the bottle until she was done.

And Mars felt even more incompetent since there was something else he would not have known to do. "Why do you pat her on the back?" he asked.

Mrs. Warbler answered. "It eases any intestinal vapors."

Intestinal vapors?

"So they don't have stomach bloat," Mrs. Summerall added.

You had to unbloat babies?

Dora finished the bottle. Miss Taylor carefully removed it from her lips. Dora made sucking movements and then with a soft sigh, seemed to fall deep into sleep.

And Mars wished he was holding her.

Mrs. Warbler spoke up.

"Who is the mother?" Of course she would ask. The matrons would be alive with curiosity.

"No one of importance," Mars answered and could feel their frowns of disapproval. He kept his gaze on his daughter.

Mrs. Summerall said in her gentle clergyman's-wife way, "My lord, we are not unsophisticated women. Your activities are well-known."

"Aye, we have known you as a randy one for a long time, my lord," the always direct Mrs. Burnham agreed, half laughing.

Such was life in Maidenshop. "I keep my business to myself," he answered, unrepentant.

"Not any longer," Miss Taylor murmured. As Dora had nursed, he'd moved deeper into the room to watch. Only now did he realize he stood right by Miss Taylor's shoulder. He took a step away.

"Have you given any thought to what you are going to do with Dora?" Mrs. Warbler asked.

"Thought?"

"Are you going to farm her out?" Miss Taylor sounded angry. She referred to the practice of passing off unwanted children to yeoman's families and the like. Many a nobleman had used the practice for their bastards. It was considered a responsible action . . .

"No," he answered, genuinely insulted. "She is *my* child."

The tension eased in the room. Mrs. Burnham got a silly grin on her face. "Miss Eddington. I like it."

Mars did, too. Miss Dora Eddington.

He also had a sense that, at last, he had

done something that earned the approval of the ladies in the room, including Miss Taylor.

"Well, then," Mrs. Warbler said, "you shall need a nurse for this child."

He nodded. He would.

"And I have the right person in mind," Mrs. Warbler continued. "Miss Taylor."

Clarissa Taylor? Under his roof? Where he would see her daily? Mars's first instinct was a resounding, *No.*

Except before he could answer, Miss Taylor said in that crisp, matter-of-fact voice of hers, "That is a terrible idea."

"Terrible?" Mars was offended.

She shot him a look. "You don't like me. I don't like you."

"Although she is very good with the baby," Mrs. Summerall pointed out. The three matrons were lined up on the opposite side of the table from the two of them. Mars was the only one who stood. Well, save for the maid Jane who lurked in the doorway, her facial expressions giving away that she sided with the women.

"Also there isn't anyone available to take the position," Mrs. Warbler observed.

"Miss Taylor has turned the position down," Mars pointed out. "I shall send to London."

Mrs. Warbler hummed her feelings before saying, "I wonder how long it would take to find a good nurse?"

"Even from Cambridge, a week, maybe two?" Mrs. Burnham answered.

"Longer than that if one searched in London," Mrs. Summerall agreed.

"And what will you do in the meantime, my lord?" Mrs. Warbler asked.

Mars didn't know.

"He will *manage*," Miss Taylor retorted, except he didn't know if he would.

Mars was also still offended that Miss Taylor had turned her pert nose up at his employ.

Then Mrs. Warbler delivered what he sensed was a coup de grâce. She said to Miss Taylor, "Except, if you don't take the earl's position, where will you go? Oh, wait, I believe Squire Nelson and his wife could make room for you. Again."

"You said I could stay here." Miss Taylor sounded dismayed. It was no secret that the Nelsons had been relieved when she'd finally left. Apparently Miss Taylor had felt the same.

The wily old lady shook her head in regret. "I've been thinking, my dear, there is barely room for Jane and me."

"I don't take up much space." Miss Taylor sounded desperate.

Mrs. Warbler shrugged as if the matter was out of her hands.

"And you *are* very good with this baby," Mrs. Summerall observed. "Look how sweetly she is sleeping in your arms."

"Very good," Mrs. Burnham echoed, giving Mars a look as if to say he'd be sorry if he didn't hire Miss Taylor.

He was beginning to think she might be right.

It *would* take a fortnight to hire a good nurse. In the meantime, Dora would be in the care of Nelson, Gibson, himself, and whatever milk-maid or other available female he might find. This was unacceptable for *his* daughter. He understood the effects of having an uncaring mother. Dora had already been through too much.

Besides, he sensed that Deb had deliberately left him without a bottle or clothes or clouts because she wanted him to feel like a fumbling fool. That was part of her retaliation.

Without Miss Taylor's help today, Deb would have had her revenge. The matrons had been helpful, except it had been Miss Taylor who had known exactly what to do—and wasn't that what he wanted for Dora?

Against his better judgment, he knew he had only one choice.

He looked to the matrons. "Would you ladies give us a moment? Miss Taylor and I should discuss the matter in private."

Chapter Four

Women rarely respond to reason.

—*Book of Mars*

*T*alk in private? With *him*?

Oh, no, that was not going to happen. "There is nothing to discuss," Clarissa answered swiftly. "I am not interested in such a position." And she wasn't. The last few days had been the most troubling of her life. She had found the energy to handle Dora . . . but there were limits.

Except her friends were already leaving the room. "No, don't go. Wait. *Come back here*," she begged. She tried to rise, making as if to follow them, except her arms were full of baby. She couldn't move as quickly as they did. They went quietly out the kitchen door, closing it, and deserting her.

Clarissa stared hard at that door, struggling with her temper—which she must *never* allow herself to lose. The righteous should not indulge in heated words, as Reverend Taylor was fond of saying.

Still . . . how dare Mrs. Warbler rescind her offer to let Clarissa stay with her. Why, over the years, Clarissa had done a hundred favors for her friend.

And Mrs. Summerall! She and her husband had taken over the parsonage, forcing Clarissa from the only home she'd ever known. There had been commiserating looks but never once had they expressed regret over kicking her out.

Both matrons had been involved in moving Clarissa in with Squire Nelson and his family because *they* had decided what was best for her. Even Mrs. Burnham had played a role.

Lord Marsden broke the silence that had fallen. "Your friends believe you should take a position in my employ."

"They don't know what is right for me." Her throat was tight with resentment.

He moved into her line of sight, reaching for the chair adjacent to hers from the table. She had drawn hers out to make it easier to feed the baby. He now turned his so he sat directly in front of her. She could not avoid looking at him without appearing ridiculous. He leaned forward, resting his forearms on his knees, a very *male* way to sit. No gentlewoman would have been allowed to be so casual. It also made him seem "earnest."

Please, God, save her from earnest men.

"I know you mildly disapprove of me—"

"Mildly?"

Lord Marsden's eyebrows rose. Perhaps at

her tone? Perhaps no one *dared* speak to him that way?

He then conceded, "Noted."

"As what?" she challenged. She was in no mood to be conciliatory. She'd had a hard two days of travel after disappointing months of working for the most miserly, mean-spirited, whiney woman in this whole country. And she hadn't even touched on her anger at Mrs. Emsdale's lecherous grandson.

"As, that you don't like me," he answered. "For that matter, I don't like you either."

"You've said that already. In front of the others no less. You don't need to repeat yourself. Besides, I've been aware of your lack of respect for me for a long time." She was proud she sounded calm, distant.

Still, his statement hurt. That was, if she allowed herself to be hurt. Being the village charity case, she'd learned long ago to maintain her composure when others spoke with little regard to her feelings.

And that was what it would be like for this sweet baby. Soon all would know the circumstances of Dora's birth and whisper about her.

Although, *Dora's* father would protect her. She would grow up knowing him, and even who her mother was.

Clarissa was startled by the jab of jealousy she experienced.

"Then let us clear the air between us," Lord Marsden suggested. "We are both adults. We can discuss our differences reasonably—"

She swallowed back the "ha" of doubt she

wanted to throw in his face. He would have ignored it anyway. They were all going to pressure her into their way of thinking. *Again*.

"—because the truth is," he continued, "the matrons are right—although you are the last person I would ever choose—you are the most suited for caring for *my* daughter. Look at her. I doubt if she was ever so peaceful even with her mother."

Dora slept as if exhausted. Clarissa had seen this often with babies at the foundling home. They might not understand the uproar in their lives, but they knew when they were safe and could sleep deeply at last.

"She certainly wasn't like that when she arrived," he said. "I can hire another nurse, but that will take time and I need one immediately. I also need someone who can teach me what I should know."

"Know about what, my lord?" she asked, so lost in the peaceful beauty of Dora's sleeping, she barely gave him her attention.

"My daughter," he repeated as if it should be obvious, except it wasn't. Clarissa had never met a man who seemed interested in the details of caring for his child. Especially when it came to changing a clout. She had to give him a bit of credit . . . begrudgingly.

"So," he continued, "in the interest of Dora's well-being, let's clear the air between us. What is it you don't like about me?"

"Are you mad?" She couldn't tell him what she truly thought about him.

"I don't believe I am," he said as if seriously

considering her question. "I mean, not completely mad—yet. Is that what you don't like about me? My madness?"

She narrowed her gaze at him. "You know what I meant. And, no, I will not tell you what I think."

"Why not? You certainly haven't held back your disapproval of me before."

Yes, she *had*. She had said several things, but not her *true* thoughts. Just the general rash things that came to one's mind when truly provoked, and he could provoke her.

She decided her best course was to ignore this invitation of his.

He sat waiting. Tall, handsome, insufferable. His fingers started drumming on his leg. There was no sound, but it annoyed her. She stiffened her back, willing to wait him out—

"Never mind, I'll start," he said. "I think I know why you do not care for me—"

"You are going to tell me how I feel about you?" She couldn't believe his presumption.

"You have always been as clear as a pane of glass."

"No, I am not."

He was silent, although his expression said louder than words that she deluded herself.

Clarissa's temper was ready to snap. She didn't need his nonsense. "Very well, what *do* I think of you? Pray tell me."

"That I am uncommonly handsome, well-spoken, and intelligent."

His statement startled her so much, her reaction had to be quite comical because he laughed, and she rolled her eyes in disgust. Why had she believed he was serious about any of this?

Then, he spoke, his tone sober. "You find me arrogant."

Clarissa thought about his rudeness over the years, the white cotton dress, the verbal pokes. She went to the heart of the matter. "Aye, you are arrogant. However, what I don't like is that you believe your arrogance is excusable. After all, you are the wealthy, entitled Earl of Marsden. Why shouldn't you do as you wish, even if it inconveniences others? It is just your due."

"There is some truth here," he said as if trying hard to be conciliatory. "I am often excused for poor behavior. Although I must put forth that my behavior is little different from any other man or woman. We *all*"—she sensed he was including her—"have bouts of poor behavior. Of course, the fact I have a title can't help but make me 'entitled.'"

"Don't annoy me," she answered.

He opened his mouth. She cut in, "You asked for *my* opinion." He shut his mouth, and crossed his arms as if barricading himself.

Good.

She smiled, her expression tight. "But let me not waste time on petty complaints, my lord. What truly annoys me the most about you is that you have wasted your life."

"Wasted it?"

"There is so much good you could do. You have opportunities that the rest of us can't even imagine. Look around you. Can't you see the need? The hunger? The number of citizens of this country who have no one to speak for them? You don't even contribute to the leadership of this parish—"

"I'm a member of the Logical Men's Society," he grumbled, letting her know her comments were hitting their target.

"The Logical Men's Society?" She made a dismissive noise. "Do they even exist any longer? After Mr. Balfour and Dr. Thurlowe left your bachelor ranks, who remains who matters? Oh, yes, Sir Lionel, although he's usually too deep in the cups to be a leader in any direction except the next bottle. And you know as well as I that the Logical Men's Society was more of a drinking club than one dedicated to social welfare or justice."

A muscle hardened in his jaw. She counted that a victory.

"Any other complaints?" he asked. Tightly.

"Of course I do. I find it a disgrace you rarely warm your seat in the Lords," she said, referring to the House of Lords. "Or that you believe public intoxication is perfectly acceptable."

"I've never been intoxicated in public."

"Sitting off in a dark corner of the room counts. Sneaking out of a parish dance to tipple in someone's coach *counts*. And it is common knowledge you over-imbibe almost nightly—"

"You are wrong. I no longer indulge regularly."

"—whether you have company or not," she finished, ignoring his protest.

Oh, yes, that did not please him at all.

"Finally," she said, rather enjoying herself, "I find it disgraceful that a man who has been given so much does so little. You can't even rouse yourself to make an appearance at Sunday services—"

He sniffed his opinion. "Oh, yes, that is the epitome of a gentleman, a hypocrite who presents himself in the church each Sunday."

"It wouldn't hurt you," she answered. "Many a hypocrite has had his soul saved inside those walls."

"Well, then, they won't need my soul. There are plenty of hypocrites to keep the Church busy."

"No, you are too busy chasing your 'pursuits' in London. There are terrible rumors about you, my lord. Then again, this is the fruit of your actions." She nodded to Dora. "Look at her, my lord. She wasn't born out of love but *lust*. It is a pity."

"*Most of us* had our starts with lust," he flashed back.

Was he referring to her and the mystery of her parentage? "No one can say we are all the better for it," she answered primly.

A glint lit his eye, a sign he was ready to retaliate. "And now, I must ask, is it *my* turn?"

"You may proceed," Clarissa answered, fairly certain there was little he could justifiably find at fault with her. She worked on her flaws. She always tried her best. She was punctual, usually thoughtful, and well-schooled in her manners.

"What annoys me about you, Miss Taylor, is your strong desire to be a matron-in-training."

"Matron-in-training?" What was he talking about?

"You are judgmental and you always have been. Even when you were shorter than a stump, which was not that long ago."

"You make fun of my height? My lord, you embarrass yourself with personal complaints." Although what she really didn't like was being called judgmental. Clarissa thought herself quite open to people from all levels of society.

Well, save for *him*.

He shushed her. "It is my turn now. I find your fussiness to do everything exactly right irritating. I don't even like your given name. Clarissa. You were preordained to prissiness."

Clarissa was sorry now she'd taken the high road. "You seem to have a problem with names," she shot back, matching his disparaging tone. "You don't like my name. You don't like Dora's name—"

He laughed at that. "Again, Menadora is not a name anyone should be forced to carry through life. Although the horse is out of its stall on that one. She is stuck with it."

"Perhaps *you* shouldn't be so *judgmental*."

He did not miss her barb and she could crow her victory. She smiled. "Perhaps the true reason you don't like me, my lord, is that you aren't accustomed to women who are unafraid to challenge you."

"No, I'm not accustomed to *shrews*," he answered, sitting back in his chair as if he'd made his point.

She was made of sterner stuff than to wince over the word *shrew*. Men had been using it on strong women since time began. "No," she agreed sweetly, "you are accustomed to women who abandon their children."

The air left the room.

His brow turned as dark as a thundercloud. It took all her courage to meet his anger and hold her head high.

Then, he released his breath slowly and drawled, "Better to be wild and entertaining than dull and pious."

Dull? Clarissa's hand ached to slap him. "If you are trying to convince me to take a position in your household, my lord, you are miserable at the task."

Lord Marsden blinked as if realizing the truth of her statement. A stain crept up his neck. He stood abruptly, walked a few paces, gave her his back as if needing to collect himself.

Clarissa sat with the weight of his child in her lap. Poor Dora. What kind of father did she have?

One who claimed her, was the unbidden reply. *One who wanted to do what was right for her.*

Suddenly, Clarissa came face-to-face with her own culpability.

She could not return to Squire Nelson and his family. Although they had been kind to take her in and treated her as a family member as best as possible, she'd worn out her welcome. If she didn't find a position, even Mrs. Warbler would tire of her.

After she'd lost Mr. Thurlowe, her goal had been to build a life for herself. She'd suffered a setback with Mrs. Emsdale, still she had to remain optimistic . . . even if she wished she never had to leave Maidenshop.

And now, here was Lord Marsden offering her a position that allowed her both suitable employment *and* her beloved village.

Except, she would be a paid servant, not a member of the local society. Her status would definitely change.

Oh, Clarissa, you have too much pride. She could hear Reverend Taylor whisper those words in her ear. He'd said them several times during her childhood. He'd known how hard life was for an orphan. After all, he'd been one.

Lord Marsden returned to the table. He looked very grave and formal. She expected him to repudiate her. Instead, he said, "You are correct, Miss Taylor. I *have* been rude. Please accept my apologies."

She blinked. He was apologizing? She hadn't known Lord Marsden was capable of an apology.

And she knew how she should respond. "I have too sharp a tongue myself, my lord."

He didn't argue.

She shifted the peacefully sleeping child in her arms. All that rancor going on around her and Dora had been blissfully unaware.

"I will accept the position of nurse." It almost physically hurt to be so humble with him. So,

Clarissa buoyed her spirits by saying, "Let's discuss my wages."

He rocked back as if he hadn't expected capitulation.

Or had he changed his mind? Aristocrats were known for being remarkably touchy.

Then, his gaze fell on his daughter snuggled against Clarissa's arm. He made a low sound, one Clarissa recognized as her own conflict with the situation.

Almost reluctantly, the word "Done" was drawn out of him. "Except I don't discuss money. My man Lowton in London will handle the matter."

Clarissa didn't realize she'd been holding her breath until that moment. She hadn't even had to tell him about the terrible incident with Mrs. Emsdale and that reminded her of something. "I will expect good references for my service," she said. "No matter how long I am with you."

He shrugged as if it wasn't an issue.

Then, because Mrs. Emsdale had taught her a valuable lesson, she said, "I require twenty guineas a year, my lord."

"*Twenty* guineas?" He shook his head. "Do you believe I am made of money? I don't need Lowton to tell me that is a ridiculous price."

Clarissa had known it was a brave ask. Mrs. Emsdale had been paying her two guineas a quarter to act interested in the face of stultifying boredom. It had not been easy. Little Dora would be a joy after being in that woman's service.

Still, Lord Marsden needed her.

"As a matter of fact, you have more than enough money." The words popped out of her mouth before she considered their wisdom and he pounced on them.

"See? *That* is what I'm talking about. So high-handed, so self-righteous—"

"So very good at caring for your child," she finished for him. "And how can one set a price on that?"

He stopped, eyed her, then drolly echoed, "How can one?"

She added, her voice sweet, "In truth, I would care for Dora or any child this needy for free. The twenty guineas is the price I ask for putting up with you."

It was a cheeky thing to say. But then, she'd always spoken her mind with him.

To her relief, he gave a sharp, almost angry bark of laughter. "Touché, Miss Taylor. In turn, it will be worth twenty guineas to keep you away from the matrons. Thinking the matter over, this might be the best thing that has ever happened to you. Therefore, you are hired— because I really don't have another choice, do I?"

She didn't reply. He knew the answer. Still, she had one more matter to settle. "My lord, I will require my first quarter's wages paid in advance."

"You must take the matter up with Lowton. I don't care. Like you said, I have plenty of money. But you will have to discuss it with him. And, as long as you take care of my daughter, I'll pay whatever you wish, *when*ever you wish.

However, I expect you to not let your feelings toward me bleed over onto her. Am I clear?"

"I would never do such a thing." She was insulted by the suggestion.

"Of course not. You aren't like the rest of us mere mortals, are you, Miss Taylor?"

"Oh, I'm mortal, my lord. I make mistakes. I just don't whine about it."

"Ah, yes, there is that sharp tongue."

Guilt rose to her cheeks. She must be more considerate of him because Clarissa was realizing that not only was she employed, she was also in charge of this sweet creature in her arms. For miles around, only Clarissa had the experience to guide Dora through the attention the unusual circumstances of her birth would bring down upon her. And here would be her purpose in life—protecting Dora.

Resolve poured through her. At last she had a mission, a reason for being, a role. She would shepherd Dora and keep her safe from the innuendoes of narrow minds.

There was a shuffling at the hallway door. Mrs. Warbler peeked her head in. "So, it is resolved?" she demanded, although the triumphant light in her eyes said she knew it had been. All of them, including Jane, had probably had an ear to the door.

"It is," Lord Marsden said. "Miss Taylor will be Clarissa's nurse. I will now return to Belvoir to fetch the coach. Miss Taylor, while I'm gone, determine what else Dora needs that can be purchased in the village. Also, I have no idea of the condition of Belvoir's nursery. I shall tell my butler Gibson to set one up. The daily details will be left to you. *Lists*, Miss Taylor. I will need lists of what my daughter needs. What we can't find here, I'll send someone to Cambridge to collect." He started for the door as if he, too, had a renewed sense of purpose.

Clarissa wanted to give a glad shout. She had somewhere to go. She wasn't going to be passed around the village. She lifted Dora up on her shoulder, liking the weight of the child sleeping there.

And then Mrs. Warbler said, "Wait, my lord. There is one other matter. I will be going with Miss Taylor."

Lord Marsden had been halfway out the door. He now whirled around. *"What?"*

Clarissa could have mimicked the question. She was just as stunned.

"I must accompany her," Mrs. Warbler said as if it was clear to everyone. "Yours is a bachelor establishment. It is well-known your staff is all male. That has not changed, has it?"

He frowned.

She took that as assent. "Then," Mrs. Warbler said, not unkindly, "you will need to employ me as well until you hire more women."

"What the devil are you nattering about?" he demanded. Mrs. Summerall and Mrs. Burnham acted just as surprised as he was.

"I can be a housekeeper," Mrs. Warbler suggested. "I have always thought I would make a very good one."

"Mrs. Warbler—" Clarissa started but with a snap of her fingers, her friend cut her off.

"See here, Miss Taylor, it would not be suitable for you to live under Lord Marsden's roof without other female company." She didn't even bother to whisper as she added, "He has a reputation, you know."

"Oh. That is true," Mrs. Summerall agreed.

"I'm to take care of his child, not let him chase me around the dining room table," Clarissa answered.

"There it is. You are concerned as well," Mrs. Warbler said brightly.

"I am *not* concerned," Clarissa protested.

"And I do not chase women around the furniture," Lord Marsden said. "Besides, Miss Taylor and I do not like each other."

"*Exactly*," Clarissa agreed. "There is no danger of my smashing his fingers in the door."

"Why would you smash my fingers in the door?" Lord Marsden asked.

"You wouldn't like the story," Clarissa assured him.

"Perhaps I would. Have you smashed someone's fingers?"

"No one's," Clarissa lied. Now she was annoyed that the topic had come up and she was the one to have raised it. "You needn't worry, Mrs. Warbler."

"I must," Mrs. Warbler responded smoothly. "Why create gossip when it isn't necessary?"

"Very true," Mrs. Burnham echoed.

"I don't care about gossip," Lord Marsden answered.

"Because you don't have to worry about it," Mrs. Warbler explained. "However, Miss Taylor will not be in your employ forever. Her reputation should be important to her. Furthermore, you don't want your daughter in the center of unsavory speculation and gossip, do you?"

"I—well, no."

"And that is why I am offering my services. So that all will look well. That is until you hire a new nurse."

"Or a new housekeeper?" he said pointedly.

"Or that," she agreed pleasantly.

"Gibson will not be happy." Lord Marsden's butler was famous throughout the country for the efficiency he brought to his employer's household.

"Change is always difficult," Mrs. Summerall offered helpfully.

Lord Marsden shifted his weight. "I'm not going to win this, am I?"

"Not if you wish to hire Miss Taylor," Mrs. Warbler said.

"Mrs. Warbler, please, I—" Clarissa started, but Lord Marsden cut her off.

"Very well. It will be an opportunity, Mrs. Warbler, to see if you can do something constructive instead of meddling. How much will I have to pay *you*?"

"Oh, whatever you are paying Miss Taylor is fine."

Lord Marsden groaned . . . and then his gaze fell on his daughter. "Very well."

"Oh, and my maid Jane must come with me," Mrs. Warbler said.

"Why does a housekeeper need a maid?" he demanded.

"I have always had a maid. Jane must come. Have no worries, I will pay her wages."

"That makes me feel better," he drawled, meaning the opposite. He looked to Mrs. Summerall and Mrs. Burnham. "Would you other two ladies like to enter my employ?"

Mrs. Burnham giggled. "Oh, no, my John likes keeping me close to home. Although it would be quite a thing to be chased around the dining table." She laughed and laughed.

"Unfortunately, I'm too busy with parish activities. I'm certain you understand," Mrs. Summerall said as if seriously entertaining such a suggestion.

Lord Marsden frowned his suspicions. "Why do I have the feeling I am being hoodwinked?"

"We are just watching out for Miss Taylor's reputation, my lord," Mrs. Warbler said in the most innocent tone possible.

He grunted his response.

Clarissa tried to apologize. "My lord, you do not have to hire her. Not on my account."

"Actually, Mrs. Warbler may have a good point especially once word of Dora's presence starts being bandied about." He still did not sound pleased. "I will return within the hour. You have a lot of work to do, Miss Taylor. You'd best be on it."

On those words, he strode out the door, a far different man from the one who had arrived.

Clarissa waited for the front door to shut before she confronted Mrs. Warbler. "Housekeeper? Do you have any idea what you are doing?"

"Shush," her friend warned. "You don't want to wake the baby." Then, with a shrewd twist to her smile, she admitted, "I am creating opportunity, my girl. Just for you. Come, Jane, we must pack. And you'd best be busy, Clarissa. Lord Marsden sounds as if he will be a hard taskmaster. We must do what we can to please him." She went out the door.

Clarissa looked to Mrs. Burnham and Mrs. Summerall. They stood like two silly magpies. "Don't ask us what is afoot," Mrs. Burnham said. "You know Elizabeth has her whims."

"Well, this is a strange whim. I'd never imagine she would wish to be a servant."

"She wants to see you safe," Mrs. Summerall soothed. "Although, she does have her ways."

"Yes," Mrs. Burnham confirmed. "She does."

They shared a co-conspirators' smile. Clarissa had seen that crafty look before with respect to the matrons. They'd had that smile when they had toddled her off to live with the Nelsons. They'd smiled when they had decided the time had come for her to marry, prodding her with a *Don't you think Mr. Thurlowe would be an excellent husband?*

What could they be plotting now? It was unsettling how the lot of them didn't even need words to communicate.

And then Mrs. Summerall brought Clarissa back to her present problems by saying cheerily, "Now, what can we help you gather for the baby?"

Chapter Five

Women don't play fair. Neither do men.
—*Book of Mars*

$\mathcal{T}$rue to his word, within the hour, Mars rolled into Maidenshop. He didn't normally use his coach when he was in the country. He preferred riding Bruno, his ill-tempered gelding who usually threatened to unseat him at any given moment—except earlier when Mars had been carrying Dora in his arms. Then, the horse had shown good sense and behaved, to his owner's relieved surprise.

Now Mars arrived in lordly fashion. His coach sported the Marsden colors of red and black. The wheels were red, too, with yellow spokes. It was so well-sprung, a rider never felt the bumps and ruts of village roads.

His thoughts were on everything that had already transpired today. Yesterday seemed empty compared with all he had before him now.

What he *hadn't* anticipated was the splash

the coach would make in Maidenshop. People watched him pass and then started to follow. They called out to their family and neighbors, who left their chores or came out of their cottages for a look, and then they joined the procession. Children ran alongside the coach calling out his name as if begging for him to stop. Even the lads hanging around the smithy came walking down the road for a better look.

Of course, the horses enjoyed the attention. They were big-boned, bloodred animals who moved in high-stepping harmony and looked as if they had the strength to go all day.

The jewel on the top of the crown was the driver and footman who sat in the box. Bewigged and dressed in the splendor of Marsden livery, their shoulders were straight and their heads high. They basked in the attention.

And trotting behind them was a pony cart driven by a stable lad.

And Mars thought, if this didn't impress Miss Taylor, he didn't know what would—

Immediately he corrected himself. She would not be impressed. She'd accused him of acting "entitled" and here he was with his crest on the coach door. Except her problem wasn't with him, but with society. Earls were expected to put on airs. It made the populace happy. Look how many villagers seemed genuinely delighted to gawk at this little parade.

The coach and cart pulled to a halt in front of Mrs. Warbler's house. Of course, the women were not waiting for him. That was the way of women, he reminded himself. He remembered too clearly hearing his father grouse about his mother's tardiness—

The memory stopped him. It wasn't that he didn't think of his father. He'd been thinking of him a great deal of late, especially last night. The howling incident embarrassed him now. It was that he rarely thought of his mother.

Miss Taylor came out on the step, shifting his thoughts away from the past. The last person he wanted to ruminate on was Eleanor. Dora was still asleep, wrapped in a blanket, her head and a tired arm resting on Miss Taylor's shoulder.

The sight of Dora sent a wave of purposeful anticipation he hadn't felt in a long time. He also experienced a bit of pride that he was in front of Miss Taylor at his best. He'd even shaved. Sherry was not Port, but it had been restorative.

However, when Mars opened the coach door and jumped out, he was immediately surrounded by curious children trying to have a look inside. He couldn't even take a step forward.

"Do you like it?" he asked, bemused.

At his question, they fell back as if not wishing to be in trouble. He just laughed. "When I was your age, I would have done anything to look in such a vehicle."

They stared at him as if uncertain if he was telling them the truth.

He knelt a bit so he was on their level. "Well? Would you like to see inside?"

The older children watched him warily but

the youngest one eagerly announced that he would, tacking on "my lord" when one of the older girls gave him a punch to remind him of his manners.

"Very well," he said to them. "I must use the coach. However, if you are quick, each of you can have a turn sitting in the seat a second."

Eyes widened as if they couldn't believe their good fortune. "Here, Hodner," Mars said to the footman. "Organize this." Then he turned his attention to his daughter . . . and the woman holding her.

Miss Taylor watched him with a worried line between her brows. He couldn't tell what she was thinking. He was certain it wasn't a charitable thought toward him. Before he could approach her, a local solicitor by the name of Michaels called out his name. "My lord, a moment of your time?"

Mars stifled his impatience. Michaels was a member of the Logical Men's Society. He was short, lacked any knowledge of anything, and Mars could not abide looking at the man's brown teeth. However, he put a pleasant smile on his face as he acknowledged his fellow Society member. "Michaels, good to see you. Unfortunately, I am busy at this moment." He would have moved on, except, as he suspected, Michaels had something to say.

"My lord, we must discuss the Logical Men's Society. Several of the lads have dropped out. Why, my friend Shielding is now promised to Squire Nelson's oldest daughter."

"Yes, there are concerns. We will talk about it later." He tried to move on but a persistent Michaels stepped in front of him.

"Which is what you keep telling me. Unfortunately, we need to talk about this now. Since Mr. Thurlowe married, I have been named the leader of what is left of our small group. Most don't care about the Society the way you and I do. I need your help in organizing a meeting of all the members in good standing—"

"And you will have it," Mars promised smoothly. "Although, we are not discussing this issue right now." He'd managed to maneuver around Michaels and now moved swiftly to Miss Taylor, leaving the hapless leader to stew on his own.

"Are you two ready?" he asked. He noticed a valise and a bag holding a few more clouts and a bottle of goat's milk at her feet.

However, Miss Taylor wasn't the one who answered. "Absolutely, my lord," Mrs. Warbler said from the open doorway of her house as if she were the queen of France. She was dressed for travel with a brown bonnet trimmed in purple feathers and silly bows on top of her customary lace cap. Even her maid Jane had changed, obviously dressing herself in her Sunday clothes.

"This is so exciting," Mrs. Warbler trilled. "I've always envied you living at Belvoir and now, I shall be there as well."

Mars had to force himself to keep his smile. What the devil had he signed on for?

He did note Miss Taylor wore what she'd

been wearing when he left her an hour ago. In fact, over the past few years, perhaps since her parents died, she dressed for the most part like a drab sparrow. Or a poor relation. It was a pity actually. She had the looks that could break hearts if shown to advantage.

He kept this thought to himself. He didn't need to marry her off. He needed her as a nurse.

"You must send someone to fetch our luggage, my lord," Mrs. Warbler said. "It is at the top of the stairs."

"Tommy, go help," he said to the stable lad. "Hodner, he may need assistance."

"Yes, my lord," the footman answered. All the children had been given a turn and Hodner had been closing the coach doors.

Mars's gaze returned to Dora. He didn't need to climb the step to be level with Miss Taylor. He gently touched Dora's hedgehog-y hair with his gloved hand. "Do you think she'll have curls?"

"It is too soon to know," Miss Taylor answered. "She is, what? Perhaps five to six months old?"

Mars shook his head. "I don't even know that." He didn't know anything.

"You could ask her mother?"

"Hell will freeze over before I talk to her."

"Well, there are ways to find answers," she replied, for once not arguing with him. "If you know where Dora was born, there will likely be a register in some church with her birth date recorded."

"Perhaps." He would hire a man to seek information. He changed the subject. He was anxious to take Dora home, and to be out of the public eye. Perhaps including the matrons in his plans was fortuitous. He needed to concoct a plausible story of Dora's appearance in his life and they could help. They would also then be sworn to secrecy.

His daughter was so innocent, so completely dependent upon him. The protective instinct he'd experienced that moment in front of the looking glass in his bedroom grew stronger. He'd do anything to keep Dora safe, especially from the sharp tongues of gossips. "Are you ready?"

"I am," Clarissa said. "We have gathered a few things Dora will need and I have lists for the rest. It is a sizable list. Mrs. Warbler and Mrs. Summerall insisted on adding more items than I found necessary. After all, we can wash a bottle and use it several times a day. That is what kitchens are for."

"Have you ever seen the interior of Belvoir?"

She frowned, paused, and then admitted, "No."

"There is a bit of distance between the kitchen and, really, anywhere."

The set of Miss Taylor's mouth told him she was adding "slothful" to her catalog of his defects.

She would see.

"I do have a concern about the goat's milk," she continued officiously, as Tommy and Hodner carried a trunk out of the house. "We are going to need more very quickly. This child is hungry. Arrangements must be made with Mr. Ewan. Someone will have to fetch it—"

"I've already purchased his goat herd."

"What?"

Mars shrugged. "I purchased his goats. My man is probably with him right now discussing their care and whatever."

For one enjoyable moment, Miss Taylor looked stunned. Mars smiled.

Then, her lips went from being parted in surprise to turned down in disgust. "What will the rest of the village do if they need goat's milk? Have you thought of that?"

Did he have to?

"They can come to me for milk," he answered. The solution seemed simple enough. Yes, Ewan lived closer to Maidenshop than he did, but he could have the milk delivered to the village if it was *that* important.

"Or you could leave Ewan with some goats?"

Was she being deliberately provocative? "I could."

Her expression said he should.

"Very well," he said to her unvoiced criticism. "I will give Ewan a goat or two."

"That would be an excellent solution."

"Yes, matron," he answered under his breath, riled by her constant assumption of his selfishness.

Fire flashed in her green eyes, a sign that she'd heard him. He didn't care. Instead, he turned his attention to Tommy and Hodner returning to the house. "There is more?"

"Yes, my lord," Hodner said, ducking inside.

He had no doubt Mrs. Warbler had other motives than wanting to play chaperone. And he had an idea what her game was. He was all too aware of the measures the Matrons of Maidenshop had taken to shame one of the Three Bucks, their name for him, Balfour, and Thurlowe, into offering for Miss Taylor years ago. Thurlowe and Balfour were now out of the game since they were married. However, if the crafty old ladies thought they were going to corner him into marrying Miss Taylor, they were wrong. He could easily outfox them. He'd spent years successfully dodging matchmaking mamas.

His servants came out of the house with their arms loaded with valises and bandboxes. Mars would wager only one valise belonged to the maid.

Mrs. Warbler and Jane followed them out this time. The maid shut the door. "Well, my lord," Mrs. Warbler said, pulling on her gloves. "Are we ready?"

"Absolutely. This way, Mrs. Warbler," he said and offered his arm.

She accepted it, a bit of a blush coming to her cheeks. He knew that most of the village was watching. She thought she was going to ride in the coach. She was wrong.

He escorted her to the pony cart that was piled with luggage. There was just the right amount of room for the ladies and Tommy. He opened the door. "In you go."

Mrs. Warbler balked. "I assumed I would be riding with you, my lord."

Mars pretended a puzzled look. "Why would my new housekeeper ride like a favored guest?" he asked, before leaning close and reminding her, "We must be true to the charade."

A tight smile crossed her face. She glanced around, then countered, "We don't have to be completely accurate."

"I'm afraid we must."

Seeing he wasn't going to budge, she climbed into the pony cart with a huff and eased around the trunk. Jane followed. Tommy had already climbed in over the side.

"Hurry to the house," Mars ordered. "I know Mrs. Warbler will want to settle in so that she can start her duties."

"Yes, my lord." With a crack of the small whip he carried, Tommy set the pony off at a fast clip. So fast, Mrs. Warbler had to grab the side of the cart with one hand to keep her balance.

Mars watched them go and then he returned to Miss Taylor. "Are you ready?" He picked up her valise.

"I can take that, my lord," Hodner quickly offered.

Mars waved him away. He guided Miss Taylor to the waiting coach. There was still a crowd watching. He could see the questions in their eyes and the way their necks craned so as not to miss a detail. He had no doubt they would be the talk of Maidenshop for days to come.

It was fine. He was well-liked and his stature in the village was even higher than the Duke of Winderton's. They would talk but he was one of them and they would protect him, as he protected them over the years. Especially from Dervil.

He heard a girl ask, "Why is Miss Taylor going with my lord?"

Her mother shushed her. "I'm sorry, my lord."

He smiled and helped Miss Taylor into the coach, handing her valise to Hodner to stow. Removing his hat, he waved at the villagers and then joined Miss Taylor inside the coach, taking the red velvet lined seat opposite hers. Hodner closed the door and Mars stretched his long legs so that he was comfortable. That meant she had to scoot to the side a bit.

Miss Taylor released her breath. "That was a challenge."

"I appreciate your discretion."

She nodded and shifted Dora into the cradle of her arm. The baby didn't wake. He knocked on the roof, a signal they were ready to go.

Within a minute, the coach began moving. At the first feeling of motion, Dora startled. Clarissa held the baby closer and Dora settled against her.

Outside, the villagers stepped back to allow room for the rig to turn in the direction of Belvoir. Hands waved as the coachman called out to the smart stepping horses, and Mars relaxed, pleased with the turn of events.

After a few minutes riding, Miss Taylor

said in surprise, "This coach seems to skim the earth. I've never ridden in anything this smooth. I also understand now why the children wanted to sit inside." She patted the red velvet. "You enjoy your luxury, my lord." Her words lacked the critical edge she often used.

"We all should," he answered. Dora was still sleeping peacefully. "Is it good for her to sleep this much?"

"She has suffered an ordeal. Traveling, having her mother leave her."

"Do you think she knows?" he asked, concerned.

"Yes," was the quiet reply, and he realized that she had experienced exactly what Dora had been through. Their gazes met. She looked away.

Immediately, he regretted his question. He should have been more aware, more understanding.

Perhaps Miss Taylor was right about some of his boorish tendencies.

Then, she said, "She won't remember in the sense that she has details in her mind. However, she'll know she was left. And she will always wonder."

"I will see that she suffers no shame from it."

Again, green, all-seeing eyes met his.

This time, he was the first to look away, embarrassed. What the devil was wrong with him? It had been a long time since a woman had made him feel awkward.

Of course, Clarissa Taylor had always had that power.

She also looked exhausted.

"May I hold the baby?" he asked.

"Of course, my lord. She is your child." Miss Taylor scooted to the edge of the seat and leaned forward.

He took Dora from her, holding the baby the way Miss Taylor had. For a second he felt stiff. He sat upright, swaying with the coach. Heedless of his discomfort, Dora snuggled in against him with the sweetest sigh he'd ever heard.

And he found himself smiling. *His* daughter. He'd never been one for children but this was different. She was his.

Slowly, he relaxed, cherishing the feeling of what—? Not being alone?

Such a strange notion. He'd always been alone, even with his friends. He'd had no family since his father's death. Not one he trusted . . .

He removed his glove, using his teeth since he didn't want to disturb Dora, and then he ran the tip of his finger along her cheek. It was as smooth and soft as it looked. She made a face as if his touch had tickled and he smiled before looking up at Miss Taylor to see if she had noticed—

Miss Taylor was asleep.

Her head was tilted downward against the velvet cushion. Her shoulders were slumped, her hand in her lap. He knew she must be past exhaustion to sleep in *his* presence. He noticed what he should have seen earlier—deep circles under her eyes. No wonder she had been so touchy.

No, that wasn't right. Clarissa Taylor had always been prickly.

Just as he'd always aggravated her. They just didn't rub along well.

Still, he was glad she had been at Mrs. Warbler's when he'd arrived with Dora. She was exactly what Dora had needed.

At that moment, the coach turned up the long drive leading to Belvoir. Miss Taylor leaned with the movement of the coach and woke herself. Mars dropped his attention to Dora. He knew Miss Taylor would be self-conscious to be so human as to be caught napping.

From the corner of his eye, he saw his concerns were correct. She sat up, glanced over at him, frowned at herself. She touched her bonnet as if to check that it was straight and then looked out the window, studiously ignoring him. Which she would have continued doing until she saw something outside that made her gasp. "This is your home?"

Mars looked to see what she meant. They were reaching the edge of Belvoir's front lawn with the house stretched out in front of them at the end of the long drive. "Yes."

"I'm—" She stopped. "It's a palace."

He laughed. "It once was. Now it is just a very grand house." And much more. From the trees lining their way to the gray stone walls and row after row of windows reflecting the late afternoon sun, Belvoir proclaimed to one and all that a Person of Substance lived there.

Stately columns held up a portico that was the size of the St. Martyr's church. The steps led up to wide double doors. Stone hawks, some with their wings spread, others looking out over the world as if on watch for enemies, topped the staircase posts.

"I've never seen a lovelier building," Miss Taylor whispered, almost as if she spoke to herself.

"I'm surprised you've never seen it before."

"For what reason?"

He opened his mouth to speak and then stopped. His parents had not been ones to entertain the locals. After his father's death, he'd not thrown open the doors either. "The gardens are said to be the finest in England." He spoke with more than a touch of pride. He liked seeing his home through her eyes.

At that moment, Dora began to stir, almost as if she realized she was home. "May I take the baby from you, my lord?"

"No, she is fine."

"I think it prudent. If she hasn't wet herself yet, she will. And she'll be hungry again."

"She's fine, Miss Taylor." Mars wasn't eager for another wet clout, but he wasn't anxious over it either.

And Miss Taylor needed rest. He would have to see that both nurse and baby had naps.

Clarissa held up her hands, a sign that she would not argue. He smiled. He wondered how difficult it was for her to back down.

Probably as difficult as it would have been for himself.

As they drew closer, Mars could see that Mrs. Warbler and the pony cart had already arrived. Gibson stood on a step, directing the transport of luggage with his servants moving like worker bees in a hive, and that was when Mars noticed the other coach under the covered section of the front portico.

He wasn't expecting guests. Nor did he recognize the vehicle. He also caught a disturbed expression on Gibson's face. Either the butler was very upset over Mrs. Warbler naming herself the housekeeper or something was not right.

Almost as if it was second nature, he shifted Dora to his shoulder, a protective hand on her back. Her little face turned into his neck.

His initial thought was that Deb had returned. Well, if it was Deb, she wasn't taking his child.

His coach rolled to a stop. A footman opened the door.

Mars climbed out, leaving his hat behind. He unfolded his long frame, holding his baby close. Behind him, the footman held a hand out to help Clarissa.

Gibson hurried forward. "My lord—"

"Who is here?" Mars demanded, and then he had a horrible premonition.

It wasn't Deb.

If what he suspected was true, Deb would have been a blessing.

Dora started fussing. It was as if she sensed his mood.

Immediately Clarissa put her hands out to take the baby, but he wasn't ready to give her up. Not when he sensed danger.

And then a voice from the top of the step said, "Hello, my son. It has been a while."

My son.

The words made his blood go cold.

Slowly, he turned and faced her. She had aged since he last saw her ten years ago. Or had it been longer? Her blond hair now had streaks of silver. She was tall. He'd earned his height from her. And her bearing proclaimed louder than words that she was in charge—as all of London would agree. It had taken great skill on his part to avoid her at the few balls and routs he had been forced to attend out of obligation.

"Lady Fenton is here," Gibson announced in a low voice, finally delivering the message he'd been anxious to convey. "I did not know what you would wish me to do."

What he wished Gibson had done was toss her out on her regal buttocks.

Now it was up to him.

Of all the times in his life for her to make an appearance, today was the worst . . . and yet he allowed nothing of what he was thinking to show in his expression. She knew how to take advantage of any weakness.

His mother had remarried ages ago. Lord Henry Fenton was a renowned statesman, one of those men who lived and breathed Parliament.

She now came down the steps with the stately pace of one accustomed to holding court. "How long has it been, Lawrence, since we've seen each other. Ten years? Maybe more?"

"I truly don't care," he murmured, the sound of his given name on her lips setting his teeth on edge. "I hadn't had a desire to further our acquaintance."

"I knew you wouldn't be happy to see me."

"Yet, still you came."

"I'm known for my persistence."

"I know you for other things."

She did not like that comment. What? Had she expected him to remain the confused lad she had deserted when she'd betrayed her husband? Her marriage?

Before she could respond, her gaze fell on Dora. The baby was awake. She lifted her head, her tiny fingers grasping Mars's coat as if she, too, understood they needed to be wary of this creature. She regarded Lady Fenton with stoic curiosity.

"What is this?" his mother asked.

"She's mine." He sounded defensive, and he was. Dora was none of his mother's concern.

"Yours?" she echoed. "With all that dark hair?" She stared harder, and then her expression softened. She took another step down the stairs. "Why, she is." There was a hint of wonder in her voice. "What a sweet little face. She looks just as you did as a baby." She lowered her voice. "Does she have the toe?"

This grandmotherly attitude surprised him, not enough to let down his guard, but it was still a bit unnerving. He gave a nod, even as he gathered his daughter closer. He would not share the sordid details of Dora's birth with his mother. He did not want to give Lady Fenton a secret that could be used against him. For all her smiles, this was not a social call.

And he knew of only one way to protect Dora—parentage.

He reached behind him with his free arm, finding Miss Taylor standing close as if ready to take Dora if he so wished. He pulled her forward up onto the step beside him, keeping his arm around her.

Lady Fenton eyed Miss Taylor with a frown. "Who is this?"

"She's my wife, Mother. Let me introduce you to Clarissa."

Chapter Six

Sometimes we roll along in life;
sometimes life rolls over us.
                              —*Book of Mars*

Clarissa felt her brain freeze. *What had he just said?*

And why had Lord Marsden's arm around her tightened? As if he was afraid she would escape? Why, he'd even grabbed ahold of the material of her pelisse. He also shot her a "meaningful" look that said, *Don't speak. Whatever you are thinking, hold your tongue.*

And for a reason she couldn't ever in her right mind fathom, she obeyed. Perhaps it was village loyalty. This woman was a stranger. He might be trying to protect Dora. Clarissa could appreciate the delicacy of explaining Dora's presence, and it was obvious he and his mother were not close.

That didn't mean Clarissa was happy with her sudden promotion from nurse to wife—

and she would let him know the moment they were alone.

However, for now, she clasped her gloved hands in front of her to present the picture of a servile spouse, and as a way to keep from punching him in the side for tying her into this lie. She even attempted a smile.

"My dear," he said, the endearment sounding formal on his lips, "this is my mother, Lady Fenton."

To be honest, Clarissa had forgotten he had a mother. The village rarely mentioned his parents, especially since his father had died tragically in a duel with Lord Dervil. And what a surprise to learn his mother was the celebrated Lady Fenton, the doyenne of London's political and literary salons. The woman was always mentioned in the London papers. She moved in the highest echelons of society. What must such a woman think at having a son who was a political prodigal? Had she arrived to take him in hand?

Clarissa hoped so.

Except, it was very clear that while a baby was a pleasant occurrence, a daughter-in-law was not.

Lady Fenton raised a pair of lunettes attached to a gold chain around her neck. Feeling she must do something, Clarissa made a clumsy curtsey. Lady Fenton's lip curled with disfavor, and Clarissa discovered she was not in the mood for such nonsense. Once she and Lord Marsden were alone, she'd tell him as much, right before she beat him around the ears until they were bloody for dragging her into all of this.

The image of pounding on him made her smile.

Meanwhile, Mrs. Warbler, standing to the side, watched the scene with such avid interest. This whole conversation would certainly be shared the next time the matrons gathered.

Nor did it help her growing temper when his mother repeated, "Clarissa?" as if tasting the name and finding it not to her liking. Like mother; like son.

Then, quite deliberately, Lady Fenton gave Clarissa her back. "You've married? I had not heard. And a child as well?" There was a beat of heavy silence, before she said, almost conversationally, "Are matters between us so far gone that we know so little about each other?"

"Oh, absolutely," her son said cheerily.

At that moment, Dora decided she was tired of being ignored. She began her little whimper sounds that warned of a looming full-throated cry. She was probably hungry—again.

Clarissa reached for her. "Here, let me have her, my lord." Her plan was to take the baby and make an escape.

He gave her Dora but he kept his hold on her pelisse. "If you will excuse me, Mother, we must see to our daughter. Gibson?"

"Yes, my lord?"

"Take care of all of this, please." He waved a hand to encompass the pony cart, the coaches, the mother. "I'm certain Lady Fenton is ready to head back to London—"

"*I am not*, Lawrence," his mother said. "I came here on a mission. I *must* talk to you."

"And I don't wish to talk to you," he replied ruthlessly. "The reason you don't know the facts of my life is because I don't want you to. Now come, Clarissa. Let's see to our daughter." He started up the stairs toward the front door, practically carrying Clarissa and Dora in his haste.

But Lady Fenton was not going to let him have the last word. Her voice carried from where she stood. "You shall not be rid of me easily, Lawrence. Not until I say what I've come to say."

He ignored her, propelling Clarissa and a fussy Dora through the heavy wood door held open by a liveried footman.

However, once he was inside, in the main hall, he stopped as if both his energy and his fury had run out. That was fine because Clarissa's temper was just starting.

She was peripherally aware of the magnificence of the home's entrance. The ceiling was a huge dome fashioned out of glass. Shafts of light bounced off a giant brass chandelier and wall sconces. The walls were lined with portraits of lords and ladies, on rearing chargers or pretending to be woodland sprites, that she assumed were Lord Marsden's ancestors. At any other time, she'd be entranced by the grace of the furnishings.

Right now, she wanted the nursery and she needed privacy to throw a fit that would rival one of Dora's. How dare Lord Marsden drag her in to such a charade?

Dora had started sucking on her fists between her complaints. She was also wet. The child deserved better treatment.

Lord Marsden didn't help the situation when he leaned toward the footman and said in a low tone, "Peters, please pass the word amongst the staff that I am married."

The comment startled the manservant. "Married? Um, oh, yes, my lord. Congratulations—"

"No congratulations necessary," Lord Marsden said easily. "It will only be for an hour. However, act as if I have been married for ages."

Lord Marsden was truly mad if he expected this nonsense to work. Or that asking people to lie for him was the simplest action in the world. It was not, and so Clarissa wanted to tell him.

However, she had some dignity, even if he didn't. What she had to say should be spoken in private. But if she didn't speak her mind quickly, she was going to explode. "Peters, where is the nursery?" She actually sounded like a countess.

The man looked to Lord Marsden, who nodded for him to speak. "Mr. Gibson set it up in the Countess's Chamber next to the earl's apartments. He said that is traditionally where the nursery has been placed when a babe is small."

"Really?" Lord Marsden said, as if he had had no idea.

Peters nodded. "Yes, my lord."

"Hmm, well, I learn something every day."

"And that is *where*?" Clarissa asked, her temper already tested far too much.

"This way," Lord Marsden said and took her hand. He led her up the sweeping staircase. The carpet on the treads was so thick, Clarissa's shoes sank into it. There wasn't a worn spot to be seen.

Lord Marsden had the good sense to be quiet beside her, as if he knew she was ready to tear into him. He was not wrong.

A servant waited for them upstairs. He stood in front of the next to the last door at the end of the hall. "My lord," the man said with a bow. "The nursery is ready."

Lord Marsden nodded. "Very good. That didn't take long."

"Everything had been stored in the attic waiting for the happy day when there would be a child again at Belvoir," the man said proudly. "Mr. Gibson had it all in hand."

"Ah, well, before you show the room to us, Nelson, I must introduce you to my wife."

Clarissa could not contain herself a second longer. In a low, dangerous under voice, she said, "I am *not* your wife."

"She is pretending to be my wife," Lord Marsden amended.

"I am not *pretending* to be your wife," Clarissa said.

"My lady, this is Nelson, my valet." Lord Marsden spoke as if he was chiding a child to mind her manners.

Meanwhile, Dora's whimpers were turning

into loud whines with a renewed momentum, and Clarissa had enough.

She reached past the valet and opened the door. She charged right in—and was taken aback by the size of the room and the furnishings.

This was a nursery?

Like the rest of the house, the treatments were made of the finest stuff. The drapes were a gold brocade and the carpet as thick as what was on the stairs. The room's colors were cream, gold, and shades of blue. A chair on rockers was arranged beside a charmingly ornate crib filled with blankets.

There were also provisions for the nurse. There was a privacy screen, a small armoire, and a bed with a blue counterpane. A washstand with a pitcher and a basin large enough to bathe a baby was located between the two spaces.

At any other time, Clarissa would be quite pleased. This was far more than she had expected. She was also happily surprised to see that her bag with the bottle and clouts was already on the bed beside her valise. Lord Marsden's servants were very well trained, a compliment to Gibson, she suspected, rather than the earl.

She walked over to the bed and immediately began changing Dora. The baby was hungry and inconsolable. She kicked her feet, which didn't make unknotting the wet clout easy.

Lord Marsden came up behind her. "Let me help," he said.

Before she could bark she didn't need help, he sat on the bed by Dora's head and caught her flailing arms. The baby stopped crying to see who was interfering with her tantrum.

"Just me," he cooed to her in a silly musical tone, and Dora fell under his spell. She watched him with her wide, pondering stare, another female to fall for Lord Marsden's supposed charm—something Clarissa would never understand. Ever. Except, his presence allowed Clarissa to change the clout for a dry one.

She lifted the baby up and reached for the sucking bottle. Catching sight of it, Dora dove for the teat and latched. She made satisfied noises, her hands trying to hold the glass container, as Clarissa cradled her in her arms and took a seat on the bed to better support the baby.

"Well, she's happy," Lord Marsden said as if, together, they had reached a good outcome.

He was wrong.

"I am *not* your *wife*. I also do not believe it is right to lie, especially to your mother."

"Of course it is. It is done all the time. Especially to mothers."

The man was incorrigible. "If I had a mother, I would never lie to her," Clarissa retorted.

"No, you wouldn't," he agreed. "You are too sanctimonious."

Oh, now *that* was an insult. Clarissa abhorred sanctimonious people. They were unpleasant. Rigid. No fun.

She was past the point of boxing his ears.

No, she wanted to pull them off his head. After all, he never used them anyway. Unfortunately, her arms were full of baby. "What if she tells people she knows in London? They will expect you to have a wife. Then what will you do?"

He laughed as if the idea was preposterous. "Then we will just have to marry—oh, Clarissa, I'm teasing. Sit back down. Don't be so easy to bring to a boil."

"Easy? I've had plenty of time to be worked up. I have been *boiling* angry with you since we arrived." She moved to take a seat in the rocker, *away* from him. The baby, for her part, stopped eating and looked at her father. She gave a sweet little sigh, apparently deciding this was all their affair and of no concern to her. She returned to the bottle.

As if finally realizing that Clarissa was serious in her outrage, Lord Marsden tried to become amenable. He was not good at it. His patience was too exaggerated as he said, "If I go to London and my mother—who has *never* had an interest in me at all throughout my childhood or until this time—actually decides to announce my marriage, then I shall say she is suffering from delusions. There. Problem solved."

"Just as simple as that?"

"Absolutely."

"Lady Fenton, one of the most acclaimed minds in London, suffers from delusions?"

"My word against hers. And she is female. Your sex has odd humors."

Clarissa's jaw clenched. "Odd humors?"

"Queer notions? Do you like that wording better?"

"*I don't like any of this*," Clarissa answered. "Liars are always found out."

"Liars rule the world," he opined. "Trust me, my mother is the most skilled of them."

"Well, I'm not."

He frowned. "I forget you are a minister's daughter."

"No, it is more than that. Lord Marsden—"

"Mars," he interrupted. "We are pretending to be husband and wife. You must call me Mars. Have you not heard me call you Clarissa?"

"I've been ignoring you."

"Well, it worked for the charade."

"Lord Mars—" she started again, determined to make her point.

"No, no, no," he chided, cutting her off. "*Mars.* You must call me by my name, Clarissa."

"Very well, Lawrence—"

"Oh, no, *not* that name. I hate that name."

"I noticed," she said happily. "You winced every time your mother said it. Although," she continued philosophically, "I believe it is the sort of name a wife would use to great advantage."

"You are trying my patience," he warned. Now his jaw was tight.

"And I'm enjoying it."

In her arms, Dora had stopped sucking on the bottle and followed their conversation, her gaze going back and forth as if she understood perfectly. Then, as if siding with Clarissa, she made a soft sound.

"There, see? Even Dora agrees that you should not lie," Clarissa remarked. "You are setting a terrible example."

"When I want a sermon, I will go to church," he responded, clearly not pleased with her obstinance.

"Or take a wife," Clarissa flashed back, and was rewarded with the knowledge that she had, at last, gained the upper hand. He didn't look as if he had a reply—and then he started to laugh.

The sound began as a chuckle, as if the absurdity of the situation had finally dawned on him. The laugh grew in tone and tenor.

The unexpected thing was, Dora seemed to laugh with him. Her lips curved into the shape of a smile. Her brown eyes lit up with interest and she moved her legs as if performing a jig.

Both Clarissa and Mars stared in wonder. He even knelt in front of the rocker. "She has a personality," he marveled.

"She's a bright one," Clarissa assured him, sitting the baby up. "Curious and engaged. You are very lucky."

His chest puffed up with her compliment. Again he touched Dora's hair with an air of reverence that Clarissa found unexpected from him. He did care for this child. He might even love her the way Clarissa had always imagined a father should feel for his children.

She could also understand the attachment.

She hadn't known Dora three hours and yet she, too, felt a strong desire to protect the child, to be a comfort to her, and do everything in her power to see that Dora only experienced the best in life.

Sensing she had restored harmony between the two of them, Dora leaned forward to take the teat in her mouth to resume eating.

Mars didn't move. He stayed right where he was, kneeling in front of the rocker, his gaze on this perfect baby, but his words were for Clarissa. "I know you didn't come here to pretend to be my wife. Unfortunately, my first thought when I saw my mother was panic. She is not one to trust with sensitive information. She wouldn't hesitate to use it to gain her way. Meanwhile, Dora is still too new to me."

"She is still new to the world."

"Yes . . . and I don't want whispers to follow her. I know I can't protect her from gossip forever. But right now, she is defenseless." He stood. "And you are right. I should not have pulled you into such an uncomfortable situation without some sort of notice—"

"Or permission?"

He frowned at her interruption then finished handsomely, "It was disrespectful and I am sorry."

Clarissa didn't respond, uncertain to trust such a straightforward apology. Or really, anything he said.

"I *am*," he assured her.

Feeling prodded to good manners, she answered quietly, "Thank you."

"And we shouldn't even be arguing about this," he pointed out. "Our marriage is over, before it even started. By now Lady Fenton has left. She was uninvited and she knows I don't wish her here."

"It seems a callous way to treat your mother."

"Don't worry. She has treated me worse."

It was on the tip of Clarissa's tongue to ask how. So far, his mother hadn't done anything that made her believe his distrust was justified—but a knock on the door interrupted them.

It opened without the person waiting for an answer. Lady Fenton entered. She had removed her hat and outer garments and gave every indication that she was here to stay. Clarissa removed the bottle, setting it on the floor, and shifted the baby to her shoulder as both she and Lord Marsden stood, but there was no greeting.

"Ah, the nursery," her ladyship said expansively as if she had been invited in. "It is as I remembered when you were little, Lawrence."

He'd moved forward as if to place a barrier between his mother and Dora. "You need to leave," he answered coldly. There was no patience or gentle humor in his voice.

"Not until I've spoken to you," she replied, and then she leaned around him to see Clarissa. "There's the little one. And what a pleasure to meet your aunt, Mrs. Warbler, Clarissa. I may call you Clarissa, no? We are family—"

"We are *not* family," Lord Marsden corrected. His hands were balled into fists at his side. Clarissa had never seen him tense. He was usually a bit too carefree for her tastes.

Lady Fenton drew a deep breath as if he tried her patience before saying brightly, "I don't believe your wife realized you were this mean-spirited, Lawrence."

"And *don't* call me Lawrence," her son answered.

"Oh, yes, that is right," Lady Fenton said as if piecing something together in her mind. "'Mars.' That is how they all refer to you. *Mars*, well-known Corinthian, a man of the world, an out and outer. He has his vices and yet, they all like you. Admire you even."

"What will it take to have you leave now?" His tone had become insistent, more terse.

"A conversation. Nothing more. And then I'm gone."

His response was a sharp bark of humorless laughter. Clarissa didn't understand how such a simple request could make him so angry.

She decided if he was going to force her to pretend to be a wife, then she should play a wife's role. The words were out of her before she considered their wisdom. "Why *not* listen to her, my lord?"

Lady Fenton gave her a thin smile. "Why not?" she echoed as if Clarissa made great sense.

He stood no more than five feet from where Clarissa stood. A brooding presence. He was not pleased.

Clarissa didn't care. This was his mother.

Her request was not unreasonable and she had traveled a long way to make it. Dora made a mewing noise and Clarissa sat, picking up the bottle. "Would you wish for Dora to treat you this way?" she dared to ask.

Hard gray eyes narrowed in response, and then he said, "Very well. Speak, Mother."

If he had spoken to Clarissa in that tone, she'd have hidden under the bed. Instead, his mother's smile widened as if he had walked into a snare . . . and Clarissa began to have doubts.

"I want you to come to London," Lady Fenton said smoothly. "A challenge has been made for my husband's position as Chairman of Committees. It is a very powerful role that determines the work of our great nation. Fenton presides over the House when it is in committee and he has done so effectively for several years. Everyone admires him."

"Obviously not everyone. Otherwise, there would not be a challenger," Lord Marsden countered.

"True, but then again, this is politics," she answered as if it should be obvious. "The vote over the position will be very close." As he opened his mouth, she cut in easily, "I know you don't give a care about your responsibilities, *Mars*. I can't remember the last time anyone has seen you around Westminster. It has actually made you a bit of a joke with my set."

"Parliament is your territory, *Mother*. I avoid it to avoid you." That was a surprise to Clarissa, who had criticized his lack of involvement as arrogance. And she thought it still was, but for a different reason. She wasn't so naïve as to think that all families felt a close bond, except there was a vast and cold distance between this mother and son. And not just from Lord Marsden. His mother was far from nurturing. However, her manner said she was not going to leave until he did her bidding.

"Your title carries responsibilities," his mother answered. Had not Clarissa said the same thing to him only an hour or more ago? "In order for Fenton to retain his position, we need one more vote to put him over the top."

"If you are counting on me, he will lose."

"Then that would be a pity," Lady Fenton answered. "Because Lord Dervil will win and become the country's second most powerful man after the prime minister."

And just like that, Lord Marsden's attitude changed. His interest picked up. Clarissa was not surprised. Everyone knew he lived to thwart Lord Dervil.

His mother smiled. She knew she was using the right bait. "We can let you cast the deciding vote, if you wish. That would be good, wouldn't it? Dervil would hate you for it. It would be humiliating to him and you would finally have the revenge you've longed for."

He shocked Clarissa when he declared, "I don't want revenge. I want him dead."

"You may have that opportunity," she answered as if his stated goal was well worth the effort. "Besides," Lady Fenton continued, "you need to introduce your wife to society. You will come, won't you, Clarissa?"

Clarissa didn't know how to answer. The conversation sounded normal and yet there was no humor in Lord Marsden's wishing another man's death or his mother's acceptance. He meant what he said.

She tightened her hold on Dora protectively. The baby was half-interestedly sucking on her bottle while playing with her little hands as if they were toys. She made a sound of protest at being held closer and then went back to her busyness.

"I believe I will stay here," Clarissa murmured.

"Oh, I won't let you do such a thing," Lady Fenton countered. "London is always interesting. I have so many people I need to introduce to you."

Clarissa shot a pleading look to Lord Marsden. This woman was too forceful for her right now, and, blessedly, he stepped in.

"My wife just returned from a journey. The thought of another one so soon is probably overwhelming to her."

"Ah, hence the valise. I should have known." Lady Fenton gave another of her smiles, the sort that never reached her eyes. No, her gaze was always calculating. "Well, we can make plans over dinner."

Clarissa didn't know how much longer she could manage to be surrounded by the swirl of troubling emotions between mother and son and keep her balance. "I will not be able to join you for the evening meal. I'm quite fatigued after my trip."

"Understandable," Lady Fenton said, jumping on the suggestion of having her son to herself. "We can have a tray sent up to you. Meanwhile, Mars and I will discuss our strategy for the vote over dinner." These were not questions but orders. She opened the door. "I will be staying the night. It is too late to start my return to London." On those words, she left, shutting the door behind her.

In the sudden stillness following her departure, Lord Marsden stood quiet. He seemed preoccupied.

Clarissa took the bottle from Dora and said, "Don't trust her."

"I don't," he replied. He forced a smile, then turned his attention to his daughter. He touched the baby's head. She looked up at him with bright eyes, her little fingers laced together as if she had been completely satisfied with her dinner. He spoke to Clarissa. "You do look tired. I'm sorry for this and I thank you for being a game one."

A game one? A person who could be counted on?

And yet he was right. She would not make a fuss about the lie, not in front of the creature who was his mother. She nodded.

He leaned forward and placed a light kiss on Dora's head.

It was a gentle, loving gesture.

Again, Clarissa envied Dora. Clarissa had never been kissed in any form save for one peck on the cheek Mr. Thurlowe gave her because she'd badgered him for it. That was after two years of being promised to him. Her adoptive parents hadn't been demonstrative. There might be a pat on the hand but little else. That had been their way.

And Clarissa could pretend she was happy with her solitary life. After all, what choice did she have? Still, a part of her, one she kept tightly suppressed, yearned for *more*.

This was dangerous ground, especially around the handsome Lord Marsden, who was revealing a softer side of his nature. Was this ability to be kind the reason the man was notorious for his way with women? Was this how he lured them to him? Clarissa had never understood it—until now.

Having kissed his daughter, he still stood so close she could see the line of his whiskers, feel the heat off his body.

"Anything else?" he asked.

"Else?" she whispered, caught up in the moment.

"The bottles, clouts. I'm having Gibson scour the countryside for what you need from the list."

"Oh." Clarissa swallowed, and took a wise step away. She could breathe better over here. "We will need more milk very soon."

He reached for the empty bottle she had set on a table beside the rocker. "I'll see it is refilled and sent up," he said, taking his own step away. "I will let you rest. And thank you, Clarissa, for not exposing me for a liar. I know you wanted to." His smile robbed his words of any sting. "It is a terrible thing to compromise a minister's daughter."

"There is still time to expose you, my lord. Don't be too cocky."

He laughed and walked out the door. Outside, she heard Lady Fenton say, "Where is the baby's nurse? Shouldn't she be up here?"

Clarissa could not hear his answer, but she was certain he had a ready one. Of course he would. And now that he'd left the nursery, all the energy in the room seemed to have followed him.

A huge yawn overtook her. She *was* tired. He was an aggravating man.

She shifted her attention to the baby. A protective urge rose in Clarissa. This child needed to know she was important, that she was loved no matter her background . . . something Clarissa had not felt herself when she was younger.

Dora smiled up at her as if she knew Clarissa's thoughts and approved. Then she returned to the important baby work of trying to take off her shoe.

A half hour later, a tray was delivered with two bottles, a small pitcher of goat's milk, and some new clouts. She wondered where Mr. Gibson had found the clouts. The butler later appeared to deliver the good news that one of the footmen had a sister available to serve as a wet nurse. She lived in Cambridge and Lord Marsden had already dispatched the footman to talk to his sister and offer her a position.

Clarissa didn't know how she felt about this

information. A wet nurse was important for Dora.

But would Dora need two nurses? Clarissa didn't want to dwell on the idea of sharing this perfect baby.

Later, a dinner tray was delivered for her.

Clarissa meant to eat except that, after feeding Dora and putting her down for the night, she herself was exhausted. She washed her face and meant to move the privacy screen to separate her bed from the rest of the room. Instead, she sat on the bed, testing it, or so she thought. Before she realized it, her head landed on the pillow and she lost herself in sleep.

It wasn't an easy rest. Her dreams were muddled and confused. Lord Marsden seemed to float through them. One moment she was in a boat in a storm and he was sailing alongside her, except his boat wasn't in the storm. The clouds and high waves were only for her. Soon, she found herself on the back of a mad horse and he appeared, taking her reins to steer her to safety . . .

CLARISSA DIDN'T know what woke her. Groggily, she recognized the hour was late. No more than the middle of the night.

The air was chilled in spite of a small fire in the hearth. Its flames sent shadows around the room save for this dark corner where her bed was. She had not heard anyone come in and light it. Then again, she hadn't realized her room at Mrs. Emsdale's had a fire—

Wait, she wasn't at Mrs. Emsdale's.

Her aged employer had let her go, without pay that had rightfully been hers . . .

All the memories came rolling back—the grueling ride on the Post, the appearance of Lord Marsden. The baby.

Yes, *the baby.* Where was the child?

Clarissa sat up. Her hair was a mess and her wrinkled skirts were caught around her knees. Her shoes were spread out on the floor as if she'd taken them off in her sleep. She put her feet over the side of the bed, looking toward the crib, and then noticed the man in the rocker. He'd pulled it up to the fire.

His back was to her but she recognized those long legs that gently rocked the chair back and forth. Lord Marsden. He wasn't wearing stockings or shoes but leather slippers. At least he appeared to have a shirt and breeches on, so he was decent.

Or was this another confusing dream?

And where was Dora? The baby should have wakened her by now. Clarissa jumped up from the bed, her balance unsteady. She moved to the crib and found it empty.

For a second, she panicked and turned toward him. He'd been contemplating the fire as if she wasn't even there. He must know she was awake and yet, he gave no indication he heard her. She walked to the front of the chair.

He *held* the baby. Of course.

Lord Marsden was feeding her from one of the bottles. Dora had wrapped her fingers around one of his as if holding him in place while she ate. Her eyes were closed and yet she was busy sucking with all she had.

For a second, Clarissa didn't know what to do.

He was performing *her* duties. She had been raised to take her responsibilities seriously. She was judged by how well she performed. In fact, she prided herself as superior to him because he never seemed to be serious. And here he was, feeding his daughter as if it was no effort.

She'd never heard of a man doing that with an infant.

Clarissa pushed her hair back. There were pins still hanging in her tresses. It would take an hour to brush it out. "I can take over for you, my lord."

He looked up at her, no condescension in his expression. It was almost as if he wasn't seeing her at all. The firelight caught the shadows of his face. He seemed pensive. "I'm fine. I heard her talking. It was the sweetest little babble. She makes more sense than most adults I know. You didn't eat much of your dinner."

The abrupt change of topic surprised her. "I was too tired," she confessed.

"Understandable. Yesterday was a strange and busy day." He looked over at her. "You should return to bed. However, before you do, there is something I wish to discuss with you."

"What is that, my lord?"

He answered, "I believe we should actually marry."

Her response was swift. "Have you lost your wits?"

Chapter Seven

Sometimes, the twists and turns of the world
make little sense.

—*Book of Mars*

$\mathcal{M}$ars was not surprised at her flat refusal. As far as proposals went, it was a singularly poor one. He realized that the moment the words left his lips. He was too direct. One of his many failings.

Still, the idea had taken hold in his mind. He could see the advantages. He just had to convince Clarissa. This was a brilliant solution to all of their problems, including Dora's. "I understand that I may have caught you off guard earlier by claiming we were married—"

"'Caught off guard' is an understatement."

He continued as if she hadn't spoken, determined to have his say. "My mother's appearance surprised me and, in the moment, my only thought was to protect Dora. You can appreciate that, can't you?"

"Except the truth will come out, no matter how many women you falsely claim to be your wife."

"Clarissa, don't be so flat-footed."

"That is what they are calling honesty these days?" She grumpily rubbed the sleep out of her eyes in what was actually the most endearing gesture. Her hair was tumbled down around her shoulders in a glorious mess. She was in her stockinged feet. He always liked seeing women when they were more relaxed, more approachable.

He definitely liked seeing Clarissa this way, even if she was being stubborn, but he would bring her around.

Dora tugged on his finger, a sign that he wasn't holding the bottle the way she wished. He grinned down at her and made the adjustment. She began eating again, her brows forming a small vee. Either eating was serious work, or she was questioning his sanity, too.

Women.

Except, he discovered to his mild surprise, he didn't mind these two women.

"Open your mind for just one moment," he instructed.

Clarissa crossed her arms. "Insults are not the way to make me cooperate."

She was right. Doggedly, he continued. She had to understand, whatever her price for helping him, he'd pay it. "An opportunity has presented itself. I mean to take it."

"Are you talking about Dora?"

"I'm talking about the vote. Dervil wants

the position and I can stop him. I can rob him of what I am certain he most dearly craves—power."

Mars also knew Dervil would be furious with his interference. The last time they'd had words, Dervil had warned if Mars continued thwarting him, there would be a challenge. Mars hoped so. He'd like nothing better than to put a bullet through Dervil. To treat the man the way he had treated Mars's father.

But he wouldn't share this with Clarissa. She wouldn't understand. What he was planning was dangerous. It was possible Dervil might kill him. If so, he needed someone to take care of Dora. Someone he could rely on—like Clarissa.

Also, without a doubt, if he killed Dervil, even in an affair of honor, there would be an outcry. In many circles, Dervil was respected.

And times had changed since his father's country duel. Today, dueling was frowned upon. If Mars shot Dervil—and that was his intent—then he'd have to leave the country. At least until things calmed down. It might take years for memories to cool.

If that was the case, he couldn't take Dora with him to live the life of an exile. Who knew what dangers might be ahead?

However, as his wife, Clarissa could be counted on to keep his daughter safe, to weather the disapproval of society. After all, she'd held her own in Maidenshop. She would have the protection of his name and his fortune to help her. He'd see to it.

But he would not explain all of this to a minister's daughter. Clarissa wouldn't understand the need for revenge that burned in his soul.

Instead, he said, "You are always barking that you believe I should play a more active role in government. I thought you would be pleased I am willing to fulfill my responsibilities."

She smiled at him as if he was hopeless and for the first time he noticed her smile was a touch lopsided. She also had dimples. Small ones. Barely noticeable, and yet there they were. It was then he realized, she'd rarely ever smiled around him, even when she was laughing at him.

"And for that reason, my lord, I shall see to your best interests and not take you seriously over such a preposterous idea as marriage between us. Is your mother still here?"

"She is like an unwelcome boarder. Hard to throw out."

"Then this gives you the opportunity to tell her the truth."

"And have her disapprove of Dora once she learns the baby is the by-blow from one of my mistresses?"

"She can't believe Dora is ours. Look at our coloring. In fact, everyone in Maidenshop knows the baby is not mine."

"My mother won't listen to village gossip. She is too important in her own mind. As for the village, their loyalty is to you and me. They can be mum when they have a mind to it. Mrs. Warbler spent all of dinner waxing on about your sterling qualities and how everyone enjoyed our wedding."

"Except for us." She leaned forward. "My lord, lies always come to the surface eventually."

"I don't know where you came by that idea."

"It is universal knowledge."

"Not in my world. People lie for their own gain daily, Clarissa. As to knowledge about me, most of the *ton* haven't an idea of what I've been about."

"Your mother said they whisper about you."

"Old gossip. I haven't been in London or near an opium den in months."

"Oh, well, *months*," she echoed and then stopped, blinked, and realized what else he'd said, "Opium den?"

Mars made an impatient sound. "You can lecture me later. Right now, we have an important issue in front of us. My mother thinks I married above me. You passed muster with one of the most critical sticklers in London."

"She knows nothing about me."

"My mother is all about appearances. And it is obvious to anyone you are not a lady's companion or a nurse. You were raised to be a gentlewoman. The truth is, if I must marry someone, well, you are better than the rest of your sex."

She tilted her head as if pretending to be coy. "Why, thank you, my lord. Such strange compliments you give. I swear my head will be completely turned. You know how to please a lady."

"It is what makes me such an acclaimed lover," he answered, baiting her.

"I've never heard that."

"You haven't been around London."

"Perhaps the other lovers in London are just terrible."

That sparked a bark of laughter from him. In all the time he'd known Clarissa, he'd never seen her grovel or fawn in front of anyone. That is what made her *even more* perfect for what he planned.

She smiled as if pleased at her riposte. "I'm happy to amuse you, my lord," she responded. "However, the hour is late. Let me take Dora—"

"No, I have this." Dora had finished the bottle, her eyes half-closed. She reminded him of himself and those times when he'd lose himself in an opium dream—

He rejected the comparison. He'd never want that for her. He'd seen the women in those rooms and his daughter would not be one of them. Clarissa would see to that. He lifted her to his shoulder and began rubbing her back the way he'd seen Clarissa do. Her weight felt good.

"Come closer," he invited. "Pull up a chair. Sit here with us."

"Why?"

"Miss Taylor, so full of doubt," he mocked lightly and then said with complete seriousness, "So I can convince you to marry me."

"It won't work," she promised, even as she did as he requested. She sat. "Well?"

Dora had fallen instantly asleep on his

shoulder. He shifted her to his arms, smiling down at her a moment before realizing that if he wanted Clarissa as an ally, he must tell her a portion of the truth. "Here is my story. It is simple and it will explain everything."

She folded her hands in her lap as if sitting in church waiting for a sermon. Headstrong Clarissa. Funny, but the characteristics that had annoyed him so much over the years were the ones he needed from her now.

He began. "Lord Dervil killed my father."

"In a duel," she acknowledged. "I mean I don't agree with dueling . . . but there was some fight over property lines? It is a silly way to settle matters."

Mars ran a light finger over his daughter's fine, silky hair. She was so innocent. "I would agree"—he looked up at Clarissa—"*if* that tale was true. Actually, Dervil and my mother were lovers."

Her lips formed a surprised "oh." What was not shocking in London was very scandalous in Maidenshop.

"My father took exception to it. Can you imagine? Usually those in my class ignore such liaisons as long as everyone is discreet and after an heir is born." Which had been him.

"Unfortunately, Father was devoted to his wife. Apparently Lord Fenton is as well for reasons I do not understand."

"Love is blind. Isn't that the adage?"

"Why, Miss Taylor, you sound jaded."

"About love?" She frowned. "I suppose so. Certainly 'jaded' is agreeing to marry a man you barely know for security. I almost did that."

She was referring to his friend Thurlowe. "You did the right thing letting him go. He and Gemma belong together." Even Mars could see that.

"It doesn't make losing the only man who had ever offered for me any easier."

"That is no longer true. I have an offer on the table."

She smiled. "I turned it down."

"No, you haven't," he argued.

"When I questioned your sanity," she explained patiently, "it was me saying no."

Well, that was true, except Mars knew she truly didn't understand what she was refusing. "You would be a countess. I'm also very rich, you know."

"We don't like each other," she countered.

"I'm warming to you." And he was. He liked the way she looked, even if her legs weren't that long and her hair was the wrong color. He had found his eye straying in her direction often today, but he wouldn't tell her that. She was a true Bluestocking. They were always outraged when a man discussed looks.

Instead, he said, "I don't appreciate your straitlaced opinions, although, surprisingly, they are exactly how I want my daughter to be. I also want her to have a curious intellect and a fearless view of life. I want her to speak her own mind."

"Is that how you see me?"

"Of course. Isn't that what I just said?" Mars

continued, "I will also expect you to keep Dora *away* from men like me. She'll be an heiress. She will need a steady hand to guide her. I want you to be that hand."

"Are you going someplace?" Was it his imagination that she sounded a bit alarmed?

He was touched. "You know as well as I do that life can be hard. Relentless even."

Clarissa studied him a moment, and it was almost as if she looked into his soul. "There is more here."

Yes, there was, but he wasn't going to share it. If Clarissa didn't like dueling, she'd be set against his plan to shoot Dervil dead.

He stood and walked over to the crib. Gently, he placed Dora in it. She didn't wake. "Do babies always sleep this soundly?"

"When they are as tired as Dora was, yes. Or if they are growing. They sleep deeply when they grow."

"And here I thought the secret was a clear conscience." What a marvel Dora was. "I never thought about having children."

"Is that not one of your obligations to your title?"

"One of many. You heard my mother. Actually, I never thought that far ahead. Children?" He shook his head. No, he'd only had one all-consuming thought—revenge.

"I was home from school when the duel took place," he began without preamble. "I'd been sent down for some prank. I don't even remember what I'd done. I'm certain something foolish. I was very full of myself."

"You *were*?"

"Quick, Miss Taylor. I must admit, you never miss an opportunity." She shrugged her answer.

He continued, "Some footmen were gossiping about the duel. Of course, I knew something was afoot. My mother was in London—which was not unusual. She is a shadowy figure in my past. But Father was very distracted. He barely lectured me over my transgressions."

Mars faced her. "Have you ever had a fear grip you with a sense that something terrible was about to happen? Even when everyone is acting as if all is right?"

Her solemn gaze said she hadn't.

"Perhaps I was just fanciful?" he suggested. "My father was the one person in this world I admired. The one person who actually cared about me. I think back and wish I had stopped him from meeting Dervil—except I was very young. One foot still in boyhood and the other trying to move into becoming a man. And believing school pranks were the way to do it." He paused, realizing how pretentious he sounded.

"Go on," she encouraged, a sign she was listening to him.

That, too, was a novel experience. Mars was not accustomed to women actually paying attention to what he said, well, unless it involved money.

"I knew from the servants' chatter where it would take place. There is a circle of giant oaks between Belvoir and Dervil's land. I knew Father wouldn't let me be there, so I made a plan. I took myself off there in the dark and waited. Just after dawn, my father, Dervil, and the seconds arrived. Mr. Sexton was there as well." Mr. Sexton had been the parish doctor Thurlowe had replaced.

"Did you watch the duel?"

"Of course." He returned to the rocker and sat, leaning forward to rest his elbows on his thighs. It brought him closer to her, put them on eye level. She was so petite compared to him.

And yet, there was a core of strength about her.

"I watched them face off. Dervil seemed relaxed. My father's face was pale and he was tense. I wanted to shout out to him, to let him know I was there and present for him. I kept quiet."

"You wished you'd stopped him."

"Many times." The regret haunted him.

She leaned forward now, her expression concerned as if she understood. "Your father wouldn't have thanked you."

"No."

"What happened?" she asked quietly.

"Each man pointed his pistol toward the ground in front of him." He had never forgotten a second of this duel. "I can still remember the sound when they cocked their weapons. Lord Randall was my father's second and he was the one who gave the signal to fire. When it was done, Father crumpled to the ground."

"What did you do?"

"I shouted and ran out of my hiding place. He'd been struck through the heart. He was killed almost instantly. Now here is the important thing, Clarissa. Father had deloped."

"What does that mean?"

"It means he fired his shot to the side."

"Why would he do that?"

"To signal to his opponent that he knew there was guilt on his side as well. He was saying that, yes, Dervil had been wrong to brazenly consort with my mother so as to bring dishonor to my family, but by shooting to the side, my father was admitting that his wife was equally culpable."

"Then why fight the duel?"

"Honor," Mars answered. Seeing she didn't understand, he explained, "As a gentleman, my father had a responsibility to his family name. Dervil had insulted him by being so open about what he was doing."

"Did Lord Dervil know he was going to delope?"

"It doesn't matter. The rules are that Dervil was in his rights to carry forth however he chose. Father got off the first shot and then he had to wait. Dervil had the luxury of time and he took it. He shot Father point blank."

"And that was considered honorable?"

Mars nodded.

"But he killed a man."

"And I have *never* forgiven him," Mars admitted. "Granted, he may not have expected my father to delope, but once he did, Dervil could have shot into the ground. Dervil knew what he was doing."

"But it's murder. Why would he be so cruel?"

"You will have to ask my mother. I've wondered if she hadn't plotted all of this."

Clarissa reached to touch his knee. "She couldn't have."

"You don't know her. There is always a purpose to her actions. I have not talked to her in over a decade, and yet, she arrives here with a request to keep her husband in power?"

"Is that not a sign she cares for him? Perhaps she realizes the error of her ways?"

Mars almost laughed. "No, it is a sign she is pulling the strings of power herself. If she could be named Chairman of Committees or even prime minister, she wouldn't give two snaps of her fingers for Fenton. She is an intelligent woman hindered by society's expectations of her sex."

"But to suggest she manipulated the duel, it makes her sound very callous."

"Exactly." Mars edged forward, wanting her to understand. "Mother knows that I have spent a small fortune making Dervil pay in any way possible for my father's death. Knowing that Dervil wants this position and only *my* vote would block it? She is dangling that in front of me."

"Although Lord Dervil should be stopped. I've never met him. However, I've heard the stories. He seems a selfish man who shouldn't be given any power."

"I agree. I will vote against him. I will show up for that vote."

"Then your father's death will be avenged," she said with satisfaction, as if finishing a tale of justice.

Mars could have spit out, *Not hardly*. He'd not have peace until Dervil's life drained from his body the way he'd watched his father die. He longed to have Dervil look into the bore of his pistol, the same way his father had stared into his opponent's all those years ago. He wanted Dervil to know that death was coming and Mars planned on being the one to deliver it. *An eye for an eye . . .* a life for a life.

Clarissa would never understand such raw, angry emotion. Or that her faith in a caring, gentle world was not his belief. A man had to protect what was his. And if in pursuing justice, something happened to him, Mars needed a strong mentor to protect and guide Dora. A person with character and compassion.

Clarissa.

"When Dervil learns that I stirred myself to make an appearance only to vote against him, he will strike out," he warned her. "He'll attack any way he can. And if he hears Dora's story? Or if my mother does?" He shook his head, leaving her imagination to see the worst.

She surprised him. "Not if you are honest. So, she was born on the wrong side of the covers? Amongst your set, many are. Mr. Thurlowe was and his father acknowledged him."

"Ask Thurlowe when he last saw his father. It has been years. He's been an obligation, not a member of the family. I do not want rumors associated with my daughter. Certainly you of all people understand. Life is harder for women. Thurlowe had the opportunities of his sex. What will Dora have?"

"My lord, you can't change what has already happened. You are being unreasonable."

He came to his feet, frankly stunned. "I'm hearing this from *you*?" He paced a few steps to the hearth, shaking his head before saying, "You are a truly beautiful woman with a good heart and a fine mind. Why do you think the matrons had to force someone to offer for you?"

She rose, the movement graceful . . . befitting a countess, he realized. Although her expression was far from peaceful. "What are you saying, my lord?"

"What you already know," he answered. "Oh, come now, Clarissa. Certainly you did?"

She stared, almost as if she dared him to speak the truth. "Know what?"

With an exasperated sound, he said, "That you should have had bucks lined up outside your door mad to marry you."

"My parents were ill. I was busy nursing them."

And she was *loyal*. He mentally added the characteristic to his list of Clarissa's strengths.

"Yes, true," he agreed. "However, you also lacked fortune and—" He paused, wanting to be gentle and yet, she was the one who felt honesty could overcome obstacles. She needed to understand, that wasn't true. The world was cruel. "And your parentage was questionable."

For the longest beat, his words seemed to hang between them. Her expression barely changed . . . until she drew herself up to her full diminutive height and answered, "Yet *you* have asked me to marry you. I suppose you believe I should throw myself at your feet in gratitude."

"That is not my purpose—"

She cut him off. "I don't know how you can be the way you are. Always cynical. Always distrusting. You like being alone, don't you?"

Now it was his turn to feel judged. "I have friends."

"All male and a very close circle, no?"

True. Very true.

"You don't like women."

"I like some very much. Dora is proof of that."

"I think your mother has colored your view of my sex."

Without a doubt. Still, he found the realization disconcerting.

"So now you wish to marry me so that I can what?" she asked. "Raise your daughter with values? Serve as a moral example?"

Take care of her if I'm forced into exile or die in my quest to kill Dervil.

He kept that response to himself and answered, "Yes. Yes. And yes."

His reply took the wind out of her sails. Her chin came down a notch, but then she said, "What if I want more?"

"Such as?"

"A real marriage. A meeting of the minds. Of two souls uniting."

"Is that in the Bible?" Mars was confused. Where did she learn such nonsense?

"As a matter of fact, my lord, it is," she said, moving around her chair as if preparing to dismiss him from the nursery. His *own* nursery. "And I will settle for nothing less in a marriage. I almost sold myself short once. I shall not again."

Mars only took a moment to reach a conclusion. "Why not? Of course. We shall have a real marriage. A meeting of the minds. Two souls and all that."

"Except there would not be any love."

There was that cursed word again. *Love.* Why did women always think love was important? He had yet to understand what that useless word meant. It changed from one person to another. "Actually, we will have something more," he assured her. "We will have mutual respect and consideration."

She frowned as if the prospect was unappealing.

Whereas he believed he was being very reasonable. "You will never again have to worry about a roof over your head," he reminded her.

Her shoulders sagged. She turned from him.

He frowned, annoyed she was making this difficult. The desperate thought struck him that if Clarissa didn't agree to marry him, if something happened to him, then Deb might reclaim Dora thinking there was money in it for her. He could not let that happen. *Tell Clarissa you love her*, a devilish voice urged him. *Give her the words.*

Except he discovered he had too much respect for Clarissa to make such a declaration.

And then she faced him. "If I agree to what you propose, what sort of marriage would we have?"

"Whatever you wish." He really hadn't given the marriage part very much thought. There was a good chance he wouldn't be around any longer than a month. Perhaps even less.

She nodded as if he'd confirmed something in her mind, and Mars realized she needed time to think. He'd thrown a lot at her and here it was the middle of the night.

He moved to the door that linked his bedroom to her room. "This is my bedroom door. I'll leave you to think over the matter. If you are set against a marriage between us, say nothing. However, if you wish to accept my offer, knock on the door and tell me. I will send for a special license and we shall be married with all haste."

"What about your mother?"

"She will be leaving this morning. She can't abide being in a place that doesn't cater to her every whim. The servants side with me in their opinion of her. She also believes London and the world should not make any decisions without her."

"She will know there is nothing between us. Mothers have a sense about things."

Her excuses were sounding weaker. He smiled. "Clarissa, the only thing my mother has worried about is your poor taste in clothing. Or that I am miserly. She has instructed me to dress you better before presenting you in Society."

That brought Clarissa's brows together. He almost laughed.

"I don't like shallow people," she warned.

"Then you will have a fine time in London criticizing them all. The place is awash in shallowness."

Mars put his hand on the door handle. "Sleep on my offer. I hope you say yes. I believe it is what is best for you and for Dora."

On those words, he left the room.

And he really didn't know which way she would choose.

However, he surprised himself by having one of the best night's sleep he'd had in a long time.

The next morning, Mars sat in front of his looking glass while Nelson finished shaving him. Mars was dressed in boots, breeches, shirt, and vest. He'd already had a cup of tea and had foregone the Port. The loss of it had not seemed to bother him and Mars took this as a positive sign.

There was a knock on the nursery door. His breath caught in his throat.

He reached for a towel and wiped his face. "That is enough, Nelson. You may go."

"My lord?" The valet appeared confused.

"I need a moment alone," Mars said, pointing to the nursery door.

Nelson's eyes lit and he nodded, a bit too enthusiastically. Mars wondered what the talk was now in the servants' hall.

Once the valet left, Mars walked to the nursery door. He could almost feel her presence on the other side. She had an answer for him.

He opened the door, catching Clarissa just as she was preparing to knock again.

Her hair was completely down and brushed out. It was longer than he had imagined. The golden ale color of it made her green eyes all the more prominent. Cat's eyes. Seductive ones. The sort a man could lose himself in. He braced himself, suddenly uncertain of her decision.

Then she said one word, but it was the only word he needed.

"Yes."

"Excellent," he answered, deeply relieved. She would go through with it. Dora would be in good hands.

"However," she continued, "you said our marriage could be whatever I wished it. I have a few terms I want understood before we continue."

"Terms?" She sounded so businesslike.

"Rules, then, if you prefer that word."

And he knew she had him. He would agree to anything and he *had* offered, although he felt a stab of disappointment. She sounded like any of his mistresses. And why not? Women were grasping creatures. His mother was the queen of the lot.

"Very well, Miss Taylor, what are your terms?"

Chapter Eight

*There is always a shining moment when one
makes a decision, and then reality sets in.*

—*Book of Mars*

Clarissa was shocked by her boldness.

She'd had every intention of turning him
down.

The man frustrated her with his loose ways.
If she was the earl, she would be present for
every vote in the Lords. She'd also spearhead
laws that would help people, even down to the
orphans in the foundling home.

His laxity toward his responsibilities had
always annoyed her. Then again, the villagers
could count on him. If there was a crisis, he
was there. If a parishioner suffered bad luck,
Clarissa knew firsthand that all her father or
Reverend Summerall had to do was ask. And
Mars never boasted about his help.

Yes, he could buy up all the goats, but there
had been a time when Mr. Ewan's oxen team

had taken ill and died. Without any fanfare, a new team had shown up in his barn. Clarissa knew the earl had been behind the gift and so many other occasions when a villager needed a little help.

By marrying him, she would be allying herself with the ability to bestow those gifts that made a difference.

In the middle of her weighing all the reasons she should say no to Lord Marsden, Dora had woken. Fortunately, there was another bottle prepared and waiting. Then afterward, instead of going back to sleep, Dora had been content to contemplate the world. She'd tried reaching for her feet, babbling the most charming nonsense as she did so. She didn't know the difficulties waiting in her future. She trusted that someone would be there for her, even if those people included a mother willing to give her away. Or a father who surprised Clarissa in his readiness to accept responsibility for his child.

A father's support didn't mean that life would be easy. Or not full of questions.

As Clarissa played with the baby by buzzing her finger in the air around Dora as if the tip of it was a bee, she found herself wondering about her own parentage. She'd had a mother who had given birth to her and then left her to the care of others. And a father who had stood aside and watched. Or who had possibly died.

Of course, Clarissa wanted to pretend they had good reasons for abandoning her, that they had wished her to be happy and felt they had little other choice. Unfortunately, through her work at the foundling home, she learned some parents had *selfish* reasons for discarding a child.

That didn't mean she hadn't lain awake at night and worried about the mysteries of her birth. She sensed she had emerged from a darkness.

Once, when she had confided her fears to Mrs. Taylor, her adoptive mother had laughed them off as silly fantasies. *We wanted you*, she'd said, and yet, they never let her call them mother or father. They were always Reverend and Mrs. Taylor. Still, she knew them as parents, even if she was not allowed to use the words.

Dora would use the words, Clarissa decided as the baby grabbed for her buzzing finger. If Clarissa married the earl, she would want Dora to call her "mother," if she wished, of course. And Clarissa would protect her as fiercely as if she were her own. She already felt a protective bond with this child. When Dora had questions, Clarissa would let her ask them . . .

And maybe, perhaps, Clarissa and Lord Marsden could find common ground, but only if she married him.

"Should I say yes, Dora?" she had whispered.

The baby had caught both of her hands and raised and lowered them excitedly as if she'd discovered a new action that filled her with pride. *Or* as if she was saying how pleased she would be with the match.

And Marsden had said she could name her terms.

When Clarissa had returned to bed, sleep eluded her. Once she realized she was going to agree to this madness, she was too anxious to rest. She no longer worried whether accepting his offer was the right decision. Now her fear was that he would change his mind.

It had taken most of her courage to knock on his door this morning. She'd even rehearsed a little speech that had flown from her head the moment he'd opened the door and she saw him freshly shaven, his wheat-colored hair neatly combed. He cut a fine figure in leather riding breeches, shined boots, and a well-tailored vest. His shirt was so white it blinded her.

But she must stand her ground—for her and Dora's futures. Men couldn't be trusted to think ahead.

"First," she started in her most authoritative voice, "ours will be a marriage of convenience and there should be no expectation of anything more than politeness."

"Politeness?" he repeated. "What the devil does that mean? That I am supposed to practice good table manners? I don't eat like a wolf if that is your fear. Nor do I dribble on myself."

Of course, he was going to make her be specific. Heat rose to her cheeks, but she did not look away. Matching his blunt tone, she answered, "A fake marriage does not require *real* intimacy."

There was a laden beat of silence. Then, "Why, Miss Taylor," he drawled, "who knew you could be so direct?"

He was mocking her. "Anyone who *truly*

knows me," she replied with her own false sweetness. "I can speak my mind without being crude."

"Hmmm, *crude*. And are you saying you weren't planning to be intimate with Thurlowe if he had married you? The poor man. Did he know? I can't imagine the two of you having this conversation. I admire Thurlowe greatly but I can't picture him talking to you about having a good shag."

Shag? Clarissa had never heard such a term although she knew exactly what he meant by his tone—and it both offended and rather titillated her. Images sprang to her mind that she would have sworn she would never have entertained.

It was his shaving soap, that was what it was. He smelled clean. He smelled masculine. The fresh scent of it surrounded her, subtly urging her to step closer, but that would be folly. This man seduced women on a whim. She must keep her courage and her strong values.

Clarissa pressed her soles into the ground and held her head high, letting him know she was impervious to him, even though she wasn't. Not really. Not with him this close.

And then he smiled, as if he sensed her inner turmoil.

Her common sense came roaring back. "My arrangement with Mr. Thurlowe was far different from this one—and none of your concern," she added briskly, knowing exactly what tack he would take and wishing to nip his impertinence in the bud. "Furthermore, I have more power over our situation than I did over Mr. Thurlowe, my lord. You need me more than I need you."

The playful light left his eye. "I could turn you out right now."

"But you won't. You would have to explain your lie to your mother and I believe you would rather gnaw off your arm before admitting this was all a farce to her. Especially since you fear she will use Dora's parentage against you. Imagine a lifetime of having to do your mother's will lest she gossip about her own grandchild. I, personally, find the whole matter upsetting. However, I'm trying to help you, my lord. Please, be reasonable."

His brows came together. He gave a low growl of annoyance, and then he said, "No intimacy?"

"Yes."

"You know I'm not that sort of man."

"A chaste one?"

Her comment sparked an abrupt laugh out of him. "Exactly."

She shrugged. "You know I'm not the sort of woman who pretends what I don't feel. And, let's be honest. I'm not the sort who attracts you."

Her words pricked his interest. He leaned against the doorjamb, once again his cocky self. "You underestimate yourself, Miss Taylor. There are many things I find attractive about you."

That comment, and the way he let his gaze skim lightly over her breasts, let her know exactly what he meant. She crossed her arms against her chest, an action that made him laugh softly as if she greatly amused him.

Well, this was not a game. Her future was at stake. "I understand you have an obligation to your title to provide an heir. Will Dora be enough for you? Can you accept not having a male child?"

He studied her a moment. She wished she could read his thoughts, and then he said, "She must be."

Clarissa frowned. It could be that easy?

"Don't look so suspicious," he told her. "You said yourself I have little leeway in all this."

He was right. She brought herself back to the business at hand—security. "I will also expect you to deposit a handsome sum of money in an account under my name."

"I promised I would take care of you."

"I understand. However, if something happens to you, your heirs might decide not to part with your money. I want to know that Dora and I have the resources to live comfortably. After all, you are marrying me to keep Dora safe."

"Quite right. When we are in London, I shall see an amount is set up in your name."

"Thank you."

"I will be quite generous," he promised.

"I have no doubt you will be. I've heard stories about what you have given your mistresses. I shall expect just as much. Is it true you purchased a coach and pair for each one when you parted?"

He straightened. "Does Maidenshop have anything else to do with its time except talk about me?"

"Absolutely nothing," she assured him. She enjoyed seeing him cranky. It humanized him.

He frowned as if he saw nothing amusing in the idea and then barked, "Anything else?"

"No, that is the whole of it," she said. "No intimacy because I will not be forced to offer what is not real and true security for Dora and myself."

Lord Marsden nodded as if confirming their agreement, and then he said, "Since we are bargaining, I have a few terms of my own."

Of course, he would. The man was predictably nettlesome. "And what terms would those be?"

"Well, the first is that although we aren't planning to consummate our marriage—I did understand that correctly, didn't I?"

She nodded, wary.

"Then I wish your assurance that, for Dora's sake, we never give the impression that we *aren't* intimate. People would find it strange if we weren't behaving as married couples do."

"Strange? That I can resist you?" She scoffed at the idea. She was made of sterner stuff. She'd learned her lessons the hard way.

"No, that I would resist you, Clarissa."

His statement startled her. There it was again, the suggestion that he found *her* attractive?

Clarissa didn't know if she quite trusted anything he said, even as she felt her heart kick up a beat. And the way he looked at her—his expression intent and without any hint of humor in his eyes. Could he possibly be sincere?

She must not let her guard down. After all, she'd once believed Mr. Thurlowe had been happy to marry her. She'd nursed that fantasy for close to two years and had thought herself quite special until the brutal truth was borne home.

"Of course, we will give the impression that we are married," she replied stiffly.

"*Happily* married," he corrected. "Dora deserves happily married parents."

"I will be her stepmother," Clarissa had to point out. "No one will believe she is mine with her dark hair."

"You leave what they think about Dora to me. I'm asking you to behave as if you are my wife in public and around the servants."

"Well, of course I will." She knew she sounded cross and why not? She didn't understand why he was harping on this issue.

"Excellent," he replied as if she had given all he could ask. "Now, for my second demand."

"Another one?" Why did she sense he was toying with her?

"You have two stipulations," he reminded her. "It is only fair I have two."

"I don't think you should have any," she shot back.

"But you have already given me one, so—" He opened his arms as if showing he played no tricks.

She scrunched her nose in doubt. "Very well, what is your second condition?"

"That you start dressing better. I say, Clarissa, you have a countess's manners but your dowdy wardrobe needs great improvement. I'll pay," he added before she could protest.

Still, she was rather offended.

"My tastes are modest," she had to offer.

"Your tastes are boring. You should wear color and show off some style. You don't want Dora to be ashamed of you."

That stung. "Dora doesn't care what I wear."

"She will. Someday."

"However, you seem to wish to see me more stylish now."

He grinned at her. "I would. Or else I would never have negotiated for such a stipulation," he said with an unrepentant shrug. "Besides, Clarissa, I've seen you wear better."

That was true. Of course, those dresses had grown old and frayed at the hems. They'd also become a touch tight, especially in the bustline. If he was talking about what she wore to village dances, well, those gowns had been borrowed.

The two serviceable dresses she currently possessed had been a gift from the matrons. Clarissa had selected them because they made her feel like a proper lady's hired companion, except she didn't enjoy wearing them.

Her resistance to his request began to change. She wouldn't mind pretty things. "I will amend my wardrobe."

"Well, then—" He stuck out his hand. "Do we have a marriage bargain?"

She glanced at his gloveless hand and then

back up to his face. He acted serious. There was no telltale glint in his eye that he was mocking her.

And Clarissa knew the time had come for her to make a decision. Anyone else would have leaped for this opportunity. She would be a countess. The thought was fantastical to her.

She would never worry about money or her security again. She'd be safe. She would also be able to guide and protect Dora, a sweet baby who didn't deserve to be abandoned any more than Clarissa had. She was already more than half in love with the child. She'd always enjoyed babies but Dora was special.

Unfortunately, she had Lord Marsden for a father.

"Yes, we have a marriage bargain." Resolutely, Clarissa placed her bare hand in his.

His fingers clasped around hers. The warmth of his body flowed from his arm spreading throughout her, enveloping her.

"*Thank you*," he said fiercely. "You won't regret this. I promise."

All she could do was nod. She was overwhelmed by not only the bigness of him—Mars was a very tall man and she was petite—but also his solidness. He was all muscle. Strong, capable, protective . . . and now she was entering the circle of his protection.

"My mother left an hour ago—" he continued, but Clarissa interrupted him in surprise, glad for a new subject.

"An hour ago? She didn't come by to see Dora."

"Of course not," Mars answered. Seeing that he'd shocked her, he explained, "You have a good heart, Clarissa. Because of that, you assume others share your consideration for their fellow humans. I'll warn you right now, you've lived in a sheltered world. It's simple and the people are kind to each other. London is different. Everyone wants something. My mother thrives in that world. And what she wants is for us to be in Town by Monday. The vote will be on Thursday and then we will wisely race home on Friday."

We. He'd said "we." "I'm to go with you? What of Dora? Will we take her with us?"

He didn't let go of her hand, preventing her from running. "I may have found a wet nurse. If she takes the position and you find her amenable, Dora can stay with her."

"I don't know—"

"I'd *like* for you to accompany me to London."

"I will be of no use to you. I don't know anyone."

"I will introduce you. If we are to set up the accounts you requested, your presence would be necessary. Or are you just going to accept my word that it has been done?"

"I—"

"Clarissa, I need your steadiness. I want you there."

Oh, dear. *Needed.* No one had ever needed her. She thought of opium dens and wondered if that was what he meant by "steadiness." "I have nothing to wear—"

"I have already promised to buy you whatever you wish."

They stood very close to each other. His breath smelled of mint. He looked past her shoulder. "Dora's asleep?"

"Yes, she has been up for several hours. I just convinced her to go down before I came to you."

His gaze had traveled to the crib but now it swung down to her, practically tucked in the haven of his body. When he spoke, it was for her ears alone.

"I'm not going to set you aside, Clarissa, if that is what you fear. I'm not going to marry you as an elaborate ruse. It is important that you are widely recognized as my wife."

She nodded mutely. In truth, it was hard to think being so close to him. To even breathe.

"Believe me when I say this, Clarissa. I'm like my father. I will honor my marriage vows and your terms." Then he added softly, "You can trust me."

Did she? Did she trust anyone any longer?

Then he raised her hand to his lips and kissed the fingers. The gesture melted any resistance.

She was going to marry him. With that knowledge, she felt something hard and tight within her relax. She would become the wife of not only the most eligible catch in the parish, in England even, but also a man who was young and handsome . . . and virile. Oh, so very virile. Certainly a man beyond what a foundling like herself could ever have hoped to marry.

Clarissa had always feared she'd be stuck with a grasping man like Warner Emsdale. Perhaps that was why she had been doubly set against him. Well, that and because he was a crude bully.

However, all of that was in her past. Warner Emsdale wouldn't think of touching her now. His crotchety grandmother's meanness could no longer harm her.

Then Mars gifted her with his laziest, most handsome smile and said, "Who knows? We might even fall in love. Stranger things have happened."

She couldn't believe he'd say such a thing. Immediately, a wistful part of her wanted his words to come true, that she'd find a place in his heart. She didn't speak such silliness aloud, of course. After all, she had her pride. And she'd learned over the years not to trust the musings of others—

The moment for confidences was interrupted by a knock on his lordship's door. "My lord? I have excellent news." It was Mr. Gibson.

Mars acted as if he didn't appreciate the interruption any more than she did. However, he released her hand and entered his rooms. She followed, stopping at the doorway.

Mr. Gibson reported that Hodner, the footman with a sister in Cambridge, had sent a message. Yes, she was still nursing and would be grateful to accept employment in Lord Marsden's household.

"She's been widowed," Mars explained

to her. "Her husband was an ostler and was dragged behind a runaway team."

"That is terrible."

"Yes, but at least we can offer her someplace safe to live where she will be useful. In fact, Clarissa, this will free you from most of the nurse duties. We were going to have to hire a nurse and this makes life simpler."

He acted as if Clarissa should be happy, except she wasn't certain how she felt. The thought flitted through her mind that if this widow had appeared before she did, then the footman's sister might be marrying Mars.

Immediately, she recognized the uncharitable thought as a mixture of jealousy and the old fear that she didn't truly matter to anyone. She tried to push it away. She was better than this.

She *was*. Except she had to repeat the admonishment several times to herself.

Mars didn't notice anything amiss. Neither did the butler because men rarely noticed anything save for the direction of their own thoughts.

Her future husband was ordering Mr. Gibson to have a rider set off for the bishop. "I need a special license. We will have a wedding posthaste."

"And that means?" Clarissa asked, a bit unnerved by how quickly her life was changing.

"Tomorrow, if at all possible," he said as if the answer was obvious.

"Tomorrow?" she repeated, incredulous.

Tomorrow was too soon. She had just reached her decision.

"I took the liberty of sending a letter to Reverend Summerall with our plans."

"But you didn't know what my answer would be."

"I was optimistic. Summerall is very happy for us. I will include his letter commending us to the bishop with my request."

At that moment, Dora started fussing in the room behind her. He craned his neck to look beyond Clarissa and then he walked right past her, moving toward the crib. He picked up Dora who kicked her legs as if recognizing him. He smiled his approval. "Let me give you both the full tour of the house," he cooed more to Dora than Clarissa. "That is a good idea. After all, you two will be living here."

Clarissa still stood in shock. *Tomorrow.*

They would be in London on Monday.

And once again, her life was changing.

Chapter Nine

I am letting in the enemy, I am marrying.
God help me.

—*Book of Mars*

$\mathcal{M}$ars gave Clarissa a few moments to pin her hair up before he gave her and Dora a complete tour of Belvoir. He held the baby easily in one arm as he guided them through the main house.

There were no fewer than fourteen bedrooms, all of them named after a different color with bed linens to match, and two *full* libraries. To Clarissa's surprise, Mars enjoyed reading. The expression on her face must have given away her shock. "And here you probably didn't believe I could read," he suggested.

Clarissa did not lie. "I'd never imagined it."

"I hope I continue to surprise you," he said, obviously pleased with himself. He then explained that there was a third library in his London house. "The newer books are there."

Newer books?

Nothing brought home the advantages to marrying him like the realization that she could have *books*. Lots of books. Reading was her escape, her passion. She could have sworn she'd read every available book in Maidenshop until she saw his libraries. How could he have kept them from her?

She walked reverently into the room and ran a hand over the binding. There was literature, botany, geography, diaries—the wealth of topics threatened to overwhelm her.

Comfortable chairs were situated by the window. There was also a desk and writing implements. A leather-bound journal was centered on the desk. She glanced at the handwritten title. "'Book of Mars'?"

He actually blushed. It was a startling sight. He paused as if weighing whether to say something and then apparently decided he must. "It is my diary."

"Oh, do you keep track of your daily proceedings?" She asked out of interest. She could never keep a diary with any regularity.

"Somewhat. Mostly it is just random thoughts I have. Observations about"—he waved a distracted hand—"life. Sometimes only a line or two a day."

"I'd like to read it."

His response was to pick up the book and slide it into a slot on a shelf that was easy for him to reach, but one for which Clarissa would need a ladder. "It is nonsense actually. Nothing important." He gave his hand back to Dora,

who seemed fascinated with gnawing on his
fingers.

"Still, it is an accomplishment," she answered.

"Yes," he said with a distracted air as he
shepherded her out of the library.

She went willingly but she couldn't wait to
sneak back here to read the "Book of Mars."
There was a library ladder in the corner. She
could maneuver it to retrieve his diary. She
would just have to bide her time.

And then she felt guilty. She shouldn't pry . . .
and yet the temptation was great. What else did
she not know about him?

With Dora in one arm, he took Clarissa's
and led her through two dining rooms, one he
called a breakfast room, to the kitchen. Really,
all she had to do was follow her nose and the
scent of freshly baked bread.

The kitchen was a hive of activity. There
were so many hearths and ovens, they could
have fed all of Maidenshop. Realizing that
Clarissa hadn't eaten yet, Mars sat her at the
kitchen's center table and offered to have Cook
prepare whatever she wished.

Whatever she wished . . . the thought astounded
her. No one had ever catered to her before.

As it was, she was happy with toast, a soft-
boiled egg, and tea. She caught sight of one
footman, the one she had met yesterday, Peters,
whispering to another. Realizing he had been
caught, the man smiled, gave a small bow, and
said, "We see to the family service. I'm making
certain that your preferences will be ready for
you in the morning." He tapped his brow, an

indication that what she liked would be saved for the future.

"I'm not picky. Whatever you serve is fine," Clarissa answered, feeling a bit awkward. She wasn't accustomed to having so much attention paid to her. It seemed that wherever she went in the house, someone was watching her. She'd believed they acted out of curiosity. Now she realized the servants were anxious to meet her every need, a concept she was not comfortable with.

"We wish you to be happy, my lady," Peters said.

Had she ever been anywhere where they only wished her to be happy?

Not in a long time.

"I will be happy with whatever you do," she assured the servants.

Meanwhile, the lord of the manor played with Dora. He sat on the chair beside Clarissa and lifted the baby up into the air. Dora made happy noises and rewarded him with the baby giggles. For a second he appeared stunned and then he burst out laughing himself. It was a carefree sound, a delighted one. He sounded young, unjaded.

All the servants stopped what they were doing and looked at Mars in wonder. So did Clarissa.

The earl noticed her staring. He held up a bright-eyed Dora. "Isn't she special?"

Yes, she was . . . but so was a father who could have such pride in his daughter.

Clarissa nodded, taken with how easy he

had adapted to fatherhood. It was as if he'd found a new purpose for his life. He hadn't even balked at marrying, even with her terms. And once again the tightness of fear and uncertainty that had been her constant companion for as long as she could remember eased ever so slightly.

When Clarissa finished her meal, Dora's yawn returned them to the nursery. "We can tour the grounds later," Mars said.

On the way, they ran into Mrs. Warbler and Jane who had just come in from a walk around the gardens. The matron acted as if she was enjoying herself. "You should see them, Miss Taylor. They are magnificent. I just spent an hour learning secrets from your gardener, my lord."

"What about your housekeeping duties?" Clarissa asked archly.

"I changed that. Don't you remember? I became your aunt. Lady Fenton and I had a cozy chat last night. She is an intelligent but very intense woman. She approves of you, by the way," Mrs. Warbler assured Clarissa. "Well, after I finished telling her about your lineage."

"You will have to tell me one day," Clarissa answered. "I wouldn't wish to make you a liar if Lady Fenton questions me on the subject."

"She won't," both Mars and Mrs. Warbler said together, and surprising themselves laughed like old friends.

Mrs. Warbler finished, "She is far too interested in herself to worry about anyone else. I know her kind."

Clarissa was bemused by the earl and Mrs. Warbler's acceptance of each other. She and Mars excused themselves and went upstairs.

In the nursery Clarissa changed Dora and gave her a bottle. Mars lingered in the doorway between the two rooms seemingly content to be near his daughter. Clarissa had just put the baby down when Gibson arrived with the information that Mrs. Yarborough, the local dressmaker, was waiting for her in the Green Bedroom.

"Why is she here?" Clarissa asked, confused.

"I sent for her," Mars explained. "You will go shopping in London—after all, it is one of *my* terms. However, you need something to wear tomorrow and for traveling, no?"

She did. She held back, a bit overwhelmed. Her parents had not been rich people. Clarissa had learned how to use a needle.

But she had always dreamed of going to Mrs. Yarborough and picking out material like the other village girls did. Then, in a week, through no effort on her own part, receiving a lovely dress. She'd been jealous of those girls who'd had their clothes sewn for them. She'd longed to be one.

"Go on," he encouraged as if sensing her hesitancy. "I'll be in the next room and I can hear Dora. Enjoy yourself."

Enjoy yourself? Who was this man? He certainly wasn't the Earl of Marsden she'd thought she knew.

She was also so excited about the opportunity of a fitting, her hands were shaking. She pressed them against her skirt, nodded, and followed Gibson to the Green Bedroom. She ran into Mrs. Warbler going to the same place. "I must be involved," her friend said.

"Or does the earl not trust my taste?"

"That, too," Mrs. Warbler allowed with a pleasant smile. "He fears you will be too frugal. He knows with my help that will not happen."

Mrs. Yarborough waited with her tape measure and several dresses already made. She was a cheery, practical woman who had served Maidenshop for years.

"There is no time to make new," the dressmaker said. "Fortunately, I do have some already made up. Here, have a look at these."

Clarissa and Mrs. Warbler examined the dresses. They were made with a quality of muslin Clarissa had never been able to afford.

"The earl instructed me to tell you to purchase all I have," Mrs. Yarborough said with a chuckle. "And look at this tall looking glass for our use." She nodded to the mirror in the corner of the room. "I would like one of these for my shop."

"Why would you just have dresses already made up?" Clarissa asked, puzzled.

"I had this order from the Misses Heath." She referred to the daughters of a wealthy Fulbourn merchant. "They had them made for a country party. I thought you could use them instead."

Clarissa dropped the dress she had been eyeing. "I don't want to take these away from anyone."

"Don't you feel guilty about his lordship seeing you properly dressed or my giving the dresses to you. I have time and material to remake them. They aren't needed until next week. And, your lord is paying me handsomely. I may even ask him for this mirror. Now, what shall you wear for the morrow? I was thinking the cream muslin shot through with gold. Pretty, no?"

Mrs. Warbler held the gown in front of Clarissa. "Perfect."

It was the most beautiful dress Clarissa had ever seen. The lines were simple but the material was smooth and light against her skin when she tried it on.

As Mrs. Yarborough pinned to make adjustments, she said, "Everyone in the village is happy for you."

"They know?"

"Of course. It is high time that you had a bit of luck. To my way of thinking, you are marrying the best of the Three Bucks."

"How did they find out so quickly?" Clarissa asked.

"I heard it from Mrs. Summerall, who had it from her husband, who shared the info with the matrons—and in a blink, we all know." She sat back on her heels from where she was pinning Clarissa's hem. "What do you think, Mrs. Warbler?"

"The Misses Heath may be taller than Miss

Taylor but they are not as endowed in the bodice. Is there material to let out this seam?"

"I would think you would want it a little close right here," Mrs. Yarborough said. "Makes for a nice silhouette."

"You are right."

"*I* would prefer it loosened a bit," Clarissa said.

"Trust me, my dear, you do not," Mrs. Warbler said, so the bodice stayed. "Besides, we want the alterations to be easy. Think of poor Mrs. Yarborough's back."

"Yes, my back," the dressmaker echoed as if she was a part of some scheme—? And then it all made sense.

"Mrs. Warbler," Clarissa said, "did you come with me to Belvoir to push Lord Marsden into marriage?" She wouldn't put it past her friend and the thought was mortifying.

"Yes," the older woman said almost proudly. "Except I didn't have to prod. He saw the wisdom of marrying you all by himself. I didn't finagle anything if that is what is worrying your conscience."

"And we are all happy for you, Miss Taylor," Mrs. Yarborough declared. "Proud we are. And pleased that someone as fine as you will finally take our earl under her wing. He needs looking after, that one does. He's a good man."

"He is," Clarissa echoed and found she meant the words. Her opinion of him was changing. Was it the books? The diary? Seeing him laugh with joy over his daughter's happiness?

Or was it something deeper?

"I am fortunate," Clarissa murmured, taking off the cream muslin and preparing to put on a forest green walking dress Mrs. Yarborough held out to her.

"To my thinking, he is the fortunate one. You will make a lovely countess, my dear," Mrs. Warbler said.

The compliment made her blush. Although, she was actually pleased with this new direction for her life, and not just because she was going to marry. No, because she was going to marry *Mars*. Mrs. Yarborough was right. He was the best of the Three Bucks, although she would never have admitted it to herself until this moment. She didn't understand all that would be expected of her as his wife and countess but with her friends, she would manage.

In the end, Mrs. Warbler took over the fitting. She decided for Clarissa to take all four dresses. She also asked in that imperial tone of hers for any undergarments, gloves, and chapeaus Mrs. Yarborough might have on hand. Both Clarissa and the dressmaker were overwhelmed.

Mrs. Yarborough promised to return very early on the morrow with at least the cream muslin for her to wear and a marine blue day dress. The others she would finish altering by the following day. "And undergarments," she added excitedly. "I have a petticoat I will barely have to rework."

"Send all charges to Lord Marsden," Mrs. Warbler said, as if she was enjoying herself. She smiled at Clarissa. "You will have to become accustomed to saying that."

Clarissa didn't know if she ever would, and yet she was secretly pleased to have such lovely clothes. She couldn't remember when she'd had a new petticoat.

She returned to the nursery just as Hodner, the footman, brought his sister to meet her. Mars stayed for the interview as well. Beth Rucker was younger than Clarissa with a toddler she had been nursing. She assured them that it would not be a problem for her to take care of Dora and her own young one. She struck Clarissa as very honest and desperately in need of a position. Dora acted relieved to finally have a breast to suckle and hence, Mrs. Rucker was hired. Provisions were made to bring in a small bed for her daughter, Vivian, and another chest.

Clarissa ended up moving her things into the Green Room. She was uncomfortable with not helping with Dora—until she remembered Mrs. Yarborough's admonishment to not feel guilty.

That evening, she had a quiet dinner with Mars, Mrs. Warbler, Jane, and Dora. They sat in the kitchen at the huge center table. She was relieved that Mars was not one for formality. It was also interesting that, now that he and Mrs. Warbler had set aside their animosity, they actually had quite a bit in common.

After Dora had been delivered to Mrs. Rucker to be put down for the night, the earl walked Clarissa to her bedroom.

"You haven't asked about the license," he said.

"I assumed if there was a problem you would let me know."

He grinned. "You are right. It arrived this evening. Gibson has it."

She nodded. They stood in front of her door. She placed her hand on the handle, but she didn't turn it. Instead, she said, "You know you don't need to marry me." She couldn't look at him as she spoke. The paneling on the door was easier to focus on than his face. What if she saw that he agreed with her? "Mrs. Rucker is here now and your need for me—"

He turned her face toward him, tilting her chin up. His expression seemed certain. "My need for you continues," he said quietly. "Dora must have someone fierce to protect her. That is you. I sent a letter to my secretary Lowton to draw up paperwork, so if anything happens to me, you are Dora's guardian with a generous allowance and privileges at Belvoir. We will sign it in London."

"What would happen to you?" she asked, the import of his words setting off an alarm inside her.

His smile was calm, reassuring. "Nothing, Clarissa. Nothing will happen. You are here and all will be right."

And then he did something miraculous. He kissed her.

It was not a dutiful peck on the check, but a true kiss. Her *first* kiss. The sort of kiss a man gives a woman that he—

Likes? That word seemed too tame for the erratic beating of her heart.

Loves?

There was a word! He'd raised its specter many times today with his kindness. And now a kiss? A meaningful one?

His lips were warm as they fit with hers. There was no hardness, just the delicious sensation of an invitation to something more.

Clarissa had always feared she wouldn't know what to do when she had her first kiss. Instead, she discovered, she knew exactly how to respond. She reached for his jacket, gripping the material for balance, and rose up on tiptoes to make it easier for him. To her delight, the kiss deepened. His arms gathered her close. Her breasts flattening against him.

He was holding her now. She felt the hardness of him, a hardness for *her*. She'd never been this close to a man and she was curious—

Mars broke the kiss. She wasn't ready to finish. She leaned forward, her eyes shut, not ready to stop. He gently pushed her away, keeping her at arm's length. She opened her eyes.

He appeared as amazed by their kiss as she felt. Their gazes held, his breathing as hurried as her own.

"Well," he said, pushing a curl that had escaped from her pins back into place.

"Well?" she echoed, wanting to lean into him. Except, his arms held her from him.

"If I am to honor your terms for this marriage, I'd best take my leave now."

Yes, *her* terms.

His kissable lips spread into a slow smile. "We will do *well* together, Miss Taylor. Very well. And now, good night, Clarissa."

She nodded like the good minister's daughter. "Good night, my lord." She entered her room.

WHO WOULD have thought Clarissa Taylor could spark such reaction out of a man, especially himself?

Mars felt a bit dazed.

She may be an innocent but she was responsive, and obviously not that set against him. He'd desired nothing more than to sweep Clarissa up and take her to his bed. Except, that would be the wrong thing to do. He was the *new* version of himself. The responsible earl.

The one who had promised he'd not touch her . . . although after that kiss, Mars knew he could work his way around her. He'd also won her promise to act as if they were man and wife. He could win her to his bed.

He was also rather proud of the woman he'd chosen. Did she realize how tempting she was? How her response to his kiss, coupled with her fierce independence, offered a challenge few men could resist? He'd always considered marriage a punishment. Now he found himself looking forward to the wedding bed.

Because there would be one. He knew it, and so did she whether she realized it or not.

Clarissa deserved to be cared for. She had given much of herself to others over the years. She'd always been active in charity work around the village. There wasn't a soul she wouldn't help if she could, just as she'd helped him with Dora. She would actually be the very image of a benevolent countess.

Yes, he was pleased with himself. Marrying Clarissa was a good move.

In the past, his success would have called for a celebratory drink. Besides, the moon was still full. Mars had always liked drinking under a full moon. There had to be something heathen in his soul. A full moon set his blood running.

However, tonight, her kiss had done that.

Alone in his room, he went over to the window and looked out upon Belvoir's carefully manicured gardens in the moonlight. The other night, he'd seen this scene and had bayed like a mad animal.

Tonight, he was a man in charge of his world.

It had been a long time since he'd experienced a sense of peace.

For once, his dreams were as he wished. He dreamed of the duel, only he was the one who faced Dervil, not his father. And Mars was the one who walked away alive.

The next morning, he woke clearheaded and ready for another kiss.

Chapter Ten

There is nothing like a wedding to make one feel as if
he is standing on a precipice before an endless fall.
—*Book of Mars*

$\mathcal{A}$ knocking at the door woke Clarissa.

She opened her eyes, startled by the sound.
Her first thought was a panicked one—*Why
hadn't she heard from Dora?*

Sitting up, she looked around the room and
suffered momentary confusion. This wasn't
the nursery . . . and then she remembered. She
was marrying today.

And last night, Mars had kissed her. A kiss
that had kept her humming with, well, she
wasn't certain what all she'd thought about. It
had been a mix of yearning and thankful relief
that, finally, she'd been kissed—and by a man
who knew how to do it well.

No wonder she'd had a fitful night until the
very wee hours of the morning—

The knock at her door grew more insistent.

Clarissa climbed out of bed. She wore her heavy cotton gown. It was the only nightdress she owned and quite worn from years of use. She cracked open the door.

Mrs. Warbler stood there holding several dresses. Behind her was Jane with a tray full of covered dishes. "Open up. Come along, missy. We don't have all day to prepare you."

"Prepare me?"

"For your wedding." Mrs. Warbler pushed on the door and Clarissa stepped back. "We have much to do and little time. Lord Marsden invited all of the matrons for the vows. And then there will be the wedding breakfast afterward. It shall be a feast."

"He invited the matrons?" What a stunning turnaround.

"I know," Mrs. Warbler agreed, her tone reflecting Clarissa's shock. "When Jane and I saw him in the hall a few minutes ago, he was humming. Can you imagine? Humming."

"We are talking about Marsden?" Clarissa had to ask.

Mrs. Warbler nodded. "He was carrying the baby. He is quite taken with her."

"Enough to marry for her," Clarissa answered, honest enough to admit his motivation.

"Nonsense. A man like him does not like to marry anyone. Jane and I were talking—"

"Umm-hmmm," Clarissa said, knowing that when Mrs. Warbler took that tack, it meant that her friend had spoken and the maid listened.

"*We* were," Mrs. Warbler insisted. "And *we*

feel that perhaps part of the—I don't know what to call it, discord?—between the two of you was an expression of his interest."

"Interest?" Clarissa laughed. "His disdain was genuine."

"Only because you don't wish to see what is plain to the rest of us. You are far too humble, Clarissa. The time has come to stand tall. And Jane and I are here to help you. Now come. We must be busy."

"What time am I marrying?" Clarissa had been so preoccupied between the baby, the tour, and *him*, she hadn't asked.

"Eleven at St. Martyr's. And it is already half past seven. Jane, place the tray on the table by the window." Mrs. Warbler laid the dresses on the bed and then started to reposition the full-length glass in the corner of the room. "Clarissa, sit and eat. You will need your strength. The bath will be here shortly."

"The bath?"

"Oh, yes, my girl. Jane and I are giving you the royal treatment this morning. Now eat. The footmen will be coming up with the tub and water and you don't want to be seen wearing that—" She stopped, paused to consider the nightdress. "What is that? You can't be planning on wearing that for your husband."

"I have nothing else." Nor did she want to share that it wouldn't matter. Their marriage would be in name only.

"Nothing!" Mrs. Warbler said, seizing on the word and popping herself on the head. "Why am I worrying about what you will be wearing? Marsden won't care. No, he won't. Let's put our energy into turning you into the loveliest bride in the parish. And one ready to be a *countess*."

There was a soft-boiled egg and toasted bread on the tray, along with strong tea. There were also several buns, cheese, and fruit. "I can't eat all this," Clarissa worried.

"You don't have to. That is for Jane and me." She and the maid were pulling out a privacy screen from its place along the wall.

Clarissa had just taken a few bites of her breakfast when there was another knock. Mrs. Warbler went to the door. "Hide yourself behind the screen." She then let in a parade of footmen with a tub big enough for two people and buckets of steaming water.

Mrs. Warbler had several bars of the soap Gemma made. "You won't believe how it will make your skin feel. The woman is a marvel. Each is scented. Pick the one you wish to use."

Clarissa realized that for the first time she was hearing Gemma's name and not wincing. She chose the soap that smelled of lavender and something else she couldn't quite name. Gemma had a gift for creating fragrances.

Soon, she was in her bath. Clarissa couldn't believe the luxury of it. She'd never once imagined a tub this big. Then again, it would have to be a huge size for Mars. While she enjoyed bathing, Mrs. Warbler and Jane visited the baby. They returned with the report that Mrs. Rucker was a true find and Dora seemed very content.

Clarissa had a chance to see for herself when she threw on her old gray dress and ran down to the nursery for a few minutes before Mrs. Warbler insisted she dress for the wedding. The baby was happy to see her and some of the tension in Clarissa relaxed at knowing Dora had not forgotten her. Little Vivian seemed quite sisterly with Dora. Vivian was a talkative child who seemed to have adapted as well as Dora had to this new turn in life.

"Would that we all have the resilience of children," Clarissa said to Mrs. Rucker, who agreed. Then, giving Dora a kiss, Clarissa returned to the Green Room.

Jane styled her hair, piling it high on her head with loose curls falling down her back. Clarissa had never looked so fine. Or had the chance to wear such elegant stockings. "The earl didn't pay for those," Mrs. Warbler said crisply. "They and the gloves are gifts from the matrons. We are all so happy for you."

Clarissa pulled out a pair of black leather shoes with rounded toes. Mrs. Taylor had insisted on purchasing them for her almost five years ago. Clarissa had taken good care of them. They were worn for Sunday services and the parish Cotillion Dance. Now they would see her marry.

Finally, the women helped Clarissa don the cream muslin, slipping it over her hair and shoulders with the care of handling a work of art. The dress fit perfectly. Mrs. Yarborough had also generously sent a yard of emerald green ribbon for Clarissa to tie under the bodice.

Clarissa looked at herself in the glass and couldn't remember ever appearing so regal. She even felt taller . . . and wondered if it would make a difference to Lord Marsden to see her this way.

Mrs. Warbler came behind her and placed her hands on Clarissa's shoulders. "He will consider himself a lucky man," she predicted. "And he is. But there is one thing you need to complete the ensemble. Jane, will you please leave us?"

The moment the door shut, Mrs. Warbler surprised Clarissa by, with great solemnity, placing a long gold chain with a small medallion around her neck.

"What is this?"

"The chain is another gift from the matrons."

"You all have already given me so much," Clarissa protested.

Mrs. Warbler turned her around. "My dear, we are so proud of what you have become."

"You wanted me to marry Mr. Thurlowe."

"Mr. Thurlowe is the one who offered. However, I will at last confess that your suspicions were correct. When Lord Marsden appeared the other day with the baby and acted so completely at sixes and sevens, well, I secretly hoped this would happen. There has always been something between the two of you."

"Yes, dislike."

"Sometimes dislike is a stronger attraction than we give it credit. And it isn't such a stretch of the imagination for an earl to choose a godly minister's daughter—"

"Are we talking about the Earl of Marsden? The man who refuses to step inside a church?"

"He is today. To marry *you*. Nor am I surprised, although this is definitely a quicker timeline than I saw coming, and yet, I believe all will be good for the two of you. Now, please sit. I have something to tell you that may be upsetting."

Clarissa took the chair next to the desk, both curious and alarmed. Mrs. Warbler pulled the other chair up so that they were next to each other, cozy-like.

"You are making me nervous," Clarissa warned, touching the chain's small medallion resting against the soft material of her bodice. The weight of it felt comforting.

"I *am* nervous," was the response. "I wish to speak to you about your mother."

"My mother?" Everyone had always claimed they knew nothing about her parentage.

"She owned the medallion that is on that chain."

Startled, Clarissa lifted it up to look at it better. It was no bigger than the nail of her little finger and seemed very old, the color dull compared to the newer chain. There was a faint engraving. She turned it toward the light in the window. She could make out a *P* on one side in a lovely script. On the other was the outline of a flower. A lily.

"What do you know about my mother? Did Reverend and Mrs. Taylor know? Why has no one told me anything?" Clarissa couldn't believe that people she had known all her life had kept this secret.

"Reverend and Ivy Taylor didn't know anything because the dowager"—she referred to the Dowager Duchess of Winderton—"and I kept it all a secret." Mrs. Warbler looked at the tray of half-eaten foods in front of her as if wishing there was sherry. Then, with a heavy sigh, she said, "She died, Clarissa." Mrs. Warbler's voice was as gentle as she could make it.

Died. Of course. Why else would she not have come for her baby? There had been many times in her childhood that Clarissa had dreamed about her mother striding into Maidenshop and claiming her. That she hadn't meant that she couldn't. And yet some mothers could give up a child. Such was Dora's lot. Still, death—?

Clarissa discovered her feelings about this piece of information distant and somewhat vague. "Did you know her?"

"Not at all. And we didn't withhold this information as a jest. The duchess suggested it best to keep the news to ourselves." She sighed heavily again and said, "A young woman was found wandering on Winderton lands. She was delirious and holding a wee babe. The old duke was out of town. The current one hadn't even been born yet. Lucy was still new to her title and she sent for me. She was concerned the woman was going to die."

"What was she ill from?"

"She had a fever . . . *and* a broken heart."

"A broken heart?"

"Yes, apparently she was in Maidenshop hoping to reunite with the father of her baby."

The father? Clarissa leaned forward. "Who is he? Who was she?"

Mrs. Warbler placed a hand on Clarissa's arm. "We don't know. She refused to tell us. She wouldn't even give her name. Most of the time she was delirious from the fever. From what little she did say, we learned she'd come to Maidenshop to meet her lover, except he already had a wife. The poor girl had been betrayed. She was horrified by her situation." Mrs. Warbler did not hide her disgust. "Apparently, she had been staying with her brother, waiting for her lover to come for her. When he didn't and she started showing, her brother turned her out."

"That's shocking." And yet, Clarissa knew it happened.

She was also upset to realize that her mother had been discarded by the man who had fathered her. "My father was dishonorable."

Mrs. Warbler nodded her agreement. "It was obvious to Lucy and me that your mother was gently bred. She was a lovely girl. Younger than you are right now. Life had played a cruel trick on her. Mr. Sexton tried to save her but she went very quickly." She reached for the medallion. "She pressed this into my hand and begged me to see to your care. She offered it as payment but, of course, money was not important. The dowager and I were beside ourselves when she died." Tears welled in Mrs. Warbler's eyes. She reached for a kerchief she had tucked in her bodice.

Clarissa sat very still, her mind racing over what she'd just learned. She picked up the medallion, turning it in the light. "Did Reverend and Mrs. Taylor know of my mother? They never said a word. They claimed I had been left on the church step."

"And you were. I put you there."

That was startling news. "Why?"

"As I said, the duchess and I both agreed that your mother was from a good family. She thought about taking you in, except as I said, her marriage was new and the duke was a stickler. As was Reverend Taylor. I feared he wouldn't be sympathetic to your plight if he knew you were a child born from adultery. So, we decided on a little ruse. We would present you to the community as a foundling, abandoned on the church step. We hoped a family would take you in. We didn't expect it to be the reverend. We were pleased that he and Ivy did because it allowed us to watch you grow."

"What of my mother?"

"The duchess told Reverend Taylor that her people had found a young woman's body on the estate. A stranger—and she was. Like I said, even ill, she was very close-lipped. Well, all save for one thing. Your name. She told us you were Clarissa. Yes, you were named by your mother. I tied a note with your name to the basket before I left you on the step. The duchess and I were pleased that the Taylors kept your name. We didn't know what we would do if they didn't. Reverend Taylor was a hard man to dissuade once he made up his mind."

He had been . . . . "No one even told me that my mother chose my name."

"My dear, you can't believe the number of times over the years that the duchess and I debated what we should tell you."

Clarissa turned to the older woman. "So, why now?"

"Because your life is moving into a new direction. We felt you could understand, especially after your compassion for Dora."

Clarissa placed her hand around the medallion, wanting to feel some hint of her mother's presence. "All my life I've had questions. I used to pray that I could dream about her." She looked to Mrs. Warbler. "Did she suffer much?"

"No, she left us in a matter of hours after she was found wandering in the cold. Mr. Sexton truly did try to save her, but it was almost as if, once she had you someplace safe, she could . . . leave. Like I said, she was not only very ill but heartsick as well."

Clarissa could all too easily put herself in her mother's place. A young woman abandoned and alone, yearning to believe a faithless man's promises . . .

Pressure had been building inside of Clarissa right behind her eyes and tightening her throat. She was strong. She didn't give in to self-pity, and yet this was her mother. A mother she'd never known. She looked down at the medallion, the graceful *P* blurred—

Mrs. Warbler put her arms around her. "Cry, my dear. I have for your mother over the years. She would be so proud of you."

When the tears came, they weren't a torrent. Instead, they slipped silently over her cheeks.

"I do wish we had sherry," Mrs. Warbler muttered.

The words broke Clarissa's grief, because they were so Mrs. Warbler. She pressed a hand against her cheeks. "Thank you for letting me know," Clarissa murmured. "It is hard news to share."

Mrs. Warbler leaned close. "Everything your mother did was for you."

"Except stay alive."

"My dear, you know that sometimes life beats us down too hard. Any of us can lose hope. But you are stronger than she was. More resilient. After all, you slammed Warner Emsdale's 'bits' in a door."

The reminder sparked a laugh from Clarissa. "Not the important bits."

"But you put him in his place well enough. And now, you are going to take Marsden in hand. You will be a brilliant countess. I predict that you will have a wonderful life. And that is all any of us, including your mother, hoped for you."

She reached for Mrs. Warbler's hand. "Thank you. Thank you for the gift—" She touched the medallion. "Thank you for being a godmother to me in more ways than I could possibly have known. You and the duchess gave me a chance, and I know you did all that you could for my mother."

"We take such pride in you." Mrs. Warbler blotted away tears with her kerchief and then visibly took hold of herself.

"Do all the matrons know my story?"

"Just the dowager and myself."

"So, it truly is a secret."

"You know we won't say anything."

And her mother's life would never be acknowledged. "We don't know my mother's name?"

"No. Her clothes were well-made. The leather on her shoes was excellent, so she had to come from money. Her hair was the same color as your own, and that is all I remember. The duchess hired a man to make inquiries for a missing young woman. She never learned answers."

"No one cared about her. What happened after she died?"

"A funeral was held. She is buried in the churchyard."

"She's buried there?" Clarissa had grown up playing amongst those graves.

"Yes, close to the yew. The headstone is a small block with the letter *P* on it."

Clarissa knew that grave. She'd always thought it was the resting place of a child. "Thank you," she said, meaning the words.

At that moment, Gibson knocked and announced, "Your coach waits to take you to the church, Miss Taylor."

"Is his lordship here?" she asked. Both women stood.

Without opening the door, Gibson said, "He has already left."

"You are going to tell him, aren't you," Mrs. Warbler said.

Clarissa nodded. "I must. He deserves to know who he is marrying." She picked up the shawl Mrs. Warbler had lent her and drew on her gloves. "Are we ready?"

"Don't tell him," Mrs. Warbler advised.

Clarissa didn't answer, because what she would have said was that she was done with secrets in her life. She believed she owed it to Mars to be honest. And those words might make Mrs. Warbler regret sharing the story. Instead, Clarissa left the room, taking a moment to peek in on Dora. Mrs. Rucker had matters well under control. Vivian was playing on the floor while Dora watched from Mrs. Rucker's lap. She closed the door.

What if Mars was not pleased with marrying a woman who was the child of adultery? There were many, including Reverend Taylor, who believed the sins of the parents were visited upon the child. She didn't believe Mars would have those notions, but, in truth, she knew so little about him.

What she did know was that she did not want to give Dora up. She already loved the child.

"I should never have told you," Mrs. Warbler declared out in the hall.

"I am grateful you did." Clarissa meant the

words. "I've had too many unanswered questions in my life." She touched the medallion. "And I appreciate this. I wonder what the *P* stands for? Or the lily?"

"It sounds as if now you have more questions," Mrs. Warbler said grumpily.

"I may." Such as the identity of her father, except did she really want to know a man who could betray a young woman as callously as he had?

She thought not.

REVEREND SUMMERALL was waiting on the church step as the coach approached. He was not alone. Curious villagers waited with him, hoping for a glimpse of the bride. They were not to be disappointed.

The minister opened the vehicle's door himself and then took a step back in pleased wonder. "Ah, Miss Taylor, you make a lovely bride."

Clarissa did not move from her seat across from Mrs. Warbler's. "Thank you, sir. Is Lord Marsden here?"

"He is waiting inside."

"Please send him to me."

"You can see him if you will come along."

"Or, you may send him to me," Clarissa said.

The reverend frowned, but then went off to do her bidding.

From the seat across from her, Mrs. Warbler said, "You don't need to do this—"

"*I do.*" She could not marry Mars under any

false pretenses. "And I wish for us to be alone when I explain it to him."

Mrs. Warbler was not pleased. "Clarissa—"

"I know my own mind."

There was a beat of disgruntled silence and then Mrs. Warbler said, "Very well." She climbed out of the coach, just as Mars arrived. After a word of greeting to the older woman, he took her place, filling the coach with his presence, and for a second, Clarissa couldn't breathe let alone think.

He cut an elegant figure in black breeches, polished boots, and black jacket over a snowy white shirt and figured silk waist vest—and in that moment, Clarissa so wanted to be his.

These past few days of working together had let her see another side to him, a side she respected and admired. And with respect and admiration, could she not love him?

For his part, his eyes had lit up at the sight of her. "You do the dress more than justice, Clarissa. I doubt if Maidenshop has ever seen a lovelier bride."

His words, a compliment every woman longed to hear, made her heart even heavier. She hated doing something that might ruin her chance to live a life that was beyond her imagination, even if their marriage was in name only.

"I learned something today that you should know," she started.

He immediately grew concerned. "Is Dora all right?"

"Yes, of course. Why would you think otherwise?"

"You appear so serious."

His response brought her overwrought sense of responsibility in line. He was actually marrying her for Dora. She must not forget her place. She pressed on.

"Everything is fine. I received some news and I believed you should be informed."

"What is it?"

"Mrs. Warbler told me about my mother."

His interest picked up. "She knew something?"

"She and the dowager found my mother ill and wandering Smythson. She was carrying a baby in her arms."

"You?"

Clarissa nodded.

He did not recoil in horror. Instead his brow furrowed. He leaned toward her. She sensed he would have taken her hands if she wasn't tightly clasping them in her lap. "What happened?"

"My mother had come to Maidenshop to find her lover. She had a brother who had turned her out when he learned she was pregnant. She didn't say much before she died but that my father was to come for her. He never showed."

"So she came looking for him? Do we know who he is?"

"No, she wouldn't even tell the matrons what her name was, let alone his." Clarissa paused and then added, "Mrs. Warbler believes that, although my mother had a fever, what she really suffered from was a broken heart. She learned when she arrived in Maidenshop that my father was already married."

Mars sat up straighter. Clarissa braced herself for some condemning statement, but that isn't what he did. "The poor woman. To be abandoned by everyone who should have taken care of her."

Clarissa appreciated his understanding. "She named me. She wouldn't give her name or my father's, but she told Mrs. Warbler and the dowager the name she had given me. The name you don't like." She said this proudly, almost daring him to make a comment.

Instead, he took her gloved hand. Holding it as if he understood what this information meant to her in a way she didn't fully understand herself.

She looked down at their joined hands. Her throat seemed to close as tears threatened. She forced herself to speak. "I would understand if you would choose not to marry. I mean, with my background and unknown parentage—"

He cut her words off with a kiss. He leaned across the close space between them with a hard, no silliness kiss. It was different from the one the night before and more effective.

It settled her, brought her to him, to what they were about to do. Her hands went to his arms as if she reached to keep her balance.

The kiss broke. His face was so close to hers she could make out the flecks of blue in the grayness of his eyes. Kind eyes, nonjudgmental ones.

"Clarissa, I'm a modern man. I don't believe

in superstitions such as a person having bad blood because of their parents or whatever it is you fear taints you. Your mother is not you any more than my mother is me. Unfortunately, this is hard news to receive on your wedding day. Are *you* all right?"

He worried about her? She looked up at him, a bit overwhelmed by his acceptance, and said truthfully, "I don't know. All my life I wondered about her, and now this? Makes me wonder if it is a warning of sorts."

"A warning?" He frowned. "Like spilling salt and having bad luck? I told you I don't believe in foolishness, and I am surprised you do."

"I believe in signs."

"How is something that happened decades ago a sign of this moment here and now?"

He was right.

Still, "If your mother learns of this—"

"My mother assumes that we are already married."

"You could be honest with her. You can apologize for a lie. That you were caught up in the moment." She realized she was testing him, giving him the opportunity to run.

He gave her a mock frown. "What? And rehabilitate your opinion of me?" He laughed, his teeth even and white. "No, Clarissa, I shall not leave you at the altar. I expect you to go through with this deed today. I am marrying you for Dora, but," he added as if coming to a realization of his own, "I am not against the match."

He wasn't?

The words seemed to hang in the air between them. She didn't know what to make of such a statement. She felt she had to talk sense into him. "But what if you meet someone else you wish for a wife? Someone from your class." *Someone you could love.* "Someday you will need an heir."

A look crossed his face she couldn't define. Annoyance? Guilt? He took her gloved hand and squeezed it tightly. "Clarissa, you are the only one I trust. The future of my title is not that important to me."

"It should be."

"I have other goals."

She frowned, not understanding what he could mean—and then realizing, he'd made his choice . . . and he'd chosen her.

Sitting in the coach with his presence filling every corner, his expression sincere, she realized that if she'd had a choice of husbands, *he* was the one she wanted.

Mrs. Warbler was right. She was letting her sensibilities run away from her. Mars had reached his decision, now she made hers.

"Then let us marry," she said.

Chapter Eleven

I took the step off the precipice.

—*Book of Mars*

They spoke their vows in the quiet church with Mrs. Warbler and Mrs. Summerall as witnesses. Before he pledged his troth, he asked her to remove the glove on her left hand and then he placed a good band bearing the signet of the Earls of Marsden on her bare ring finger. It fit perfectly and was a daintier version of the one he wore.

The ring felt foreign on her hand, and yet, it made everything very real.

Reverend Summerall pronounced them man and wife in a booming voice. Mars placed Clarissa's hand on the crook of his arm and walked her out of the church where the villagers waited.

At the sight of them, a cheer went up along with shouts of congratulations and a few good-natured comments about this being the end to the Logical Men's Society. If Mars was bothered by the suggestions, he gave no indication. He was the very model of a solicitous groom.

He helped her into the waiting coach and they rode through Maidenshop as if they were royalty. Mrs. Warbler and the Summeralls followed in a barouche provided by Belvoir while a stable lad brought up the rear on Mars's horse Bruno.

"Do you like the ring?" he asked.

"I do. I haven't put my glove back on."

He smiled as if pleased. "It belonged to my grandmother. She valued being the countess. I hope you do as well, Clarissa."

At the house, most of the guests had already arrived for the wedding breakfast. These were people Clarissa had grown up around, and included the Dowager Duchess of Winderton. There was also a good number of the former and present members of the Logical Men's Society, though their numbers were dwindling. They didn't seem to regret losing Mars as a member—well, Sir Lionel grumbled but he couldn't say much since he was a widower himself. At one point he had donned the parson's noose. He groused about that as well.

Their neighbors, their friends, their mentors toasted Clarissa's health, Mars's health, and called for their future happiness. Clarissa could not recall ever feeling so included.

At one point, Mars fetched Dora. She had just risen from a nap and her cheeks were rosy red. Her hair went every which way, but no one criticized because she looked so precious with her inquisitive brown eyes and cherub lips.

The matrons all gathered around her. Mrs. Burnham announced that they would be her "grannies," a phrase that caused the dowager's lip to curl in dislike and the others just laughed.

The laughter startled Dora. She began fussing, her worried gaze searching the room—and then she saw Clarissa. Dora held out her arms, begging to be transferred to Clarissa's care. It felt good to take the baby. She hid her face against Clarissa's neck as if she was shy. Eventually, she gained the courage to survey the room as if she was the princess of Belvoir until Mrs. Rucker came and took Dora back to the nursery.

Several times throughout the day, Clarissa's breath would catch in wonder at how magically her life had changed. It was like a story in a child's tale. She was the disgraced heroine and Mars the huntsman who rescued her.

She was determined to live up to the vows she had shared with Mars. She was going to be the best wife he could *ever* find. While she wasn't certain of all the details of running a stately home like Belvoir, she was certain that she could successfully learn. She'd helped Reverend Taylor manage the parish. Could the servants be more difficult than the parishioners? She doubted it.

Later, after the wedding breakfast guests left sometime around midafternoon, Clarissa and Mars visited Belvoir's granary, the large hall where grain was threshed and stored. At this time of the year, it was empty and a good place for the servants to hold their party in honor of their earl's marriage.

Families were included and Mars had given them kegs of good ale and thrown open the larder. By the time the earl and his new wife made an appearance, most were in very good spirits. The others, Mr. Gibson, the footmen who had served the wedding breakfast, and the kitchen servants were ready to be included and making up for lost time. This was a far more raucous event than the breakfast had been. It was obvious her husband was well-liked amongst the members of his staff.

They stayed longer than Clarissa anticipated. The servants' party was fun. There was much drinking and eating but there was also music.

At one point, calls went up for she and Mars to dance together, something they had never done before. Even at the Cotillion Dance, the highlight of Maidenshop's social calendar, Mars had never asked her to dance.

He offered his hand with a smile and a small shrug as if to say that they had no choice. She was self-conscious as he led her to the dance floor.

The other dancers moved back, leaving the floor to them. The music started. It wasn't one of the high-spirited country dances they had been playing.

Instead, it was a lilting ballad that she recognized but couldn't place the song title. And before she could really grasp what was happening, she found Mars's gloved hand at her waist, her other palm in his as he swept her up into a waltz.

Clarissa had never waltzed before. Many of the matrons had thought it scandalous although it had been quite popular at the last two Cotillions. Still, she'd never been asked to dance it.

Now, in the arms of a man who was an accomplished dancer, she found herself lost in the moment. Even with their difference in height, Mars didn't make her feel awkward. Instead, his hand at her waist helped guide her, and she let him, giving herself over to the magic of music and movement.

When they finished, there was an explosion of applause. Clarissa felt herself embarrassed until Mars looked down at her and smiled as if he was proud of her. Proud of *them*. Heat rushed to her cheeks . . . and to other places. Clarissa had never experienced such complete harmony with another soul as she had in that dance. It was almost as if she—trusted him?

Apparently sensing her confusion, he said, "Smile, nod to them." She did and he led her into the crowd with the servants shouting their approval. At the edge of the gathering, he turned, placing his hands on her shoulders as they watched the dancing continue. She liked the weight of them there, of being so close to him.

"These people know me better than anyone," he admitted. "In many ways, they raised me from boyhood." There was a beat and then he said, "They are pleased with our marriage."

"Are you?" She had to ask. She couldn't help herself. She was cautious by nature and he was very quickly stripping her doubts away. She could barely remember thinking him an enemy . . . and that had only been a week ago.

"I am." And then, to her shock, she felt him kiss the back of her neck, brushing her skin in the most sensitive of places.

Anyone could notice what he was doing. Her breath caught in her throat at his audacity. Still, she held herself very still, almost afraid to breathe, caught the exquisite sensation of his touch.

"Are you ready to return to the house?" His voice was deep, low, seductive.

She nodded mutely. They should leave before she forgot her "terms." Before she threw all common sense to the wind. What she needed was space—and the privacy of her own room.

He reached for her gloved hand. It seemed the most natural thing to let him take it, to feel him clasp her fingers and lead her away, pausing to say a word here and give a nod and a wave there. The people around them acted as if it was normal to see she and the earl so close.

Under a waning moon, Mars led her through the back garden toward the house. The grass was thick beneath her slippers. Music from the party drifted behind them. The night air cooled her skin.

Belvoir stood tall and silent in front of them—almost as tall and silent as the man by her side.

She and Mars had worked well together today. She believed he was pleased with her first performance as lady of the manor. Of course, he'd helped. He'd been all she could have wished. He'd introduced her, staying by her side, quietly guiding her. Not once had she felt awkward.

Lilies, sweet herbs, and roses lined their path. In the darkness of a branching tree, a nightingale serenaded them. She trailed a step behind his, content to let him lead the way.

Mars opened a back door where there was no servant guarding it. She walked in. He followed, the door falling closed behind and they were in a hall's darkness.

"Clarissa," he said. She turned just was his arms came around her.

And then he kissed her. Here, in the shadowy privacy, where no one knew they were . . . and she leaned into him, her arms banding his waist. This was different from the kiss last night. It was hungry and hard and she reveled in it.

New impressions flooded her senses—the hard planes of his body against her softness, the heat building between them, the touch of his tongue and how kissing him was easier than breathing. She wanted to climb inside of him, to be one with him.

A low growl formed in his chest and before she realized what he was about, he swung her up in his arms. He began carrying her up the back stairs, their lips not separating until they reached a stairway door.

She felt him extend his hand to open the

door but it was awkward with his arms full of her. She was the one who leaned to open it. They practically fell into the hall. Mars kicked the door shut and returned to kissing her. Candles flickered on the wall sconces but any servant left to guard them or answer the needs of the family had ducked away for a moment or wisely made himself scarce.

Clarissa expected him to turn to the left and carry her to the Green Room even though she didn't want these kisses to end. Mars was making every bone in her body melt with the amazing things he could do with his tongue.

Instead, he turned right, in the direction of his set of rooms.

A portion of Clarissa's brain was aware that she needed to stop kissing Mars and pay attention. It was not the portion in control of her faculties. And she told herself she was not against checking in on the baby. In fact, she fully intended to do so.

So, it only made sense that she keep kissing him until they reached the nursery and then, somehow, before she realized it, he'd walked past that door and into his quarters.

He shut the door behind him with a shoulder and started walking toward the turned-down bed.

A thousand clanging alarms started going off inside her. She'd been serious in her "terms" and, while she was fully involved in these kisses—especially after such a romantic day—she hadn't lost her wits. She knew she must be careful with this man who was now her husband. It was well-known he did exactly as he wished.

But then, he began kissing her jawline, moving toward her ear, and Clarissa couldn't think, let alone protest.

All she wanted was more of what he was doing. Every part of her being, from the very hard points of her breasts to the curling of her toes, was focused on what he was doing. A shoe dropped off her foot. She didn't care.

And she wanted to do it back. She wanted his whiskered jaw beneath her lips—

Her rump landed on the bed . . . with her husband following.

He lifted himself to reclaim her lips, his hand going to her breast—

Her breast? His hand was on *her breast*.

And she liked it. It actually felt good there.

That was the frightening part. She was enjoying everything he was doing to her. Her senses swirled with the pleasure of it.

However, in another minute, he'd have her skirts up and all her good intentions toward maintaining her honor and her dignity would be destroyed.

The last thing she was willing to do was to become another plaything in the long line of the Earl of Marsden's conquests.

The thought brought her to her senses and Clarissa, acting out of desperation, doubled her fist and gave this giant of a man she'd married as hard a blow as she could.

One would think she wouldn't be strong enough to bring him in line, although Clarissa had put plenty of energy behind her blow. Fortunately, for her, she'd struck him right where he would notice, against the side of his head.

"Ouch," he said, pulling back and rubbing the space between temple and ear.

Clarissa did not miss a beat. She rolled away from him, grabbing a pillow to hold protectively in front of her as she stood up on the mattress and confronted him. "This is not our agreement," she accused.

He frowned and looked around as if he was rather surprised by where they were. The thought flitted through her head that perhaps he might have been caught up in the moment as much as she was.

Except another concern claimed her attention—her dress, her beautiful dress. She'd been in danger of hopelessly wrinkling it.

Clarissa patted her skirts before walking across the mattress with unsteady balance and jumping to the floor, only to fully realize one shoe was missing. Her *good* shoes. She'd have to find it, and that made her even angrier.

"How *dare* you," she snapped out. "You promised no intimacy."

He sat in the middle of the bed looking almost comical in his boots and fine jacket. "There hasn't been any intimacy," he grumbled. He was decidedly not in a good mood.

"There would have been—a complete violation of our agreement."

"An *inkling of intimacy* does not violate our agreement. There is a line. We haven't crossed it. At least not how I would have crossed it."

His last comment incensed her. "You *promised*. A gentleman's word should be his bond." She had to throw that last in. She didn't want a husband who broke his word.

He scowled his opinion and pushed himself off the bed. It was a huge bed. A person could be lost in it. Although she had to admit, she did admire the furnishings in this room. They weren't ostentatious and suited her tastes. She'd rather like living in a bedroom such as this.

Standing, he pulled at the knot of his neckcloth, and said, "I did not violate our agreement."

"You wanted to," she flashed back.

His brows came together. "Excuse me, I kissed you. I believe you kissed me back."

She had.

Clarissa shook her head, scattering the loosened pins that had held her curls in place. He was being deliberately obtuse. Still, she must be honest. "I may have become a bit carried away."

"A bit?"

He was baiting her. "You should have taken me to the Green Room. That is where my things are."

Mars walked to the end of the bed and leaned against the bedpost. "Actually, your things are here."

"No, they aren't," she declared until she

looked around and realized he was right. Her brush was on the dressing table. She opened the armoire close to her and found her sensible shoes and new dresses hanging beside his clothes.

Why, he'd never intended to honor her terms. She whirled on him. "This is appalling. I trusted you."

He tossed his neckcloth onto a side chair. "I've honored your terms." He shrugged off his fine coat. "I stopped when you let me know you wished to stop. It was hard. *Damn* hard. *I'm* damn hard," he muttered in an under voice. The coat joined the neckcloth. She thought it disgraceful how he treated such excellent material.

"*I* should not be in this room," she insisted. "I should be down the hall in the Green Room or the Blue Room or the Rose Room. Anywhere but *here*."

He stopped from pulling his shirt out from his breeches. "No, you agreed to being here. That was one of *my* terms, that we give the impression that ours is all that a marriage should be. There are appearances that must be maintained."

She had agreed to that. "But I didn't think it meant we needed to stay in the same room."

"Of course it did. We are newly married. People would think it strange if we stayed apart. And I don't want the servants talking." He began pulling his shirt off over his head.

The servants would talk.

And she understood what he was saying all

too well. "You *tricked* me." And then, *"Why are you undressing?"*

He threw the shirt on top of his jacket. "Because I'm going to bed. Marrying is hard work. I'm tired. I'm surprised you aren't."

She was. "You can't undress."

"I can undress. I'm going to bed." He spoke as if she was a simpleton, and that sparked her temper enough that she whirled on him.

"You are making a mockery of our agreement." Dear Lord, he was half-naked. Embarrassment, and outrage, roasted her cheeks.

Mars spread his arms in exasperation. "Clarissa, sweet little minister's daughter, you are trying my patience. We made an agreement that we would behave as husband and wife. Husbands and wives share the bedroom—"

"Not all of them. Not of your class. Why else would they have a separate Countess's Chamber in this house if the earl and his wife are to share a room?"

"The Countess's Chamber is now the nursery, as it has been since the beginnings of my family, or so Gibson has informed us."

"It doesn't matter. I will sleep with Dora." She would have marched off except he wagged a finger at her. She hated having a finger wagged at her.

"No, you will not, Clarissa. Mrs. Rucker has the bed in there and if you squeeze her out, then the servants and everyone else will know the marriage has not been consummated and that ends the impression that we have agreed to create."

And everyone would know their business. They would think her addlepated for not going to her husband's bed. She could just hear the matrons rattle on about it. They had all been so proud of what they had believed they had orchestrated for her . . .

And yet, she knew she must not share a bed or even a bedroom with him. Theirs wasn't truly a marriage. Not an honorable one in the religious sense of the word . . . even though she actually felt closer to Mars now than she ever had to Mr. Thurlowe, and she would have shared his bed.

A part of her wanted to do exactly that right now. Mars had slipped past her defenses. She was growing more than fond of him.

But another part of her, the part that felt battered after years of pity and being badgered to do others' will for her, resisted. It was about pride, she realized. And respect.

Was it wrong to insist on waiting until *she* was ready?

While she'd been wrestling with conflicting emotions, Mars sat on the edge of the bed and started tugging off a boot. He dropped it to the floor and reached for his other.

She took one look at his stockinged foot and turned toward the door, ready to bolt— but then realized she didn't want the servants gossiping either. They would dislike her stance against an employer of whom they were obviously fond. Their acceptance of her could change in a blink.

Clarissa was trapped. She could leave the

marriage, except she would be leaving Dora and this newly appreciated sense of security.

Mars placed his boots near the chair, showing at least a touch of neatness. He pulled off his stockings. "Well, what are you going to do?"

Was this the same man who had kissed her so passionately? He acted aloof, as if the decision was completely hers to make—

He was unbuttoning his breeches.

Right there, in front of her.

"What are you doing?"

Mars shook his head. "I've told you, although it obvious. I'm preparing for bed."

"But you are undressing *completely*."

"Of course, I am, Clarissa. I sleep in my altogether."

Clarissa felt her eyes cross. He planned to be *naked*.

She'd seen a naked man here or there. She'd had to help around the parish when people were ill. She'd nursed Reverend Taylor. Although he always wore a night rail that reached past his knees, nursing was very personal. She'd received a glance of his bits a time or two and had taken it all in stride. She understood the human form and believed it designed by the Almighty and therefore perfect—although, she'd never seen a form quite as perfect as her husband's.

Her husband. He was no old man. Or a sickly one.

She had the right to look at that form, and yet, when he slipped his hands into the waist of his breeches and started to shuck them off, she dropped her gaze to the floor. Her eyes strayed to his bare toes. Who knew toes could look so masculine? Or that she would find them attractive?

He was trying to snare her into setting aside *her* wants and her desires. That is what he was doing. He was toying with her, and the idea made her furious.

Well, two could play a game.

Except she knew better than to be naked in front of him. She'd experienced the heat from his kisses. His arousal had not been hidden from her and, right now, it was a war of wills. She must be true to her values.

Stoically, she looked away as he sauntered his bare buttocks right past her and headed toward the privacy screen.

Clarissa couldn't draw a breath until he was out of her presence. Then, she dived into the armoire, throwing clothes this way and that. She adored the dress she was wearing too much to sleep in it. She found her heavy nightgown folded on a shelf and pulled it out. She ducked around the armoire and quickly changed.

While she was doing that, he was going about his ablutions in a loud and unruly way. It was as if he wanted her to know what he was doing. When he started to pass water, she sniffed. He'd thought to embarrass her. She was a country girl. She'd heard people relieve themselves before.

Although, she would prefer him to be a bit more discreet.

By the time he came out from the screen,

she was in bed with the sheets up to her neck. He'd been right. This was a very big bed. Four people could sleep in it without touching.

She tried not to look below his shoulders, because she didn't want any temptation.

He came to a halt. "What is that?" He pointed to the bed and the divider she had fashioned out of pillows to separate her side of the mattress from his.

"It is a wall. Between us."

"It is a flimsy wall." He walked—no, he *strutted* around the bed to claim his side. Clarissa was not immune to his strong, long legs and broad chest. The man could have been carved out of stone.

She also had a problem. She realized she needed to duck behind the privacy screen as well. He'd know what she was doing.

Then again, a woman could not be faint of heart and married to Marsden.

Without a word to him, she slipped out of the bed and ran for the screen. She attempted to be discreet, and was happy to see that Nelson had placed a few of her personal items on the washstand as well.

Feeling much refreshed, she blew out the candle in a sconce there, came out from the screen, and then stopped. Mars had removed her "wall." He waited for her, his head propped on one hand, a triumphant grin on his face, and the sheet just barely covering his "bits."

But then he sat up in surprise, the smirk vanishing. "What the devil are you wearing?"

"My nightclothes," she said.

"A nun's habit is what it is."

The frown on his face gave her immense pleasure. Clarissa made a little curtsey. "I wish to keep us both honest to our agreement." She picked up a pillow that he had thrown on the floor and crossed the room to the desk with its upholstered chair large enough for a man of his size. It would do well enough for a bed for her.

"Oh, Clarissa, no," he said as he understood her intent. "Come back and sleep here. I'm not an ogre. I can control myself, especially since you appear swathed from head to toe in a sail's canvas."

"I'm fine here," she said primly. But she wasn't. This would be an uncomfortable way to sleep, and, in truth, she was tired.

"What is it?" he asked in exasperation. "I'm not a terrible man. You like kissing me. There was something there between us, Clarissa. I felt a spark when we were dancing."

He was right.

"Explain to me why we can't be man and wife the way we should be. Doesn't the Church have some sort of teaching that you are honor bound to obey?"

"One you would know if you attended services?"

He almost roared his frustration at her jab. "Clarissa, this is not natural. Or are you just afraid *you* might not be able to resist me?"

Now she was the one to make a maddened sound. "All right, you are correct. I find you handsome. You are a most attractive man."

Especially when compared with Warner Emsdale. She'd seen his bits, too. "And what you are doing for me is generous. However, I've spent my life beholden to others and being expected to do all the right things. Is it wrong that I need time to understand exactly how I feel about our marriage? To learn to trust you? To know that you are not just one more person who believes I should be grateful that I'm under your roof?"

For a second, they both seemed surprised by how passionate she'd sounded, how frustrated, and yet she'd not call a word back. It was all true.

Clarissa threw her hands over her face. She wished the chair would close around her. It was never good to be so emotional. Or brutally honest. However, he'd taken her to the wall.

And now what would he do? She didn't know.

There was a long moment of silence and then he spoke, his deep voice measured and quiet. "You can rebuild your wall of pillows, Clarissa. Just come back to bed. I promise I won't touch you, not unless you ask me to. I want you to believe that you are safe with me. No matter how much I tease you."

She lowered her hands. Was he serious?

As if recognizing she didn't trust him, he shrugged one shoulder, then said, "Good night." He blew out the room's only candle, lay on his side, giving her his back, and there he stayed.

Clarissa sat, her eyes adjusting to the moonlit shadows in the room. Today had been full of surprises when it came to Lord Marsden. There had been his empathetic acceptance of her mother's death and now this.

It was almost as if he cared for her.

But could she trust him?

Finally, she knew there was only one way to find out.

She rose from the chair, rebuilt her wall of pillows, and lay on the bed, conscious of his even breathing until she fell asleep.

CLARISSA HAD finally relaxed enough to sleep. Mars rose up on the bed and looked over her "wall." She looked young and defenseless. When she was awake, she was too distrustful to be so vulnerable.

Or so he'd thought until her speech tonight.

He'd assumed like many others that she was content with her lot. Now he knew differently. His petite countess had the devil's own pride, and that meant life as a subject of local gossip and pity had been hard for her.

Mars understood. He'd hated the years after the duel when the whispers of busybodies followed him. His parents' marriage and the exact number of his mother's lovers over the years had fueled discussions in numerous London drawing rooms, discussions that had been carried back to school. People adored judging other people's behavior while turning a blind eye to their own. Was it any wonder he was so cynical?

But Clarissa was not jaded. Yes, she'd been hurt by what people whispered, even though she tried not to show it. Instead, she believed if she was good, then she would earn the world's approval.

He knew differently. No "score" was being kept with the high points going to the kind and moral. She could be pleasant to all and they would still laugh at her behind her back. In fact, the more she tried, the less "they" would respect her.

And in those feelings of the world being unfair, of trying one's best and still not being accepted, he and his wife were more similar than he'd ever imagined.

It was now his job to protect her. He'd made that vow in her beloved church, and so be it.

Mars lay back down. He wished there weren't any walls between them, even pillow ones. Then he could put his arm around her and let her know she wasn't alone any longer.

Except one day soon, depending on the outcome of his challenge against Dervil, she would probably be alone again.

All he could do was stand up for her now. He would defend her, even from himself.

Chapter Twelve

I may have married a better woman than I deserve.

—*Book of Mars*

Clarissa woke the next morning feeling more rested than she had in ages.

And then she remembered. The wedding. The dance. The fight.

The bed.

She rolled over to discover her pillow wall intact and the other side empty—

"Good morning."

Mars's voice startled her. She turned to find him sitting fully dressed in the upholstered chair by the desk. He held Dora up as if the two of them had been waiting for her. "Watch this." He lifted Dora in the air and made an astoundingly funny face at her while mooing like a cow as he brought her toward him.

The baby laughed and laughed as if he was the funniest thing ever, and Clarissa realized the sound of Dora's laughter had been what woke her. She found herself smiling.

"Here, let's do it to your mother," he said to Dora. He rose from the chair, carrying the baby as if she were flying toward Clarissa. "Be prepared to moo," he ordered.

Clarissa was a bit taken aback, not by the baby coming toward her but how easily he had said the word *mother*. She took Dora from him and mooed. Her moo was not as deep and loud as his but Dora didn't care.

Clarissa found herself laughing as well.

"She's an amazing child," he declared, sitting on the edge of the bed a respectable distance from her. "So happy."

Clarissa had to agree, especially when Dora decided to entertain herself by grabbing her stockinged foot and moving it toward her mouth. "Oh, no, not that," Clarissa said, trying to lightly block her. Dora protested any restraint, trying to do as she wished with her foot.

"She is like you," Clarissa said.

"Aye, headstrong."

"And healthy," Clarissa had to add. "She is just perfect."

He beamed his pride in his fatherhood, and then said, "The first night of our marriage wasn't so bad, was it?"

It wasn't. His bed was remarkably comfortable . . . and he had been well-behaved.

Instead of answering his comment, Clarissa said, nodding to his clothing, "Please don't tell me Nelson has been in here while I slept."

"Believe it or not, I can dress myself. I shaved myself as well."

"I'm impressed. I didn't realize earls were so resourceful."

"This one is," he answered, taking Dora back just as the baby gave a huge yawn. "We've been playing," he explained. "Mrs. Rucker warned me she would tire out, but I think her color is very good, don't you? She likes it here. Come, Dora, let us put you down for your nap."

"Is it that late?"

"The morning's half gone." At the nursery door he stopped. "Do you ride?"

"Enough to stay on." She'd only ridden cart horses and farm nags. Nothing like the stock in his stables.

"Good. I thought we would go for a picnic today after Dora's nap. The staff is decidedly under the weather." He made a drinking gesture with one hand to let her know what he meant. "A picnic will make it easy for everyone."

"I'd like that."

"Then dress," he said as if it was decided and took Dora into the nursery.

Three hours later they were meandering their way across Belvoir's fields. Mars wasn't riding his huge horse. "He isn't well-mannered enough for Dora," he explained, indicating the baby he had cradled in a sling across his chest. "Although Bruno likes her. He smelled her all over."

"You didn't let that horse nibble on that child."

Mars grinned. "He just had some snuffles. Bruno likes to snuffle people."

Because he was the better rider, he had Dora. He carried the child in a sling across his chest. It was the sort of thing a farmer's wife would wear. He wore it without embarrassment.

They couldn't be out long because of Dora's feeding schedule. Clarissa had insisted on bringing a sucking bottle just in case but they both agreed the services of the wet nurse would be better for their daughter.

Daughter. Another word that made Clarissa's heart sing.

The day was lovely and bright. The summer sun warming without being terribly hot.

Mars led Clarissa down to a bank of the Three Thieves that ran along the boundary of his property. She spread out the contents of their picnic on an expanse of grass where they dined on good bread, cold beef, fruit, and a few of the sweets from their wedding breakfast.

It was companionable time. Dora was their go-between. She kept the atmosphere light, even when they discussed whether to take the baby with them to London the next day or not.

In the end, they both concluded it would be best for Dora to stay at Belvoir. Mars worried about the London air. Clarissa sensed the child had had enough of being passed around. She knew children were resilient and yet, considering they did not plan on being in London more than a week, she agreed it best to keep Dora at Belvoir.

It felt strange and comforting to have Mars

ask her opinion and to reach a consensus with him. He also kept a respectful distance from her without making a fuss about it. Instead, he acted more relaxed and natural around her than he ever had before. That didn't mean he ignored her. His gaze would stray to her hair, her ankle, her breasts—but he, Lord Marsden, rakehell extraordinaire, kept all respectful.

And at some point in the conversation on this beautiful summer day, she wished he would kiss her. The thought rose in her unbidden. In truth, the kisses they'd shared were never far from her mind.

She looked over at him. They lay on a blanket with Dora between them. He held a long piece of grass and tickled the baby's cheeks and neck. Dora tried to reach for it.

Mars caught Clarissa watching him. "What?" he asked.

Kiss me. She didn't speak the words. Instead she said, "We have come a long way from when I fell into a mud puddle, ruining my lovely white dress, and you laughed at me."

"I didn't."

"You did."

"What were we? Eight?"

"You do remember." She was surprised. "I was six."

"Ah, a time of tender feelings."

"It was my best dress."

"Clarissa, boys laugh at everything. I mean you stood up and you were black with mud from head to toe and a funny sight. I also re-member I wasn't the only one who laughed."

He was right. Now, with him bringing the memory alive, she could recall there were several other children around.

But he'd been the only one who had mattered.

Mars leaned toward her, arching his long body around Dora. "Will you forgive me?"

He was so close. If she leaned forward, she could kiss him. She felt herself blush with the thought and he immediately leaned back as if he might have upset her.

Clarissa sat up. "I don't bear grudges," she said, thinking perhaps he thought she was angry.

"No, you just remembered a day almost two decades ago, isn't that right, Dora?"

The baby made a squeal as if she agreed.

"I wasn't even thinking about the mud day," she said in her defense. "At least, not just then." But she had nursed the memory of her wounded pride.

His gaze strayed to her lips as if he had truly known her thoughts, but then he rose to his feet. "We should be heading back." He picked up the baby and offered a hand to her.

Clarissa put her palm in his. He lifted her to her feet as if she weighed nothing. They packed up the remnants of their picnic. He placed a yawning Dora back into the sling and helped Clarissa mount. She noticed he didn't touch her any more than necessary in helping her.

Adjusting her skirts and her seat, she took the reins from him and had to confess, "I mean,

I did hold a grudge against you because of the past."

He looked up at her. It wasn't often she was taller than him. "Why? Certainly not because of a childhood incident?"

Clarissa swallowed, seeing her own culpability. "Maybe."

He nodded, accepting that one word. He moved to his horse and mounted, giving great care to Dora . . . and Clarissa realized she'd perhaps always been wrong about him.

Not about his arrogance. He was arrogant.

But he wasn't callous. He also wasn't completely selfish. Although he could be rude.

They started riding back to the house. He began giving her a description of the land beyond what she'd seen.

She listened, but her thoughts were on what he'd said. She'd always valued the truth and now wondered what to do when the honesty made her sound petty.

At last she couldn't take it any longer, she said, "You never danced with me at the Cotillions." The Cotillion was Maidenshop's most important village dance. From the time she'd been sixteen, the earl had always attended. "You danced with everyone else," she had to add.

He halted his horse. "We never danced?"

"Not until yesterday. I always had the feeling that you avoided me and, well, you made that comment the other day about my being a matron-in-training."

He sat a moment, his expression stoic, and

then he said, "I remember you sitting with the matrons when you first attended."

"The Taylors were ill. They insisted I attend . . . but I didn't dance with anyone. It would have been unseemly."

"Unfortunately, it made you very unapproachable."

He was right. She didn't dance with anyone during her adopted parents' illnesses. "And then," he continued, "your parents died so you were in mourning. By that time, you would scowl at me as if I was a disreputable highwayman. In many ways, I was. Disreputable, that is. Not a highwayman. You were too good for me, Clarissa."

"I didn't think that." And then she said, "I just assumed you didn't like me."

"You didn't like me," he countered.

"Maybe . . . I was wrong?" Her voice lifted on the last word. "I didn't mean to give that impression. Of course, then I was promised to Mr. Thurlowe and—"

And dancing with the handsome earl would have seemed a bit like being unfaithful to the good doctor. Or a disloyal. After all, they were best friends.

Then again, last year at the Cotillion, Mars had been the one to force her to question whether she should marry the doctor. She hadn't liked Mars much for it. He'd made her feel shallow for wanting a marriage because she had nowhere else to go. She'd counted on the marriage to Mr. Thurlowe to give her stability, even when she realized his heart belonged to another.

And in a contrary way, probably no one else but the earl could have made her see what was obvious to everyone else.

"Sometimes," she said, "you make me think in ways I don't want to. You prod my conscience. I haven't always appreciated you for it." This was easier to say than *you are too handsome for me. Too bold. Too worldly. Too, too, too.*

She'd said enough. She kicked her horse forward and rode on. A beat later, he followed. He didn't say anything, but she could feel him watch her—and she wondered what he was thinking.

Dora was asleep by the time they reached the house. They gave her over to Mrs. Rucker before enjoying a light supper the staff had recovered enough to prepare.

Clarissa noticed that Mars barely touched his wine and didn't request Port after dinner. Instead, he suggested they adjourn to the library and she quickly agreed.

To her surprise, Mars wore reading spectacles. Clarissa was charmed to know this detail. She also thought the wire frames made him appear quite scholarly, and there was a strong appeal to that.

Several times, she almost brought up their earlier conversation. She didn't have the courage until they were in bed.

This time, he had undressed behind the privacy screen. She certainly heard all the same noises, but they didn't embarrass her as much. He came out wearing his breeches.

"Your turn," he said pleasantly. "Nelson hung your nun's habit on a hook behind the screen."

Clarissa had been wondering where it had gone off to. Nelson had been busy packing for them both. Her fear had been that he had packed her nightdress and she hadn't been certain what she would do. She could have slept in one of her old dresses although she was growing heartily sick of them with more lovely gowns in her wardrobe.

While she was changing behind the screen, Mars said, "We need to hire a lady's maid for you in London."

"I don't need one," she answered, rinsing the tooth polish out of her mouth with water from a pitcher on the washstand.

"I argue you do. Nelson will not like seeing after both of us."

Clarissa came out from behind the screen, no longer embarrassed to be this undressed in front of him. As he had pointed out, the material of her night clothing was thicker than anything else she owned. She didn't even feel bothered by her feet being bare.

"I can take care of myself," she informed him, noting that he had built her pillow wall on the bed, and appreciating him for it. "You aren't the only one who can dress herself."

"I am certain you can," he said from his side

of the wall. He was on his back, the sheets up to his waist. His bits well covered. She had looked, guiltily. "However, we will need a temporary abigail in London for whatever my mother has planned. London is full of the very critical who will judge you by your style."

She'd forgotten what all the trip to London would entail. "A temporary lady's maid might be wise."

"Thank you," he said as if she had granted a request. "Ready for me to blow out the lamp?"

She climbed into bed, not worrying so much whether he caught a glimpse of ankles or a bit of leg as she did so. "Yes."

The room went dark.

"Good night, Mars," she whispered.

There was a stretch of silence where she thought he might have fallen asleep. Then, he said, just as quietly, "Good night, Clarissa."

And then, she had to ask, "Do you still dislike my name?"

He sat up, looked over the pillow wall at her, and she saw him shake his head in the dark as if she was hopeless. "Do you remember everything?"

She admitted, "I'm trying to let go of grudges."

He laughed. She felt him lean against the pillow wall as if reaching for her, but he did not touch her. Instead, he said, "I'm starting to think your name is lyrical. Lovely actually."

She fell asleep with a smile on her face.

Chapter Thirteen

The Goat Inn, St. Albans. On road to London—
watching Clarissa sleep: I envy her peace.
I'm as hard as an iron pike.

—Book of Mars

The next day, Sunday, promised to be a good
one for travel. They planned to leave for London after Sunday services since Clarissa insisted she must attend and wished to take Dora
with her. She secretly had hoped Mars would
accompany them.

He didn't. Instead, he said he had to see to
some paperwork.

His decision was unfortunate because the
matrons and everyone else in Maidenshop
were in attendance and they fussed over Dora,
who behaved like an angel. No mother could
have been prouder.

After the service, Clarissa took a moment to
search out the marker of her mother's grave.

Dandelions and grass were encroaching on it. She bent down, setting Dora on the grass before pulling the weeds away.

A moment later, a footstep came up behind her and then a woman cleared her voice, asking for Clarissa's attention. Clarissa looked up to see the Dowager Duchess of Winderton, holding her reticule in front of her with two hands as if she felt awkward.

Clarissa picked up Dora and rose to give a curtsey to the older woman. The dowager was truly the unofficial leader of the Matrons of Maidenshop. She and Clarissa had greeted each other in church but the dowager was now searching her out privately.

Dora immediately reached for the gold chain around Clarissa's neck. She seemed fascinated by the medallion and had teethed on it through the services.

"She likes it," the dowager said, nodding to busy Dora.

"As do I. Thank you, Your Grace." Clarissa had thanked her at the wedding breakfast but knew her manners and did so again.

The dowager waved her words away before saying, "I wanted a moment alone."

It wasn't a question. Clarissa answered as if it was. "Yes, Your Grace."

"I've taken great pleasure at seeing how well you turned out. In many ways, we've all felt like your mothers."

"I've appreciated your wisdom and support, Your Grace."

"I sought you out to tell you how pleased I am with this marriage. You and Marsden have much in common, you know."

That comment caught Clarissa off guard. "That we are both headstrong?"

The duchess laughed. "You are both resilient souls, and speaking of souls, I saw you couldn't encourage him to come to services."

"He is resistant."

"Marsden hasn't entered the church doors since the duel. His father died in his arms. Very sad. He was at that age where young men take everything hard. I know. My son lost his father at about the same age and he has been a challenge since." She spoke the last more to herself. Clarissa thought it wise not to comment.

The dowager drew a deep breath and released it. "You are going to be good for Marsden. You have both been adrift in the world. It is hard to be alone. My widowhood has taught me that. Take care of him, my lady. Men can be somewhat fragile creatures. They don't always understand what is important in life. We women have to gently lead them to it."

"I believe it would be hard to lead Marsden anywhere he doesn't want to go."

"Oh, you will manage. You are a handsome couple. It was almost as if you were meant to be. And, if you will take advice from an older woman who also had her marriage arranged for her, then let me urge you to let down your guard. He's a good man. Even when he charges off in the wrong direction. We all do from time to time."

On that note, she walked away at a stately pace, moving toward the headstone marking her husband's grave.

He's a good man. "She might be right," Clarissa whispered to Dora. The baby was too occupied with the chain to answer.

But Clarissa knew what the answer was.

She walked toward the waiting carriage and returned home. Mars waited for them. He was ready to travel. The coach had been packed and all was ready.

The hard part of leaving was Dora. It broke both their hearts to have her stay at Belvoir. She'd become a conduit between them. The decision to leave her behind with Mrs. Rucker and the staff was a sound one, except now, Clarissa and Mars were on their own.

To her surprise, Mars chose to ride in the coach with her. He wasn't even taking his horse, saying they wouldn't be in London that long. His words made her happy. She had only bad memories of her short time with the Emsdales in the city.

It was also nice to have a traveling companion. The coach was stocked with food, drink, and books. They also had cards for something different although she discovered they were both not that interested in games.

At first, his long legs and broad shoulders took up most of the room. However, as the ride progressed, she stopped worrying so much about carefully touching him. She even pushed him to move once when he started to nod off over his reading and leaned against her. He settled into the far corner of the coach.

A few minutes later, she found it more comfortable to nestle in next to him. Instead of reading, though, she found herself caught in studying him. *He's a good man.*

Well, he may be a good man but Clarissa would be lying if she claimed she didn't like the set of his features on his face—the strong nose, the jawline, the *lips*. She did like the lips. They were thin but sensual.

And she admired his hands. He wasn't wearing gloves. It was too hard to turn book pages in them. She was tempted to trace the line of his fingers, starting at the knuckles and going to the tips.

Instead, she reached down and kissed the back of his hand—

Mars started, waking.

Clarissa quickly sat up, lifting the book in her lap.

"Did I fall asleep?" he asked somewhat sheepishly. "That was rude of me."

"Not at all," she answered. "I've been entertained." She held up her book.

He nodded, straightened, and stretched. This was the way of married couples, she thought. They shared space. They watched over each other. She'd even used some of his mint pastilles that morning after she had polished her teeth.

And she liked being this close to him. Her

doubts were ebbing, and yet, the dowager was right, she and Marsden both had a good deal to learn about trust.

"We should be in St. Albans shortly," he said. They were spending the night there and would continue their journey in the morning. "You will enjoy the innkeeper's roast hen. It drips with butter."

Clarissa smiled. He did like butter and his favorite color was blue. Those things she knew and hoped to learn much more.

The innkeeper, Mr. Lloyd, was pleased to see them. They dined in a private room. Their supper had been waiting for them. The hen was tasty.

Mr. Lloyd gave them the best room of his establishment. The bed was not as big as the one at Belvoir. She and Marsden would be very close. A pillow wall might not even be effective.

Nor was she certain she wanted that wall up. It had felt good to burrow against him in the coach.

Mars noticed the lack of wall immediately. He had stayed in the tap room, giving her privacy while she readied for bed. He'd sent Nelson on ahead to London with the majority of their luggage. They each had a small valise for this overnight sojourn. She was under the covers by the time he joined her.

He stared at the bed. Then said, "I can sleep in another room."

Clarissa found it hard to meet his eye. She curled and uncurled her toes, making the sheet move, before she said, "I would rather you slept here."

It wasn't an inviting offer. Still, it was all she could say because, well, what if he refused? She didn't know what she would do if he teased her.

Instead, Mars blew out the candle. She listened to him undress in the dark. A sliver of moonlight came through the shutters and gave her a glimpse of a long thigh and a bare hip.

The mattress gave to his weight. He stretched out and she'd been right. He did take up most of the bed.

Clarissa turned on her side, giving him more room. She was comfortable but sleep was elusive. All she could think about were his hands, that glimpse of bare skin, and his kiss.

"Mars?"

He didn't answer.

She rose up to see if he slept. His face was turned away from her. He was on his back. She gathered the pillow under her head and watched him breathe until she fell asleep.

The next morning, Clarissa woke to find herself snuggled in beside him, her arm boldly across his chest. He had gently been trying to wake her.

"We must be on the road."

She sat up, embarrassed and a bit disoriented at discovering she'd set the boundary *and* had been the first to break it. "I—"

He shushed her, placing his fingers on her lips. "It is fine, Clarissa. You may be uncomfortable with my touch, but I do not mind you touching me."

She opened her mouth, ready to tell him that she was not uncomfortable, except a new thought struck her. "You are deliberately keeping a distance from me?"

He frowned as if she was silly. He rolled out of bed, reaching for his breeches.

For once, his nudity didn't faze her. No, she had a new idea. "What have I done? Does this mean—?" She stopped, not knowing what she wanted to ask. Then said, "You don't like me."

He'd been on his way to the privacy screen but stopped. "What?" He was by her side of the bed in an instant. "No, Clarissa, that wasn't my thinking."

"So, you are avoiding me."

"I'm not avoiding. We are in the same coach."

She shook her head, all of her uncertainties rising. He grabbed her hands and held them together, kneeling on the floor. "Clarissa, I want you to be comfortable with me. If that means waiting, then I will."

Waiting?

"For intimacy." He let go of her hands and exasperatedly raked a hand through his hair. "Remember, you said no intimacy."

She had. "But we kissed."

"Yes," he drawled out. "And then I thought a bit better of it. It is hard to be so close to you and not be able to—"

His voice broke off.

He wanted her?

"You like me?" she asked the question hesitantly, afraid of the answer either way.

He surprised her when he said, "What is not to like? To admire?" He shrugged. "I just want you to know you are safe. Besides, you are obviously naïve about all of this."

"All of this? Do you mean a 'shag'?" she asked, daring him with that crude word he'd used on her. "I'm not that naïve."

"Oh, you are terribly naïve or else you would have understood what a rough night I had. Or how throwing such a word around is an invitation to most men."

"Most men?"

"Save for me. I'm a bloody gentleman," he replied, grabbing his shirt and throwing it over his head. "And we must be on the road. Hop up and dress." He tucked his shirt in his breeches.

But he had sparked Clarissa's curiosity. "But do you want to kiss me?"

His response was to throw her dress in her face. "Now you are being a minx. Dress, Clarissa. You are tempting me and that isn't fair since I've decided to be a paragon of virtue. Isn't that what minister's daughters want? Paragons? Virtue? Well, I warn you, I'm no bloody saint." He said all this while sitting on a side chair and pulling on stockings and boots.

"I'm not certain what I want," Clarissa answered, and then said with complete honesty, "I did like our kisses."

He groaned. "You are killing me, woman."

Mars had called her a woman. The title rather thrilled her . . . because *he* saw her as one.

Tugging on his last boot, he looked over to her. "You are chewing on what I said. I can see it."

"I'm trying to understand."

He shook his head as if weary. "Rissa, perhaps I want you to want *me*."

The explanation stunned her. She had a say? Had she really expected him to honor her terms about intimacy? And what was this "wanting"?

And why did she like hearing him call her Rissa?

"It's intimacy," he said as if sensing her confusion. "I think I'm beginning to want more than just to bed you. There's something about you. You are good. And honest—" He shook his head. "You need to dress. We should be on the road."

He stood and started for the door. "I'll wait for you downstairs. Hodner will come up for our valises." He would have left but she stopped him with a question.

"Mars?" He paused, a hand on the door. "What if I wanted you to bed me? What do we become then?"

Her husband studied her as if weighing her request. Clarissa felt as if it was suddenly hard to breathe. *She'd* asked that question. It was so bold. She'd always been the one to react, never act—and yet, here she was opening herself to being more vulnerable than she had ever been with another person.

Mars took his hand off the door. "We can be whatever you wish. The decision is yours. I'll wait as long as it takes." On that note, he left the room.

Clarissa stared at the closed door. He would let *her* choose for the two of them?

She rose slowly from the bed, feeling as if a new person was inhabiting her body. He wanted her. The Earl of Marsden, everyone's favorite rake, had admitted he wished to bed her. But the final decision would be hers.

And how would she decide? If they did this, if they became husband and wife in the truest sense of the words, could she trust him not to hurt her?

It was the unanswerable question.

And she knew he would want one.

THEY REACHED the city by late midday.

Neither of them brought up the conversation they'd had that morning. Instead they had continued as the day before with books and cards . . . and yet there was a wealth of unspoken words between them.

Of course, his London home was on Grosvenor Square, the most fashionable address in the city. His house's façade was painted white brick with a stately black lacquered door and window boxes overflowing with hyssop and delicate periwinkle blossoms.

A hive of servants came running out to welcome them. They lined up inside the door to pay their respects to Clarissa.

The front hall of Marsden House was much smaller than Belvoir's. What it lacked in size, it made up for in the quality of decorations and furnishings.

This was the home of a very wealthy family. The floor was a pattern of gray and white marble tiles. More portraits of Mars's ancestors decorated the walls. *They are everywhere*, Mars had warned her shortly after they married. *Portrait after portrait of people looking like me*. She understood what he meant now.

The butler was Dalton, a surly looking man with an eye patch. He was not as tall as Gibson and appeared a bit scrappy. Still, Clarissa caught a twinkle in his eye as he welcomed her and sensed the two of them would manage well together. He offered the staff's congratulations on their marriage.

In contrast to Belvoir, this house had a housekeeper, a Mrs. Williams, who greeted Clarissa and offered a tour of the premises when she was ready.

Mars's secretary was Lowton, the one he claimed always took care of everything for him, including wages. Lowton wore spectacles on the end of his long nose and practically jumped with joy at the sight of Mars.

"I'm beyond thankful you are here, my lord," he said. "Lady Fenton has been breathing down our necks." He spoke with such relief, Clarissa surmised that he'd had his doubts that Mars would make an appearance. "And may I say, my lord, you are looking particularly well."

"Thank you, Lowton. And before you begin chiding me over matters I've ignored, I want to introduce my wife to you. You will find in her a willing ally in seeing that I meet all of my obligations."

Lowton bowed deeply. "My lady. It is an honor."

He was so formal, Clarissa almost forgot herself and curtseyed. She was saved by the squeeze of Mars's hand on her elbow, a reminder of sorts. "It is a pleasure to meet you, Mr. Lowton."

"You have prepared the paperwork I requested for my wife and me to sign?" Mars said.

"I have, my lord. I am ready to present it at your convenience."

"Let us see to the matter on the morrow. Meanwhile, Dalton, send a tray to our room. I'm famished." Mars took Clarissa's hand and led her up a curved staircase. "I have something special to show you," he told her.

But first, he brought her to their quarters. There was a family sitting area as well as separate dressing rooms for the earl and countess. Nelson had already unpacked them.

There was also a water closet. Mars gave her a moment to freshen herself and then he directed her down the hall. He opened a door with great fanfare.

The other library! This one, like the rest of the house, was smaller than Belvoir's, however the shelves went from floor to ceiling and every one was stocked with books. She stepped inside as if entering a holy room. There were two windows for light, several lamps for reading, and chairs built for comfort. A desk was tucked beneath one of the windows.

"My grandfather started this collection," Mars said with pride. "Some are over a hundred years old. These shelves over here"—he directed her attention to the ones in the corner by the window where the light was good—"are where I have Lowton place the most current books. I have a standing order with several booksellers. Byron's are here because no one seems able to escape him, now he is all the rage. Shelley, Robert Owen," he continued, tapping book spines, "and, of course, Miss Edgeworth." He said the last name proudly, as if he believed he'd surprised Clarissa.

Her only response was to ask, "Could we move the bed in here?"

Mars laughed. The sound rose to the high ceiling, full-bodied, masculine, magical.

Dalton had come to the door. He'd been about to interrupt them but instead his mouth opened in surprise as if he'd never heard his lord laugh.

It was a short-lived moment, because Lady Fenton had been right on the butler's heels. She entered without fanfare, waving Dalton away. "I don't need to be introduced."

Mars's laughter stopped abruptly. "Mother," he said in a heavy voice.

"And your stepfather is here. Come along, Fenton. Don't linger in the hallway," she ordered.

Lord Fenton entered the room. Clarissa recognized him immediately from the satirical drawings that had circulated about him over the years, drawings that had even made their way to Maidenshop. He was portly, with birdlike legs that weren't shown to advantage in knee breeches. He combed his gray hair up and over his balding pate. He had a large nose and pointed chin. When he was younger, those features probably showed to better advantage than they did now.

He appeared a weary man past his prime. Clarissa could understand why some would wish he stepped down from positions of authority, especially when he spoke and there was a wheeze behind his sonorous words. "Pleasure," he said, drawing out the word, "to see you, Marsden. Happy to have your support in this fight. I can't believe Dervil is challenging me."

His lordship offered his hand and Mars took it. "Fenton. You are looking fit."

"I age, my lord, I age. Fortunately, I have my wife to guide me straight." He turned to his lady, extending his hand as if to call her over to him.

Lady Fenton appeared not to notice her husband's summons. She had pulled a book off the shelf and seemed to study it, although Clarissa was not fooled. She believed the woman heard every word and nuance and chose to ignore her husband.

While pushing her son to vote in his favor?

His mother's behavior didn't make sense . . . until one realized Lord Fenton was at least a decade older than his wife. And while Lady Fenton had an air of vitality, her husband appeared ready for a nap.

He endorsed Clarissa's suspicions when he said, "Marsden, may I sit?"

"Please do," Mars answered, offering him the most comfortable chair in the room. When his guest was seated, he said, "You have yet to meet my wife. Clarissa, this is my stepfather, the infamous Lord Fenton."

His lordship laughed at the description. "My infamous days are over," he assured Clarissa. "Pardon if I don't stand. Gout has robbed my legs of strength." He pointed to his right leg. "Unfortunately, they seem doubly bad today."

"Fenton," his wife said in warning, "no one wishes to hear about ailments."

"Ah, yes." He gave Clarissa a slightly embarrassed smile. "I should have stayed home. Wanted to welcome you to the family."

"Thank you," Clarissa said.

Lord Fenton barely heard her. He became interested in other things. "Marsden, my throat is parched. May I trouble you for a small glass of ale."

"Of course." Mars moved to the door where Dalton lingered outside.

The butler had heard the request and was turning to a footman to fetch it when Lady Fenton spoke. "We don't have time for you to drink," she informed her husband. "You are due at Lord Rockland's within the hour for the finance discussion. You need to know what is going on."

"Except I do know," Lord Fenton said. "Or at least you know and that is the same thing, isn't it? They will wait for me. Besides, it isn't anything formal."

"Well, *I'm* not waiting for you. I shall be at the meeting."

Lord Fenton made a vexed sound but he stood, needing a moment to manage his balance. Both Mars and Clarissa put out hands to help him. He waved them away. "The wife would not approve," he said in a mocking whisper. "She wishes me to be as strong as Hercules."

"My lord, the coach is waiting," Lady Fenton said. He started to offer his arm to her. She rejected him with a wave of her hand. "I will be along in a moment."

He was not pleased to be dismissed. He forced a smile, looked to Clarissa and Mars, and said, "Married life, eh?" He moved out the door with as much dignity as a man could muster after being shamed by his wife. He favored his right leg.

Mars nodded to Dalton. "See him out. And be certain he receives the ale for the ride." Another waiting footman took action and fell in behind Lord Fenton.

There was silence in the library until his lordship moved down the hall, and then Lady Fenton said, "I suppose, Clarissa, you find me cold." Before Clarissa could respond, Lady

Fenton shrugged. "I didn't handle that well. I just wanted him gone."

"No one expects you to do things well, Mother," Mars answered. "And do you truly believe he is fit to run such an important committee? He's aged since I met him last."

"He has been running it for years," she replied.

"Has he or have you?" Mars asked.

She made an impatient noise. "The other members of the committee are older. With worse gout. Most of all Rockland."

"Then this country is in trouble."

"Not as long as the Tories have power."

"And there aren't younger, healthier Tories?" Mars asked.

"Dervil. Do you wish to vote for him?"

"You know I won't."

His mother smiled, the expression far from comforting. "Good." She put down the book. "In truth, I prepare all of Fenton's papers and his speeches. I control that committee and I make him sound like the statesman he wishes he was."

"The truth is out," Mars replied without surprise.

His mother shot him a look of annoyance. "You have no idea what it is like to, because of one's sex, be forced to watch others make a hash of matters."

"Except, your husband doesn't seem well," Clarissa dared to suggest, feeling empathy for the man.

"He is well enough for Parliament, especially

the Lords," Lady Fenton answered. "Trust me, he'll eat a plate full of beefsteak tonight, down two brandies, and sleep well. As for the two of you"—she gave them a stern but haughty look—"I would be careful of what you say and how you say it . . . because I am no fool. You weren't married that day at Belvoir."

Clarissa immediately experienced guilt. She had feared Lady Fenton's reaction if she learned the truth.

Mars didn't even blink. "We are married now."

"I know that as well. Your countess is that abandoned baby that everyone in that village was in a lather over. Odd that out of all the more suitable women in England you could have married, you chose her. But then, you always favored your father. Your decisions aren't logical."

"Thank you," Mars answered coolly.

"I also know that the child is not yours, Clarissa. She is Mars's by-blow."

"Whom I recognize," he stated, again, surprising Clarissa with his calmness. It was almost as if he had anticipated this reckoning. "As well as recognizing Clarissa as my wife and Dora's mother. Lowton has prepared the proper paperwork to give Clarissa full authority." The two of them sounded as if they were throwing down gauntlets at each other.

"I don't care what you do," Lady Fenton replied. "I just want you to keep my husband in power."

"You mean, keep you in power. I will do that, Mother. But only because otherwise Dervil might win."

She smiled, her expression almost warm. "And I, in turn, will deliver as promised. You shall be the decisive vote against Dervil."

He gave a short bow.

Lady Fenton gathered her shawl around her. "Well, enough of this. I shall expect you tomorrow evening at Lord and Lady Harrison's rout. You should have an invitation already. I've told her you are coming. Everyone will be there." She smiled at Clarissa. "I pray you have something decent to wear, Countess?"

Clarissa stumbled over a reply. The woman was so bold. No wonder he didn't like his mother. Clarissa wasn't so naïve as to believe all mothers had loving natures. But this woman? She thought only of herself.

And the blue dress Mrs. Yarborough had made was perfectly lovely.

However, Lady Fenton didn't require a reply from Clarissa for her blunt comment. "Please don't show me out. I know my way." She left, gliding out the door as if she was Someone of Importance. Clarissa didn't believe she could spend another moment in the woman's presence without losing her good manners—

Mars grabbed her by both arms, pulled her against him and bussed her on the lips. He let her go as abruptly as he'd grabbed her. "What is this about?" she wondered.

"That you are not my mother," he answered.

"I'm glad I'm not either," Clarissa agreed. "Although, now I understand why you don't trust women."

"Don't trust them?" He frowned. "I like women."

"For friends?"

That stopped him, and then he said, "I like you."

He liked her . . . and he wanted her.

Before Clarissa could frame a response, Dalton knocked on the open door. "My lord," he said, seeing that they had noticed his presence, "I meant to offer this earlier." He held out a letter.

"I know, you were waylaid," Mars said, excusing him. "My mother is a strong personality." He took the letter. "It is from Balfour." He happily broke the seal, and read the letter. "He congratulates us on our wedding. The news has traveled fast."

Clarissa was not surprised. The matrons were remarkable in their ability to spread news.

He continued reading, and then looked over to Clarissa, his eyes bright with good news. "Balfour designed the sets for a production of *Antony and Cleopatra* opening at Drury Lane this evening. They asked us to join them in their box."

"I would like that." Clarissa had never been to a play other than the performances Mr. Balfour's wife, Kate, had presented in Maidenshop last year. Kate had headed her own traveling troupe and she had certainly stirred up the village. Clarissa liked her very much.

"They invited us for dinner before the performance as well. What do you think?"

"That would be nice."

He folded the letter, holding it a second before saying, "Thurlowe and Gemma are in London as well. They will be members of the party."

Thurlowe, the man she should have married and would have, except he was in love with another—Gemma. By all accounts, they were deeply in love.

Mars watched her as if gauging her reaction. As if her response mattered to him.

Did he worry that she had feelings for Mr. Thurlowe or that Gemma's presence would bother her?

"We don't have to go," Mars started, and she realized he was forming his own conclusions.

Quickly, she said, "I believe we should. They are your friends and I would like to see Kate and Gemma."

Gemma's name had been hard to say, but looking at Mars, Clarissa realized she just might be married to the better man.

Especially when he smiled as if relieved there wouldn't be any problems. "Well, then, I will send word that we accept."

Chapter Fourteen

I will kill Dervil.

—*Book of Mars*

*T*he Balfour residence was in a square as coveted as Grosvenor and was as well-appointed as Marsden House. Clarissa wore her wedding dress, the one of cream muslin shot through with gold.

The dinner party was intimate and the conversation light and easy. Mr. Balfour insisted Clarissa call him Brandon because she was now one of their number. Toasts were made in celebration of Mars and Clarissa's marriage and everyone acted genuinely happy for them.

Was it strange to see Ned Thurlowe after the passage of time?

Actually, it wasn't. Indeed, conversation seemed easier because Clarissa no longer felt she had to please him. She'd always liked Ned. She admired him. He was a good doctor with a keen interest in natural philosophy, geology, and other academic endeavors. The lecture series on those subjects that he had started in Maidenshop was of benefit to the village.

And Gemma truly was the perfect wife for him. She, too, was a healer. She had studied herbs and their remedies. She had taken over The Garland from the Logical Men's Society and made it into a tea garden that everyone in the village enjoyed.

She'd also been a good friend to Clarissa before she fell in love with Ned.

No one asked questions about the quickness of Clarissa's marriage to Mars . . . but then he surprised her by sharing with his friends the story of Dora.

"You? With a child?" Brandon said.

"He runs from our Anne," Kate confided to the others.

Mars discounted their grievances. Choosing instead to talk of Dora and how she was either happily babbling or gnawing on anything like a dog with a bone, including his fingers.

"Does this mean we should have Nurse bring Anne down for you to pay your respects?" Brandon teased.

"When I first met Anne, I didn't know what to do with a baby," Mars claimed. "I've changed. Here, fetch her and I shall hold her on my knee. I've had much experience, including wet clouts."

"Is that true, Clarissa?" Brandon asked in disbelief.

"He is a remarkable father." Her answer impressed everyone. Mars reached over and covered her hand in her lap with his own as if he appreciated her support. It was a small gesture, the sort of thing a true husband would do when he was pleased with his wife. A wife he liked.

"Well, I wish we could test this new version of our friend the earl," Kate answered. "Unfortunately, Anne is asleep. She is the perfect baby. She is in her bed early and sleeps soundly. Of course, she is up very early as well."

"Fortunately, Nurse and I are early risers," Brandon said. "I do my best work then. Nurse will bring her to me and we enjoy our breakfast together."

"So you aren't an early riser?" Clarissa surmised, looking to Kate, who shook her head vigorously, mouthing the word *No*.

The time had come for them to withdraw from the table and head to the theater. They crowded into the Marsden coach. Clarissa enjoyed being included in this group.

And she felt as if her place was at Mars's side. She didn't hesitate to slip her arm in his and let him escort her. A time or two, he had referred to her as "Rissa." She liked the name because he was the only one who used it.

A huge crowd milled outside the theater. Clarissa clung to Mars's arm as he worked his way through the press of people. If she had been alone, she would have been lost. Instead, she leaned on him and he was there to guide her. She didn't let go of him when they reached the private box. He moved his chair closer to hers and she held his hand resting on his leg.

The play was all she could have wished. It was bigger and finer than one of Kate's productions in Maidenshop. Clarissa lost herself in the story of ancient Egypt and was frustrated when they paused for intermission.

Mars suggested they fetch refreshments for the ladies. The men rose, promising to return.

"They are pleased to see each other," Kate observed. "And we are all happy you and Mars have joined us in London, Clarissa. I don't know how you convinced him to come here. Lately, he has been set against visiting the city."

Before Kate could say more, a well-dressed woman wearing diamonds and ostrich feathers entered their box calling her name. Kate jumped to her feet to greet her warmly. She introduced her friend as Mrs. Bennington, "a wonderful patroness of the arts," before the two of them escaped to a corner of the box where they might have more privacy.

That left Gemma and Clarissa alone.

They sat for a moment. It was awkward, and then Clarissa realized she didn't want it to be.

She turned to speak just as Gemma leaned close. "Is that man in the box across from us staring? I think he is looking at you. I mean, I don't want to alarm you but, his manner is, well, uncomfortable and quite rude."

Clarissa glanced to look in the direction Gemma indicated. A man of some fifty years of age or more was literally gawking at her. He had iron gray, short-cropped hair and a lean, athletic build. He'd even put a glass up to his eye to ogle her better.

Something about the man disturbed her. Clarissa almost found it hard to breathe and not in a good way. She didn't understand her reaction or why he displayed such outwardly poor manners.

"You've made a conquest," Gemma said.

"Not by choice. Anyway, perhaps he is interested in you."

"Oh, no, he is definitely eyeing you."

"Let us go out into the hall," Clarissa suggested, wanting to escape. "That way, Kate and Mrs. Bennington can have a bit of privacy." The two signaled to Kate where they were going and made their way out of the box. Right before they left, Clarissa cast a look over her shoulder. The man was no longer across the theater from them.

Perhaps it had been their imaginations?

Still, it felt good to move. They didn't go far because the hall was a crush of people visiting with each other.

However, the moment gave Clarissa the opportunity to say to Gemma, "I hope we can be friends the way we were."

Gemma's smile was grateful. "We still are, Clarissa. We always have been although I've been concerned that Ned and I hurt you."

"I'm the one who gave him up, remember? It was obvious he loved you."

Gemma leaned close. "I believe Marsden is a lucky man to have you for a wife. And Kate is right. He acts happy."

"I don't know if I'm the one making him happy. He adores Dora."

"I think he adores you."

Clarissa wished that were true . . . because she was falling in love with him.

The realization rocked her slightly. She and the Earl of Marsden. They were an odd couple, and maybe, perhaps, perfectly suited for each other.

"Here are the gentlemen," Gemma said.

Clarissa looked up to see her tall, handsome husband holding two punch cups to keep them from being jostled and spilled by the crowd. He caught her eye and smiled, and, in that moment, she knew her suspicions were correct—she was in love.

It was as if he was *her* person. The only one who said exactly what he thought around her and pushed her to do the same. Who truly *listened* to her and behaved as if her wishes mattered to him. Was any woman more blessed?

Gemma spoke as the men joined them. "We had the strangest experience," she said, taking a sip from her cup. "There is a gentleman in the box directly across from us who was staring to the point we felt we needed to move."

Clarissa sensed a change in Mars. He seemed to grow tighter, harder.

"The man was staring from across the theater?" Ned asked.

Gemma nodded. "Right at Clarissa. It was obvious."

"I didn't see him," Brandon said.

"I saw him, and they are right," Mars answered. "He was staring at us."

"You noticed him?" Brandon asked.

"I always notice Lord Dervil," Mars answered.

Clarissa almost dropped her punch cup. *Lord Dervil had been the staring man? Did he know why Mars had come to London? Was that why he was so rude?*

Gemma spoke. "So it wasn't us he was staring at but you, my lord?"

Mars smiled, the expression cold before addressing Clarissa. "Are you ready to go back in, my lady? I believe the next act is about to start."

The group all went inside to take their seats. Mrs. Bennington acknowledged everyone, made her apologies for claiming all of Kate's time, and then left them alone.

Brandon explained to Kate what had happened.

"Dervil? Here?" she said. She looked across the theater to Lord Dervil's box. He was not there.

Gemma leaned forward. "I don't like him. He has an unsettling intensity about him. I think you should be wary, Mars. Something terrible may happen."

"Believe her," Ned said. "Every time she utters a warning, I listen. Apparently, ominous feelings are something else she received from her Gran."

"And you call yourself a man of science," Mars chided. He put his arm on the back of Clarissa's chair.

However, Clarissa's enjoyment of Shakespeare's tragedy of love and politics was dimmed.

At one point, she leaned toward Mars. "I can't wait to return to Maidenshop."

He laced his fingers with her hand. "I can't either." Those should have been comforting words, except the stoniness was still with him and there was a bleakness in his expression, a conflict. Or was it a resolve?

Clarissa was suddenly afraid. She didn't have the gift of sight, but something was not right. It was as if Lord Dervil threatened this fragile world she and Mars were building.

"Let us go tomorrow," she pleaded, "I miss Dora." It was an excuse, the lure to have him agree with her. "Someone else can cast the deciding vote against Lord Dervil."

Except, he didn't answer, and she sensed he was no longer watching the play either.

So Dervil had thought to taunt him by discomforting Clarissa.

Mars would make him pay for that insult as well. The moment their paths crossed, he would use it as a reason to challenge the man. He really didn't care about the vote. He had one purpose for being in London. Clarissa had almost made him forget. He should thank Dervil for the clarity.

He tried not to be distracted by his thoughts. He smiled, nodded, commented as if interested.

But he was going to kill Dervil, no matter the cost. He might miss years of Dora's life if he was in exile, but she would be safe with Clarissa.

He reached for his wife's hand. They were all crowded in the coach, returning his friends home. He kissed the back of her glove.

Clarissa glanced up at him. Their gazes held.

Did the coach grow quiet? He didn't know and he didn't care. His thoughts were dark as he stewed over Dervil's ogling his wife as if she were one of the actresses on the stage and free for his taking.

They dropped Balfour and Kate home first. Then carried Thurlowe and Gemma to their hotel.

Finally, they were alone. The only light in the coach came from the lamps outside the door. She hadn't moved away from him as he anticipated she would now that they had more room. Instead, she leaned into him.

"Mars?" He forced a smile, ready to say something pleasant, except she looked up at him, her eyes reflecting the lamps. "Your whole manner changed when you heard about Lord Dervil. But then, you knew he was there from the very beginning of the play, hadn't you?"

"He should not have behaved toward you in such a common manner." Anger welled up in him again.

She placed her hand on his thigh. "Please, don't dwell on it. I was not insulted. Think nothing of it."

"You forgive too easily," he challenged. Her body was pressed against his. Her hair smelled of the soaps she favored. Lemon, lavender. Spicy, sharp, evocative.

His wife.

"Perhaps I have something else on my mind." There was a huskiness in her tone. It brought his attention to her lips.

Before he could question her meaning, the coach rolled to a stop as they reached his residence. Hodner opened the door and Mars climbed out, offering his hand to his wife.

She took it, her movements graceful. He followed her into the house and up the stairs, admiring the gentle sway of her hips.

For the past several days, he'd begun to notice the little things about her that he'd never considered in other women. When Clarissa read, her lips would move as if she argued with the book. Her eyes always widened when something sparked her interest whether it was one of Dora's expressions or an unexpected new idea, or experience—like this evening. She'd all but disappeared into the play.

He envied her clarity about life, her faith in people. Her example was pushing him to be a better man.

Or so he had thought until he'd noticed Dervil directly across the theater from them shortly before the intermission.

Mars hadn't been interested in refreshments. He'd suggested going out for them because he wanted to move closer to where Dervil was without drawing attention. He actually hoped to put himself in the man's path and perhaps provoke a challenge there.

Instead, Dervil had struck at Mars by making Clarissa uncomfortable. He'd treated Mars's wife in an insulting manner.

The bloody bastard would pay for that . . . along with his other sins—

"You've left again," she said, interrupting his thoughts. She'd reached the top of the stairs. "What is on your mind? You looked so hard. One moment I think you are with me and in the next, it is as if your mind is someplace else. An unpleasant place."

Mars nodded to the servant on the floor, Ellis, giving him permission to extinguish the wall sconces and turn in for the night. He took her hand, moving her toward the bedroom. The door was open and a candle burned. He'd already told Nelson not to wait up.

"I'm sorry for my distraction." He kissed the back of her fingers before confessing, "I'm not ignoring you. I was thinking about Dervil."

"I know, and you shouldn't," she said. "He means nothing to us."

"Clarissa—"

"*No.* Mars, you give the man too much power."

"You don't realize that staring in that manner was an insult."

"Not if I don't take it as such. You are going to vote against him and prevent him from getting something he wants. Please, don't ruin this evening. It has been amazing."

She was amazing.

They had reached the bedroom. The sheets had been turned down. The candlelight gave the room a welcoming glow. He shut the door behind them.

Their separate dressing rooms were on opposite sides of the bedroom. Mars started in the direction of his when he heard Clarissa softly say his name. He stopped. "Yes."

She had pulled her gloves off. She stood next to the bedpost, a petite, regal figure. The candlelight played off the gold threads shot through her dress—and he realized he would always remember her exactly like this. No artist could capture her beauty in this moment.

Clarissa was precious to him. *She mattered.*

If Dervil did anything to harm her, Mars would kill the man with his bare hands—

She started as if reacting to the dark direction of his thoughts. "My lord, please. He isn't worth your anger. Not when we are alone."

Mars nodded mutely. She didn't understand his need for justice. He went into his dressing room, removing his clothes and preparing for bed. He gave her time to don her heavy night-dress and be in bed first. But it was damn trying.

His wife was more than just some delectable bit of muslin. She'd easily fit in with his friends, although he'd not doubted she would. Clarissa was intelligent, insightful, and caring.

And he was very much waiting for the day when she decided her rule against intimacy was no longer important, and, please, God, make it soon.

Yes, he wanted to make love to her, to see if she was as passionate and clever in bed as she was about everything else. Other women could not compare.

He opened the dressing room. Clarissa was in bed. Because of the warmth of the day, the windows were open. What was left of the moon fell across the covers—and that was when Mars realized there was no pillow wall.

Perhaps his good behavior last night had convinced her it wasn't necessary to be so cautious.

Could he lure her across the imaginary line in the bed? She'd crossed it in her sleep last night.

He dearly wanted to make love to her . . . and yet, he was practicing discipline. He wanted to prove to her that he could behave, even though he was already hard. Hopefully she couldn't see that in the moonlight.

Mars hopped into bed, pulling the covers up to hide his excitement—and then froze.

Clarissa had pushed up on the bed as if to welcome him. Her hair formed a curling curtain around her, but he could see that she, too, was in the buff.

"Mars," she said, "I think I want to change our terms."

He didn't trust himself to speak. Had he been hard a moment ago? It had been nothing compared to what he felt now.

Mars opened his mouth to speak but his blood was thrumming through his veins and he found it hard to form words.

Then she moved closer to him and said, "If you don't kiss me right now, I don't know what I'm going to do."

He reached for his wife.

Chapter Fifteen

*It will be harder to leave Clarissa than
I had ever imagined.*

—*Book of Mars*

He was touching her. Holding her.

Clarissa had begun to regret her high-minded "terms."

Kisses were what she wanted. Kisses, this man, and everything about him.

She had been standing in her dressing room when she'd realized her doubts about him had been silly. Of course, he was arrogant and entitled. He was also generous, protective, and rather fun.

Clarissa had enjoyed this evening. At one point, Kate had been teasing her husband and Clarissa had looked over at Mars. Their gazes met, and she'd known exactly what was going through his mind, a quip he dared not speak aloud. He'd lifted his brow as if asking if she agreed and she'd had to stifle her laugh.

Clarissa was also tired of always being cautious. She'd married him. For better or for worse, she'd tossed her lot in with Mars. So why deny all he had to offer?

Besides, she was tired of eyeing his naked buttocks and not being able to let herself touch him.

So, she'd left her "nun's habit" hanging in the dressing room. She hadn't bothered with stacking pillows because she wanted him beside her.

She wanted *him*.

Still, it had taken courage to tell him that she had changed her mind, and now she was glad she had spoken up. He took her in his arms, her skin against his, warm and vibrant, and kissed her in a way that robbed her of reason.

"Rissa," he whispered into her ear before nibbling the line of her jaw. She adored hearing him use that name. No one else could call her that, just him.

Her hip bumped against his. He ran a hand over the skin, pulling her leg over his.

And she was free to kiss him. To let her hand move across the hard planes of his body, including those buttocks she'd admired.

Yes, he was taller and broader than she was, but it didn't make any difference in bed.

The heat of his mouth over her breast almost sent her through the ceiling. When he traced the inside of her thigh, his fingers reaching the most intimate places, she would have panicked if not for her trust in him. He was an accomplished lover, which was a handy skill at this moment.

As for herself, Clarissa was acting on instinct and, for once, she wasn't being shy about being greedy.

She didn't hesitate to pull his lips to her mouth. The taste of him excited her. She was a starving woman at a feast and she wasn't going to stop until she had her fill.

He rolled her onto her back, showing her how to cradle him with her thighs. She felt the hard length of him and curved her hips to nestle him

Mars looked down at her. He balanced most of his weight on his arms. "This might hurt, Rissa."

She nodded. She'd heard the whispers. Her life had allowed her to move in many circles and country women did not hold back their opinions and teasing about what happened between men and women. Some said that they had screamed. Others that it had been a mere pinprick.

Clarissa didn't care. In this moment, her body ached to have him inside her. And she knew losing her virginity would be a momentary discomfort. Then there would be, as one lusty wife had declared to her, *just the fun of the rolling around*. She wished to reach that point.

He pressed against her. The worry did go through her mind that she might be too petite for him there, and yet women smaller than her had birthed babies.

His lips took hers. His arm slid under her hips, raising her. She felt his tongue. She liked kisses this deep and she rose as if to swallow him whole—just as he thrust forward.

It was shocking, that thrust.

For a white-hot moment, she felt as if she was being torn asunder. She cried out in shock, a sound swallowed by their kiss.

Mars went very still. Her arms were wrapped around him and she held him tight, while she cataloged the pain, the tightness, all the feelings.

Almost as swiftly as the pain had come, it ebbed. Tight muscles relaxed. She liked the sensation of him inside . . . and then he began moving.

There was pure pleasure in his movement. She wrapped herself around him. He whispered in her ear that she was lovely, that no one could compare to her, that she was "his life."

And all the time, a need built inside her. A yearning for release that she didn't understand, but he did.

He was guiding her. Taking care of her. Driving her until, suddenly, Clarissa felt deep muscles tighten, followed by a sense that she was falling into an abyss, right before the most indulgent, whirling sense of sensual gratification took hold of her.

She cried his name. His arms tightened and then, in one hard thrust, he joined her, releasing his seed to flow through her. She arched, her head on the pillow, reveling in the sensation of taking him in.

It was done. She was his wife in word and in deed. They had become one. And that was the miracle of all this. They were one. He belonged to her; she belonged to him.

Mars fell to his side, rolling her over on top of him. Her hair spilled over his shoulders. She lay on his chest, unable to move, the aftermath rolling through her until she was spent, her body as boneless and languid as a cat.

He took her hand, kissed it, and pulled it up over his head. Their lips met. The kiss was sweet as if they were savoring this moment.

Finally, "Is it always like this?" she had to ask. At last she understood why poets sang love's praises.

His gray eyes met hers. "It's never been like this."

Clarissa swelled with pride at her lover's praise.

He leaned over, gently lowering her to the mattress. "How do you feel?" He sounded anxious.

Clarissa stretched. "I feel . . . as if that is the most wonderful thing to do ever."

Mars acted as if he'd held his breath in worry, but at her response, he burst out in laughter. "It is," he assured her. "The most wonderful thing ever."

Then he gathered her into his arms, his legs intertwined with hers, and they fell asleep.

And that was the most wonderful thing ever as well.

THE NIGHT before, Kate had offered Clarissa a dress to wear for the Harrington rout. She claimed to have dozens of gowns in her dressing room, and one of them should work for Clarissa with a few alterations, such as a shorter hem.

It was also a good time for a cozy chat with a person whom Clarissa admired very much.

"You and Mars act happy," Kate said as they went through the gowns. "And is it my imagination or do you seem to have a bit more of a twinkle in your eye than usual?"

Clarissa couldn't reply. All she could do was grin. She felt like a fool being so silly. Still, that morning, she and Mars had lingered in bed as late as possible. She couldn't have her fill of touching him, holding him, feeling him inside her. Or, as she confessed it to him, she dearly enjoyed a good "shag," a comment that had made him laugh with pleasure.

Oh, yes, that word. She thought it the best word in the world, especially since their lovemaking seemed to bind them all the more to each other.

There was a playfulness about their joining. An excitement in the joy of discovery. In fact, she couldn't wait to be done with this dress expedition to return to his arms.

The distrust and resentment she'd once nursed against him had been replaced with faith. He was not the ogre she'd once thought him. His love for his daughter had let her see a softer side to him. Now, she held hope for their future because she'd found where she belonged in this somewhat callous world—and that was in his arms.

"You love him, don't you?" Kate said.

"I don't even know what love is," Clarissa had to say. She wasn't ready to answer questions. It was all still too new.

"Love is what gives your face that funny, melty look whenever you are around him."

"Do I look melty?"

"*Very* melty. He appears a bit melty, too."

"Do you think?" Her friend's observation pleased her and softened her voice.

"Oh, absolutely," Kate said. "Brandon even said last night that he thinks Mars has met his match. And we are happy for it. He has needed someone by his side for a long time."

But did Mars feel for her what she felt for him?

Love was a big word. A scary one . . . and apt description for what Clarissa felt. No, Mars was not perfect, and she wouldn't want him to be anything other than himself. But the man he was made her happy.

Kate hugged her. "Don't be afraid of it. He is a good man, one of my favorites."

"And you trust him?"

"Without a doubt," Kate answered, taking the question seriously.

"I have no idea how to be a countess," Clarissa blurted out. "I mean, tonight, I won't know anyone save for Lady Fenton . . . and I don't think she likes me. I know I don't feel comfortable with her."

"Don't worry what she thinks. Be yourself. You have wonderful manners, your heart is in the right place, and you know exactly who you are."

"Who I am is a foundling. I have no family and my parentage will always be a mystery." She didn't share what she'd learned about her mother. The information was still too new.

Kate said, "Clarissa, Mars will love you if he doesn't already. He won't be able to help himself. All of us, Ned, Brandon, myself, already see signs of it. He was more relaxed and open last night than any of us could have anticipated. And," she said, pulling an emerald green water silk from her closet, "I don't believe he will be able to resist you in this dress. You most certainly will appear every inch a countess."

She was right. The emerald was perfect for Clarissa's coloring. "When you return to London for a longer visit, I'll take you shopping," Kate promised.

"I don't know when we will return. I'm ready to go home now," Clarissa answered. "I'm not one for the city. I can't wait until this vote is over and we return to Dora."

"When will that be?"

"Thursday. It can't come soon enough."

"Well, let us see how to make you the talk of the town this evening." Kate called in her lady's maid Mary who had been in charge of costumes for the acting troupe. Mary was good with a needle and pinned up the hem.

Mary stood, admiring her handiwork, and then said in a mock whisper to Kate as if she were a guest at the Harrison ball, "They say she is the new countess."

"She's lovely," Kate answered in the spirit of the moment. "Incomparable! No wonder Marsden married her without fanfare! She's a beauty!"

Clarissa laughed, even as she blushed. She didn't see herself as all that attractive.

But Mars did. He'd called her lovely.

Maybe, perhaps, she might believe it to be true?

"How must we finish her, Mary?" Kate asked.

They spent the next hour discussing hairstyles, ribbons vs. feathers vs. velvet caps, gloves, and shawls. Kate insisted that Mary must go to Marsden House that evening to style Clarissa's hair and plans were made. Mary would also bring the altered dress with her.

On the short ride home, Clarissa caught herself thinking not of the dress or the evening ahead, but of the question of love. What was she to Mars?

At the door, she asked the footman where the earl was. "In his study, my lady."

The study was located on the ground floor toward the back of the house. It had a view of a small side garden. The room was tiny compared to Belvoir standards with an even closet of a room to the side for Mr. Lowton. Fortunately, the secretary was away and she found her husband studying a stack of papers on the desk in front of him.

She knocked on his open door.

He looked up with a frown which quickly turned to a welcoming smile.

"Am I interrupting?" she asked.

"Thankfully so," he said, pushing away from the desk. He motioned to the papers. "These are Lowton's assessments on what issues I should be aware of. The man is more pleased than you are that I am at last taking on a few of my responsibilities. Who knew there were so many votes? Or so much information to be taken in?"

"You would have, my lord," Clarissa said, "if you had been paying attention over the years. Of course, now that I've met Lady Fenton . . ."

"You understand," he finished and then laughed as if the two of them were in perfect accord. "Did you find a dress?" he asked.

"Yes, Kate was most helpful."

"I would buy a shop full of dresses, but I like you undressed best of all." He gifted her with a lazy beautiful smile that sent more heat through her than his words. "Come here," he said.

Clarissa shyly obeyed and he kissed her fully and deeply, pulling her into his lap. He wrapped his arms around her—

There was a footstep out in the hall. She jumped up a second before Mr. Lowton, looking very officious in his spectacles, appeared in the doorway. "I've returned, my lord. Oh— I'm sorry. I didn't see you were busy. I beg your pardon, my lady. I'll just go, I mean, I'll do something else. That's what I will do."

He obviously suspected this was not a good moment to interrupt. Did it show on her face? Clarissa would have dashed out the door in embarrassment except Mars held her hand. "No problem, Lowton. I'm glad you are here. Let's have my wife sign those papers you prepared."

"Yes, my lord," he answered, moving to Mars's desk where there was a leather sheath holding several papers. The documents inside gifted Clarissa with a handsome income of five hundred pounds per year while Mars was alive and a substantial settlement of thirty-five thousand pounds in the event of his death.

The numbers were staggering. She had never imagined such wealth. "It is too much."

"Not to worry, my heir, who is a cousin I can't abide, will inherit more. However, this should see you and Dora happy."

"Dora and I would be happier if you live a long life."

His gray eyes met hers. She expected him to be pleased with her avowal, instead, a shadow seemed to pass over him. "Whatever happens, I promised that you would have security, Rissa. And so you shall. Lowton will oversee everything."

"I'm honored," the secretary answered. "You are also going to receive rights to live at Belvoir for as long as you choose."

"This is almost too much, Mars," Clarissa said.

"Actually, I don't know that it is enough," he answered. "If you don't wish to live at Belvoir, you are free to choose another home. All I ask is that you take care of Dora . . . and yourself. I want you happy."

"We are happier with you, my lord."

"Spoken like a dutiful wife," he answered. His tone was light, teasing almost, and yet it disturbed her. He signed the papers and handed the leather file to Lowton.

"I shall take this to the lawyers at once," Lowton said, excusing himself.

When they were alone, Clarissa said, "Thank you."

"You are more than welcome. We had an agreement to this marriage, Rissa. You asked for security. Wasn't that one of your terms?"

"I'm overwhelmed by your generosity. I just—" She stopped, words failing her. She was sitting in the chair across from his desk where he stood. She looked at her hands. She'd removed her gloves to read the documents. "You have humbled me, my lord. I did not expect such largesse."

He moved to the chair next to her. "You deserve this and more."

"We have not been married long—"

Mars pulled her up and kissed her.

This kiss was different from others. It was more solemn, almost like a benediction. Or a farewell.

When it broke, she looked hard into his eyes. "Is everything all right?"

"It's perfect, Clarissa. Perfect."

She wasn't certain she understood. Something deeper seemed to be brewing inside of him.

And then she said, "I love you." The words just flowed out of her. Perhaps Kate had planted the seeds, but she could not deny the truth of them. "I've misjudged you all these years and now that I know you—" She paused uncertain. He stared her, his hands dropping to his sides.

If she'd slapped him, his reaction would have been no different.

She waited a moment and then continued quietly, "I know you may not have strong feelings for me . . . but I couldn't have given myself to you if I hadn't lov—" She caught herself. She already felt uncomfortable. "If I hadn't had feelings for you."

A small furrow had formed between his brows.

She wished she knew what he was thinking. "Mars?"

He shook his head as if realizing he must say something. He raised his hands, touching her hair as if framing her face. She covered his hands with her own, bringing them in front of her, holding him.

"You don't have to make a declaration to me," she said. "We aren't a love match. In fact, we agreed we don't owe each other anything."

"Other than our terms."

Yes, the terms. Had what she'd asked for out of a need to protect herself now present a barrier between them?

"You are my wife, Clarissa. I'm pleased."

As far as declarations went, that one was decidedly flat, and yet Clarissa valued honesty. In spite of the tightening in her throat, she nodded.

"You don't understand," he said, his tone hollow. "I can't love . . . love is what killed my father. He loved her too much."

She released his hands. "I'm not asking you to love me back."

"Clarissa—"

"No," she said, interrupting him. "I'm not insulted or angry." And then she realized a truth. "My feelings for you don't demand tribute. I'm here, Mars. If you need a friend, I will be one. If you want a lover—" She touched his arm and then lowered her hand. "I'm here. I'm so very here." She stepped back. "Always. And I thank you for your generosity. But in truth, Dora and I hope you are with us for a long time." Forever. She wanted to be with him forever. "Now, you must excuse me. Kate's abigail Mary should arrive shortly to help me dress."

Her inclination was to race out the door. She forced herself to be dignified, to prove she didn't need for him to return her love. After all, this was all very new to her as well—

"Rissa."

She turned. He stood where she'd left him, tall, silent . . . worried.

"Thank you," he said, the words almost a whisper.

She forced a smile. "You are welcome, my lord." On those words, she left and didn't draw a full breath until she reached the bedroom. She shut the door and walked over to the bedpost, rubbing the wood with her hand.

What would happen? She'd never felt as open and vulnerable as she had speaking her heart.

However, she had no regrets. If anything, she felt alive in a way she'd never thought possible. She *loved*. She loved *him*. Was there a greater gift?

And someday, he would understand. She just had to be patient.

MARY ARRIVED with the gown. She and Clarissa retired to the countess's dressing room. An hour later, Mary had worked magic.

Staring at herself in the glass, Clarissa said, "This is not me."

"Aye, it is, my lady."

Clarissa's hair was piled high on her head with golden curls tumbling around her shoulders. Kate had lent her pearl combs that Mary had tucked together to form a simple headpiece and Clarissa felt very regal, especially with the dress's lace framing her neckline. She finished the ensemble with a cream cashmere shawl, another item from Kate, and, of course, the long gold chain carrying her mother's pendant.

Mars waited for her in the reception room. He was in black evening dress and appeared noble and more handsome than any one man should. His reaction when he saw her enter the room was exactly as she could have wished.

For a moment, he acted speechless. Then he came over to her, taking her gloved hand. "You will outshine every woman at the ball."

The heat of a blush warmed her cheeks. "Thank you, my lord. I am nervous."

"You needn't be. I'll be there." And just like that any awkwardness between them over her earlier declaration vanished. He offered his arm and escorted her out to the waiting coach that had just returned from taking Mary home.

On the ride, he talked about the people who would be in attendance as if that would calm her. It didn't. These were names she'd only heard about in the papers.

Finally, he said, "I'm blathering. Is it helping?"

She placed a hand against her stomach. "A little."

He laughed. "Courage, Rissa. You have the backbone of a matron."

That teasing declaration eased some of the tension in her. She knew Mrs. Warbler and the others would want a full accounting of this evening.

They would not be disappointed with her story. There was no doubt something momentous was happening at Lord Harrison's residence. There were so many candles in the windows and torches by the door, the house glowed in the night.

The Marsden coach joined the line of guests waiting their turn. This gave Clarissa a chance to watch people alight from their vehicles, to see their finery, and to convince herself that she would fit in amongst their company.

Inside was a receiving line. Their hosts made her feel welcome. Apparently Lady Fenton had seen to the posting of a marriage announcement and word was spreading. Clarissa was thankful. She was starting to realize that London was very much like Maidenshop, just bigger. The announcement gave their marriage an air of legitimacy. Especially when Lady Harrison declared to one and all, "You can see why he married her, she's lovely."

Lady Fenton swooped in on them the second they left the line. "I have been waiting for you," she announced. She stood out in a red-and-silver gown. "I have people you need to meet, Marsden. Come this way—"

She stopped and stared hard at Clarissa as if just noticing her. Regal brows lifted in mild approval. "You'll do," she pronounced, and Clarissa had to hide a smile. Surprising Lady Fenton made the whole evening worthwhile. "Now, follow me." Both Clarissa and Mars obeyed.

For the next hour, Lady Fenton introduced Clarissa to so many people, she stopped trying to keep track of names. They were not young people but of Lady Fenton's age or older and obviously very important. So important they were somewhat rude.

Mars had no trouble aping their disinterest. They liked him and made a point of welcoming his vote.

Clarissa asked where Lord Fenton was.

Lady Fenton made a frustrated sound. "In the card room."

"So he is a player?" Clarissa said, making conversation because it seemed silly to have a card room at a ball.

"No, it is where he hides." She didn't sound terribly disappointed.

Soon, Clarissa could commiserate with Lord Fenton. The event was a complete crush. Just when she felt there was no room to move, more people joined their number. Wine and strong punch flowed. There was dancing although most of the attendees were milling about and gossiping. It was all a bit much.

Mars leaned close to her ear. "Not as enjoyable as the Cotillion Dance."

She agreed. "And if the matrons set up a card room, there wouldn't be a man on the dance floor for the reels." He laughed his agreement.

At one point, Clarissa had the opportunity to glance inside the card room. She was surprised to see a good number of women in there and they appeared to be playing in earnest.

That is when she noticed Lord Fenton. He was in a chair in a corner by himself and sound asleep. In the room's candlelight one could see his skull beneath his graying thin hair and he looked so tired and aged, Clarissa felt sorry for him.

Meanwhile, Lady Fenton had plenty of energy, but Clarissa was growing weary of her jibes and quips about others. The woman was too critical for comfort. It was a wonder she had any friends.

Suddenly, Lady Fenton reacted to some sort of signal from someone across the room.

She turned to her son. "Lord Roker and Sir Charles wish to have a meeting with us."

"I barely know Roker and who is Sir Charles?"

His mother made an impatient sound. "They are very important whether you know them or not. Come, we will go someplace private." She started to lead Mars away. Clarissa held his hand to follow when Lady Fenton stopped.

"Clarissa, you don't mind waiting out here? Of course not. Let me introduce you to some friends of mine who will help you feel comfortable while we see to important matters."

"She will stay with me—" Mars started, except his mother overruled him.

"This is the battle of our lives," Lady Fenton said. "If my husband is voted out, then all will be lost to Dervil. Is that what you wish?"

"I will be fine," Clarissa told Mars, not wanting to be a bother. The sooner they were done with this nonsense, the sooner they could leave London.

"What a wise woman you are," Lady Fenton said approvingly before steering Clarissa away from Mars. He started as if to follow but a man of about his age called his name, claiming his attention.

"I appreciate you letting me have him for a moment," her mother-in-law said.

"Will Lord Fenton be in the meeting?" Clarissa asked.

"I will tell him what happened. That is usually how it works. Now, here we are." Lady Fenton had delivered Clarissa to friends who sat in the matrons' section of the room. Every ball had them. A group of mothers and older women who were shuttled off to the side and out of the way. They amused themselves with gossip.

Lady Fenton made several quick introductions of names Clarissa didn't catch and then left for her meeting, the one she was attending for her husband who was sleeping in a chair.

Feeling awkward, Clarissa turned to the woman closest to her to exchange a pleasantry and found herself facing the woman's back. Apparently, Clarissa had been dismissed. After all, what was one more countess in a room full of them?

Besides, they had their conversations well established and they weren't going to change the topics because she was there. This woman was complaining about one of her maids, a subject those around her apparently found interesting.

After fifteen minutes of being impolitely ignored, Clarissa decided the time had come to ease herself away. She had in her mind to go in search of her husband and beg to let them leave. She took a step away from the matron and was almost run over by several debutantes who were full of giggles and punch. She was certain their mothers would not approve, but the young men following them had high hopes.

Clarissa stepped back toward the wall where it was safe, and that was when she noticed a window overlooking a stone portico and a night garden. Paper lanterns had been strung up in the trees and several people were already out there enjoying the evening. Fresh air would feel good after being in this overperfumed crowd.

She headed straight for the door leading outside and she was not sorry. The summer breeze was velvety warm and a balm for anyone who had been cooped inside that ballroom.

Deciding to wait for Mars here, Clarissa moved away from the couples who were walking the length of the portico and found a place overlooking the garden that was shadowed. She tucked herself in there. She hoped the meeting didn't take much longer—

"Lady Marsden?" a man's voice said.

Clarissa looked over her shoulder and was shocked to see Lord Dervil standing there.

She didn't pretend to not know him. "I don't believe I should be with you out here," she said. "I know you understand the reasons. Pray don't follow me."

She would have run for the door, except he blocked her way. "No, *please*, a moment is *all* I ask."

"My husband—"

"You are the image of someone I once knew. Someone I *loved*—"

His voice stopped abruptly. His gaze dropped to her pendant and he stared as if he recognized it.

Uncomfortable with the intensity of his scrutiny, she placed her hand over the small gold medallion, wanting to block it from his view. He raised shocked eyes and took a step toward her, before asking almost desperately, *"How did you come by that pendant?"*

Chapter Sixteen

And God has brought him right to my door.

—*Book of Mars*

Clarissa was not going to answer Lord Dervil's question. She was far too alone in this corner of the portico for her to be comfortable with a confrontation.

"I'm certain my husband is looking for me." She moved to the side to go around him.

He stepped into her path. "I know Marsden will be angry I approached you, but a moment of your time. That's all I ask." He didn't sound threatening . . . however, what if he was playing some sort of game that would hurt Mars?

"Why?"

"Because I gave that pendant to a woman I loved as a gift. If you know her, tell me, how is she? *Where* is she?"

"I don't know anything." And that was the truth.

He shook his head as if she mocked him.

"It isn't just the necklace, my lady. You are her very image even to your height and the shade of your eyes. When I saw you last night in the theater, my heart stopped. I thought you were her."

"And she is?" Clarissa had to ask. If he'd given her mother the pendant, he knew her identity. Her attitude toward him changed. Perhaps this meeting was fortuitous.

Now he was the one to turn wary. His gaze narrowed as if he was weighing her purpose. Then he said, "Priscilla Comstock. Now, how did you come by that pendant?"

Priscilla. The *P* on the medallion. Clarissa closed her hand around the gold disk and said, "It was my mother's."

Lord Dervil almost lunged for her. "*Your mother?* Tell me, where is she? How may I find her?"

And because he had given her information, because she believed he was serious in his inquiries, she said as gently as possible, "She died."

His knees buckled. He reached for the balustrade and caught himself before he collapsed. His eyes widened and became red rimmed as if he held back tears, and then he bent over, losing the battle. "God help me. God help me, Priscilla."

Clarissa leaned against the balustrade. They were actually completely alone now. The others who had been outside had gone in—and she was glad. His grief was raw, humbling. She knew he would not want others to be a witness.

He looked to her, his face contorted as it took all his will to regain his composure. "Tell me what you know. *Tell me all.*"

"I know very little," she admitted, a touch afraid of his emotion.

"Then *who* are you? It is not by chance that you are the image of her and have her pendant. I beg of you, tell me your story, my lady."

"I will, if you will tell me who was she to you?" Her heart yearned to honor his request, to know all. However, he had murdered Mars's father under the guise of a duel. Her husband lived to destroy him. She had to be careful.

Lord Dervil obviously didn't feel the same caution. "She was quite simply the love of my life." It was a heartfelt statement. Clarissa would have to be turned to stone to not feel some sympathy for him.

"How did you know her?" Clarissa asked.

He pressed gloved fingers to his eyes as if pushing back the grief, and then he spoke. "I met her at a dance. My cousin had invited me to join a group of his friends. It was nothing like this affair tonight. Just a gathering of friends, music, and . . . laughter. I remember the laughter. The moment I clapped eyes on Priscilla, I fell in love. My reaction was startling and immediate, and I pursued her passionately. So much so that my father took me aside and let me know that Miss Comstock was not suitable for my attention."

"What was wrong with her?"

"Nothing. Absolutely nothing. She had a laugh that drew everyone to her. She was understanding, kind, and adored a good jest. I wasn't the only man pursuing her. She was seventeen, barely out of the schoolroom, and right in her prime. I may have been one of a herd of fellows chasing her, but she smiled on me." He said the last as if it was something akin to a miracle. "I was most fortunate."

"Then, why did your father object?" she asked.

"Because he wanted me to marry money. He was a terrible gambler. When I say 'terrible,' I don't mean he didn't play well. He played *very* well, he just lost. Over and over again. My mother had brought great wealth to the marriage along with several estates, including the one in Maidenshop."

"You know I am from there?"

"After seeing you last night, I've tried to learn everything I could about you. Little is known of you, my lady, and Society adores a mystery. Everyone is talking."

"Talking so much that I was ignored when I was introduced to people this evening," she countered.

He laughed. "I saw you with Lady Millsaps. She can't hear. Neither can her friends. It was unfortunate Eleanor steered you there."

"Eleanor?"

"Your mother-in-law."

Clarissa had not known Lady Fenton's first name, and considering her husband's attitude toward his mother, had not been interested. That is when she remembered the reason Lord Dervil would know. "You were her lover."

He made a dismissive sound. "One of many. I was the one who was caught."

"And yet you profess love for my mother?"

"Ah, you are a naïve one, Lady Marsden. We don't live in a world of happy endings. I'm surprised you haven't learned that yet."

"I don't appreciate your condescension, my lord. Is that why my mother rejected you?"

"She *never* rejected me. She loved me."

"And yet, she left you," Clarissa hazarded. They stood not more than a foot apart from each other. A good distance for exchanging confidences.

"We were from two different worlds," he said, as if it was a good excuse. Then added, "And neither of us had money. As I said, because of my father's habits, I needed to marry an heiress."

"My mother was poor?"

"Did she not tell you her history?"

Clarissa paused and then said not unkindly, "She died shortly after I was born."

Again, grief overwhelmed him. He was a strange man, calculating in one moment and then giving in to his emotions in the next. No wonder no one trusted him.

He kept repeating the word "dead," as if he couldn't believe she was telling the truth. Clarissa studied the texture of the stone railing beneath her gloved hand, knowing she should give him privacy . . . and, yet, wanting whatever information she could glean from him.

Finally, he straightened, setting his shoulders back, attempting to compose himself. She gave him a moment before daring to ask, "Please, will you tell me the story?"

Lord Dervil closed his eyes as if the memories were almost too painful to recall, but then he spoke. "Her father was a clever man. He didn't mind my suit for his daughter's hand and I did want to marry Priscilla, make no doubt about it. Her family was not of my class. Her father had started his career as a clerk, saved his money, invested, and eventually purchased a warehouse, right on the wharves and that is how he became wealthy. Unfortunately, he was like most of us, he wanted more. He began investing in cargo ships. Little amounts at first, until he believed he knew what he was doing. Then, he put in larger amounts. I met Priscilla just around that time. I gave her that pendant as a sign of my honest intentions toward her. She wore it every day. There is a lily on the back. It was my nickname for her. I wrote a bad poem comparing her to the lily flower and she enjoyed teasing me about it."

"Did you ask her to marry you?"

He tilted his head toward her as if confiding a secret. "Yes, but we could not say anything publicly. At least not at the time. Her father understood what I was up against and the pressures my family was placing on me. He was a good man. A kind one. He also understood that if Priscilla had a good dowry, we might marry with my parents' blessings. I think he was actually tickled over the idea of his daughter having a title. You know, his grandchildren being lords of the realm and all that nonsense.

He urged me to not do anything rash that would cost my parents' approval." He paused soberly and added, "And I wanted them to accept Priscilla. I didn't want her to be an outsider. Of course, now their approval seems insignificant. We should have damned them all and run away."

"But you didn't."

"No." He frowned at the memory. "Instead, her father took a big risk. He invested a good amount of his wealth in two ships that would have delivered handsomely if they had not both been destroyed. One was caught in a storm and sank. The other was boarded by pirates and was later found in some port somewhere, without its cargo or crew."

"That is terrible."

"Aye, it was. It almost ruined him. Then his warehouse caught fire and completed the task. He hadn't paid the insurance. He'd had to use his money to pay his creditors after the ships were destroyed. He died trying to save what he could in the fire."

"Dear Lord."

"The family was ruined. Her mother took to her bed. Priscilla had an older brother who was in the clergy. He was a strict man. Unwelcoming. She didn't want to go to him. She begged me to help." He drew a deep breath and said slowly, "But what could I do? I *had* to marry money. I loved her, except I had my responsibilities. I told her I could not marry her."

Her poor mother. Not only had she lost her father and the security he offered her family, but the man she'd trusted, the one who had professed love, abandoned her. Clarissa understood too well how that felt. "How did she take your rejection?"

"Calmly, with dignity. She actually tried to make me feel better about it." He looked to Clarissa. "I knew I made a mistake almost immediately. I—"

He paused lost in the past, before saying, "Three weeks later, I went to her brother's home where she was staying. I wanted to ensure she was fine. I had to see her again. That's when I learned her mother had died and she had disappeared. Vanished."

He broke down.

Clarissa had seen men cry before. She found it a humbling sight although she'd never heard a man weep with such deep-seated regret. It poured out of him. Huge, gulping, silent tears.

She worried what would happen if someone noticed. A group came out from the ballroom to enjoy the night air. Clarissa stepped around Lord Dervil, blocking their view of him, moving him a step deeper into the shadows, shielding him. Compassion demanded she do this, even as she had little sympathy for him.

He had betrayed the woman he said he loved, probably when she needed him most. "And so you let her go?"

"*No.*" Her question sobered him. "I searched everywhere. I left word with people she might turn to asking her to contact me. I hired men to find her. No one could."

And then, Clarissa understood.

Standing there under cheerful paper lanterns and the night sky, it was as if a voice, the voice of her mother, whispered to her, telling her the rest of the story. Clarissa had always had a good sense of intuition, but this was more.

"How long did you search?" she asked.

"A good year or longer."

"In your messages, where did you tell her you wanted to meet?"

"Meet?"

"You said you left word with anyone she might have turned to. What did you want her to know?"

"Oh, yes, I told her to go to the Maidenshop house. It was a safe place. The rest of the family rarely went there."

Priscilla had tried to reach him. She was bringing her baby to him.

Then Clarissa knew. "Of course, during that time, you married."

He bowed his head. "I had to."

"Soon after she disappeared? Or later?" She wanted the details. They made a difference.

"Three months after I lost Priscilla, I married. My first wife was the daughter of a banker who held a good number of my father's vowels. I truly had no choice. Then again, the marriage allowed me to begin to build my wealth. It was part of my rise. But I didn't love my first wife. I never loved her. Or my second either."

"So, if Priscilla had come looking for you, she would have found a married man? Or at least learn that you were married."

He faced her. "*If* she'd come looking for me.

She would have understood. Priscilla knew I had no choice."

The problems of the *ton*. And it always circled around money. Clarissa imagined herself in her mother's situation. "She couldn't knock on the door with your new wife there."

"I wish she had. Arabella wouldn't have minded. She didn't like me. She was even more angry after she was with child."

"You have a child?"

He shook his head. "Arabella died in childbirth. And my second wife was barren. She died last year of a flux. I have not been blessed to be a father." He laughed, the sound bitter. "I married to protect an estate for which I have no heirs. Not one. Not even a distant cousin. When I die it returns to the Crown."

"Or you marry again and have a child," Clarissa said reasonably. She could tell him the truth, that his daughter stood before him.

She wasn't certain he deserved to know. Or her feelings about the matter.

"I don't know if that would help." He looked away. "Sometimes, I feel as if God punishes me. I haven't been a good man. Perhaps if Priscilla had stayed beside me—"

"Stayed beside you? The way you stayed beside her?"

If she had slapped him across the face, he could not have looked more stricken. Well, he deserved her harsh words.

She had no idea where Priscilla went after she left her brother's house or where she had her baby. However, Clarissa could imagine her mother receiving one of those messages from the man she loved asking her to return to him. She could see Priscilla making the hard trip to reconnect with this man she loved, only to learn he had married. "You were intimate with her, weren't you?"

He frowned. His hands balled into fists. Had her instinct been wrong—?

Then he whispered, "Yes. Before the fire. We were going to marry . . . we were young."

"That is an excuse?"

"You sound exactly like her." His expression softened. "I've thought about that night repeatedly over the years. We loved."

We loved. Magic words. She knew.

"My life would have been different if I had married Priscilla. I would have been an honorable man. I just didn't understand at the time what she meant to me. And seeing you," he said, turning to her, "the very image of her, has brought all that I lost to the forefront. I was such a fool, my lady. And I thank you for your kindness in listening to me."

"I appreciate your honesty, my lord."

"Tell me," he said. "What is your given name?"

She tilted her head, uncertain, and then decided what harm could it do? He could easily learn her name another way. "Clarissa."

He laughed as if delighted. "I knew that. Priscilla would tell me that if she had a daughter she would name her after her favorite book. She read *Clarissa* repeatedly and wept every time. She always had her nose in a book.

I never worried about where she was because I knew I could find her reading." He shook his head as if he was being silly. "Of course, you already knew that."

No, Clarissa hadn't, and this detail about her mother's love for literature that mirrored her own touched her deeply. She thought of the way her mother had died, alone and betrayed by love just like in the novel *Clarissa*.

"Ah, now see, I have made you sad." He reached up and touched the tear that escaped Clarissa's eye, and she knew she had to tell him her story, the one that included him—

"Do not touch my wife," was the only warning they had before Mars jerked Lord Dervil around and smashed a fist in his face, the force of it sending the man back against the balustrade.

Horrified, Clarissa reached for her husband's arm, lest he do it again. What was the matter with him? It was as if he *wanted* to fight. As if he desired it above all other actions. To Lord Dervil, she said, "I'm sorry, my lord. I don't know what has taken hold of my husband—"

"You will meet me for this," Mars demanded of Lord Dervil, ignoring Clarissa. "I will have satisfaction. You will meet me, sir. You will meet me on the morrow."

Lord Dervil was a bit unsteady. He touched his face and saw that he had a cut on his cheekbone that was bleeding. Slightly dazed, he looked up at Mars and didn't answer.

Clarissa had plenty to say. "What do you think you are doing?"

"Protecting you," Mars barked, his angry gaze on Lord Dervil while he opened and closed his fists as if he would happily hit his enemy again.

"You *aren't* protecting me. Mars, he didn't do anything. He is my father."

The moment she spoke the words, the true horror of them rang through her. She was the daughter of the man who had claimed Mars's father's life.

Her husband jerked around to frown at her, as if she jested and he didn't appreciate the joke. "Yes," she pressed, "it is true. I just learned the story. He said I am the image of my mother."

For his part, Lord Dervil acted as if he'd been punched again. "You are my child? Priscilla had my child?"

Clarissa looked to him. "Yes, I believe so. I'm turning five and twenty shortly. Is that not the right length of time?" In truth, Clarissa wasn't exactly certain when her birth date was. The Taylors had celebrated it on October the twenty-seventh, the date she'd been placed on the step.

"My daughter," Lord Dervil repeated, his balance steadying. "I have a child. I can't believe it."

"I know it is fantastic," she agreed. "And yet it all makes sense."

"It is also all the more reason you will meet me," Mars said, interjecting himself. "Name your seconds."

"*No*, my lord," Clarissa said, "you must not do this."

But he was not listening to her. It was as if he was caught up in his own momentum.

Lord Dervil heard. "Marsden, I shall *not* meet you. There is not cause."

"Exactly," Clarissa agreed.

"Oh, there is a very good cause," her husband snapped. "You abandoned my lady's mother, you turned your back on her—"

"*Mars, that is not fair,*" Clarissa said.

He wasn't listening to her. "I shall have satisfaction. You will pay for the murderous damage you have done in your life, on the way you prey on the weak. You left a young woman to be disgraced by her family. When they found out she was carrying your child, they tossed her out and you weren't there for her."

"Tossed her out?" Lord Dervil repeated. He looked to Clarissa for confirmation, his expression stricken.

Clarissa thought her heart would break at how callous her husband was being. But before she could answer, Mars jumped in. "Yes, she came looking for you only to learn you already had a wife. It was cruel, Dervil, but now you will answer for your actions."

And in that moment Clarissa hated her husband.

He was like a madman, charging around, throwing out insults without thought to the damage he was doing. She gave his arm an angry shake. "*Stop this*. It isn't right." She looked to Lord Dervil. "I'm sorry, my lord, I would not have told you, at least not in this fashion."

Lord Dervil's expression was tight, and then his lips twisted in a grim smile. He pulled himself upright. His eyes became unnaturally bright. "I understand, Lady Marsden. I do not lay any of this at your feet." To Mars, he said, "On the morrow, Marsden? Excellent. We might save everyone from a vote if I lose."

"Absolutely," Mars agreed. "I will await word of your seconds."

"You can't do this," Clarissa demanded. "I will not be your reason for a duel."

Mars turned to her. His face could have been carved from stone.

What? Was he going to blame her for not supporting such an obscene challenge? Instead, he said, "Shall we leave, my lady?" He offered his arm.

And he expected her to take it.

Clarissa stared at her husband and she did not like what she saw. This couldn't be the same man she had married. That man was kind and caring. That man she was beginning to love—but now?

Now she had no idea who he was, and she cut off all mental attempts to understand him. She could not love this—especially since he was using the sad tale of her mother to his own ends. He'd never had any feeling for her mother. He hadn't known her.

He also didn't have true feelings for Clarissa. Not if he would use her confidences as a weapon without regard to how she felt.

She backed away, turned, ready to run—and

realized to her shock that a crowd had spilled out of the doorway to gape at her and the two men. She paused. Had they heard everything? About her being born out of wedlock? About her mother being treated so callously? All these people who did not know who she was?

Clarissa glanced back at Mars. He behaved as if he was coming out of a spell. He shook his head and then noticed the crowd and realized the magnitude of the scene. He shot an angry look at Lord Dervil as if this was his fault.

But she knew the truth. About everything.

Finally.

She'd been the silly one to believe her husband cared for her, that perhaps they could have a true marriage. Instead, she realized she was just a means to an end.

He'd planned to challenge Dervil. He'd come to London to do this whether by sparking the lord's anger over the vote or some other means. It all made perfect sense. Mars had said as much that night in the nursery when he'd asked her to marry him. He had been completely honest about his intentions to confront Lord Dervil and that their marriage was his way of ensuring Dora was cared for because if he didn't die, he'd certainly have to leave the country. And to think she'd been flattered that he had considered her a good influence over Dora—so that he could do as he wished and leave Clarissa to be the responsible one. The caretaker. The custodian. The anything he didn't wish to be.

She was the fool.

Suddenly, Clarissa didn't care what people thought. She needed to escape. She ran, pushing people aside, shoving her way into the ballroom and not stopping until she was out the front door and into the night.

Chapter Seventeen

Women will never understand honor.
They believe reason will lead to justice.
How little they understand the male mind.
—Book of Mars

Mars frowned at the sight of Clarissa running from him. Of course she wasn't pleased with his challenging Dervil.

However, he was doing it for her.

Well, and himself as well. And *the world*. Yes, he'd challenged Dervil for the world. The world would be glad to be rid of his kind—and Mars definitely intended to see the man dead.

Although Mars knew his temper had the best of him. But he wasn't ready to let go of it.

When he'd walked out and seen Dervil standing so close to *his* wife, Mars had lost all semblance of sanity. He'd never been one to be jealous over a woman before but he'd lunged forward to protect Clarissa and to lay his claim. It was obvious to him that Dervil was taking advantage of her, probably as a way to strike back at him.

But to learn Dervil was the father who had abandoned Clarissa? The father who had betrayed the young girl who had been her mother?

Mars wanted to smite him down with the forceful grace of an avenging angel.

Oh, he could imagine it all. Dervil tossed women aside with abandon. Obviously even those carrying his child. Clarissa would understand the wisdom of Mars's actions once he explained them to her.

Dervil spoke up, his voice cold. "You have greatly insulted me, Marsden, and in a very public way."

Public?

Only then did Mars fully realize that they had an audience. A *very interested* audience.

Yes, he'd registered their presence peripherally when Clarissa had left, although he hadn't truly processed the presence of so many fellow humans. He'd been too intent on his motive. Too driven by his need for revenge.

And now?

Now he questioned if he'd been wise. No wonder Clarissa was upset.

Dervil continued. "Since I'm the one challenged, I choose pistols." He didn't wait for Mars to respond but looked over to a gentleman standing near the door. "Roberts, will you serve as my second?" Mars knew Lord Roberts. He was a neighbor in Grosvenor Square.

"I would be happy to, my lord," Roberts responded.

"Albertson?" Dervil said to another.

"Honored," Albertson answered with a bow.

For all his plans to challenge Dervil, Mars had not thought about whom he could call upon to be seconds. This was a problem.

Dervil coolly returned to Mars. "Primrose Hill. Do you know the place?"

He'd heard of it. Many duels were fought there.

Dervil pulled on his sleeve as if he was more interested in the cut of his jacket than Mars's challenge. "I shall see you there at half past six. Have your man meet with Roberts for the details. You shall provide the doctor since you issued the challenge?"

Again, Mars nodded. He hoped Thurlowe was still in town.

"Very well," Dervil said. "Tomorrow." He turned and walked with purpose toward the door. Those who had not gone running inside to spread the word about what was happening on the portico moved out of his path, and then followed him in.

And Mars was left alone.

He should find Clarissa and explain his position . . . except, he was not yet ready for that confrontation. He'd been wrong to blurt out her history, even if there had *not* been so many gossips to witness his words. She'd confided the information in him and, he realized, he had betrayed her confidence. For that, he was truly sorry. She didn't offer trust easily and he had trampled all over it.

When he talked to his wife, he knew she would be rightfully angry with him.

However, he was not a coward. He had to face her. Mars started to go inside when his mother came out the door. Her face was tight and her eyes alive with anger. "Is it true? You've challenged Dervil?"

"I'm too old to answer to my mother." He took a step toward the door, but she moved into his path.

"So much like your father." She did not mean that as a compliment. It was as if that was the worst insult she could hurl.

He nodded. "Fortunately, I'm not bound to you the way my father was."

She took ahold of the material of his sleeve. "You are going to ruin everything. This could have waited until after the vote. We have what we need to win. What if you kill him? Then we need to start from the beginning and there may be a new challenger to Fenton."

He didn't answer. She wouldn't appreciate knowing he really didn't care who was Chairman of Committees. And that, as to meeting Dervil, he was ready to pay the price, whatever it was—banishment or even his own death. He also doubted if she would care about either outcome.

Then, to his surprise, she changed the topic. "Is it true what everyone is saying? That Dervil is your wife's father? A *secret* father? You know, there *are* some advantages to being aligned with someone as powerful as Dervil—"

"I will *never* align myself with him." It was a warning. Clarissa wasn't the only one who didn't trust easily.

"Then you'd best be careful," she said as if he had asked for her advice. "Dervil has many friends. Some of them dangerous."

He frowned, not understanding her game. "Dangerous?"

"Toward Fenton's ambitions." She released her hold and brushed something off his coat. Anyone seeing them could believe they were witnessing a scene between a concerned mother and son.

"Did *I* ever matter to you?" It was a question he'd always wanted to ask, even before his father's death.

His mother took an offended step back. "You are my son."

There was no sincerity in her voice. It was merely a statement of fact. She had needed him for the vote to keep *her* in power.

And he realized this lack of a mother had always gnawed at him. He thought of his almost immediate feelings for Dora and finally understood his mother was just unnatural. Cold. Remote. For her husbands, her son—even her liaison with Dervil probably hadn't meant much to her.

He was dueling with the wrong person. She'd manipulated them all . . .

"Yes, I'm your son," he agreed. "*And*, I am also a vote," he reminded her.

"Not just *a* vote. *The* vote. Remember?" she said brightly. "That is our arrangement." She smiled as if pleased with herself for being so benevolent. "*You* cast the deciding vote. That is, if you don't kill Dervil and ruin it all."

"What if I do?"

"Then I will do all in my power to ruin you." Her tone was pleasant, boastful.

Never once had he turned to her for comfort. It had been his father who had always been there when he'd needed help.

Just like Clarissa was there for him. Clarissa, who had been brave enough to say she loved him.

He needed to speak to her. He owed her an explanation. She was right to be furious with him. He needed to apologize and ask her to understand his purpose.

And maybe, he might be truly honest with her and confess that perhaps he'd overreacted in her defense because he understood all too well the pain of a callous parent. The pain of feeling abandoned by those one should be able to trust.

That is when the full weight of what he'd done to Clarissa fell heavily upon him. She'd trusted him, and he had pushed her aside.

Without a word to his mother, Mars walked to the door and entered the ballroom ready to search for his wife. Unfortunately, he had miscalculated the interest in his affairs that he had created.

He'd not taken three steps into the room when he sensed a pause in conversations, conspicuous looks in his direction, and frowns of disapproval. Many behaved as if they had been waiting for him. Waiting to glare at him, to sneer, to follow him with their whispers.

His mother came up behind him. "Excuse me," she said as if they were strangers and made her way through the crowd. She received commiserating looks and much empathy. He watched her touch an arm here, exchange a worried glance there. She was a brilliant actress.

However, these people failed to understand that Mars didn't care what their opinions of him were.

The only person he answered to was Clarissa.

He charged forward. People moved out of his way. He could feel their stares as he passed.

Although he was accustomed to doing as he wished, this was different. He quite definitely felt on the outside and that made him want to find Clarissa all the more. She would put her hand on his arm and he wouldn't care what people said, what they thought.

He found a vantage point on a step and looked around the room, using his height to help him search for honey-gold hair amongst the guests. He didn't see her. He started for the card room. She was not there. He lingered outside the ladies' necessary room until he was certain she wasn't hiding from him. She might have been angrier than he thought. He opened a few closed doors up and down the hall. He couldn't find her.

Mars stood a moment flummoxed and then wondered if she could have left? Without saying anything to him?

He went out the front door, waving away an offer to fetch his hat. A footman was standing on the bottom step, signaling to coaches when their owners were ready. He saw Mars and bowed.

"Shall I signal for your driver, my lord?"

"Actually, I wonder if you have seen a petite woman with golden hair and big green eyes. She's wearing an emerald colored dress. She is a beauty."

"Lady Marsden."

"Right. Have you seen her?"

"Ah, yes, my lord. She took your vehicle. She said to tell you she will send the driver back shortly."

She *had* left.

Mars was stunned. "Yes, that is right. I remembered she needed to leave early," he said, as if the footman required an explanation . . . because otherwise, Mars felt like a fool not knowing where his wife was.

A little over a week ago he hadn't wanted a wife but now that he had one, he expected to know where she was.

He came to a decision. Balfour did not live far from here and the duel was only hours away. "When my driver returns, tell him I decided to walk. It is a good night for some exercise." He passed the man a coin, retrieved his hat from a footman inside, and made his way to Balfour's.

The physical act of walking cleared his head and settled his resolve. He had come to London to kill Dervil, and so he would.

After several loud knocks on Balfour's door, a footman answered. Apparently the whole household was abed. Mars didn't understand why. It wasn't even midnight yet.

Nor was Balfour pleased to be woken. He was even less happy when he learned the nature of Mars's call. Still, he was a good friend and agreed to act as a second.

"You need to contact Lord Roberts. He is waiting for word from you," Mars said.

"Didn't you just leave him at the Harrison rout?"

"I did."

"Then I doubt if he will be home."

"Send a message and we can flesh out all of the details when we meet at Primrose Hill in the morning," Mars responded. He wasn't interested in the formalities. He was going to shoot Dervil, that was where his interest lay.

"Wait, did you just say 'in the morning'?"

"I did. Half past six. You need to wake up."

Balfour swore. "Mars, this is slapdash and out of character for you. Could we not do this another day?"

"He chose the details of the meeting."

His friend groaned, before confirming, "Tomorrow?"

"Half past six."

"Damn you, Mars. Do you have pistols? Because I don't."

Mars did and he kept them oiled and ready.

He had been waiting for this moment for years. "Is Thurlowe still in town?"

"You need a doctor." Balfour rolled his eyes. "Thurlowe will not be pleased although he will agree to it. I expect it is part of my duties to make arrangements?"

"If you would."

Balfour shook his head. "Mars, why are you doing this?"

"You know why."

"Shooting that man will not bring your father back."

"It is more than that. I saw him with Clarissa—"

"That is one woman no one has to worry about being unfaithful. She is not a flirt. She is solid, Mars, a true catch. Someone who is good for you."

"There is more to it, Balfour."

There was a beat of silence. Mars knew his friend was forming his own conclusions but he'd not explain. He'd already violated Clarissa's trust enough in one evening. Balfour didn't need to know the circumstances of Clarissa's mother's death. A pity Mars hadn't grasped that point earlier.

Balfour spoke. "If you kill him, you would be wise to leave the country."

"Yes."

"Is Clarissa happy with this?"

Mars rose to his feet and set aside the glass of brandy Balfour had offered. He had not touched it. "I need to go home."

Balfour saw him to the door. "You are a fool,

man. You are jeopardizing everything. If you survive tomorrow, you will miss at least a year and maybe more with Dora."

"Clarissa will take care of her—"

"Ah, that is it, isn't it?" Balfour slumped his shoulders in disappointment. "That is why you married Clarissa. To watch over Dora after you did this nonsense."

"The marriage was good for Clarissa, too. She needs someone who will take care of her."

"While he abandons her. Don't you think that woman has had enough abandonment in her life?" He leaned against the open door. "And here I'd thought you'd actually cared for her. The two of you seemed happy last night."

"We are happy," Mars insisted. "She knows about this. I told her."

But had she truly understood?

Nor had he expected to fall in love with her—

The thought was unexpected in its randomness. *He had fallen in love with his wife?*

And yet, now that it had taken hold, he was stunned by the idea.

What did he know about love? That had been the question he'd been asking himself when Clarissa had been so open earlier.

And how could he love Clarissa? He hadn't even thought about it. It had never been his intention. He wasn't even certain he knew what love was . . . and yet the word was right there, shimmering in front of him.

"I need to go home now."

"Yes, to write out your last instructions. Truly, Mars, this is a terrible idea."

It was.

The rebellious idea ripped through him. He rejected it immediately. This was not the time for doubts. Or silliness like love.

"It's happening, Balfour, and I need you."

"I'll be there. So will Thurlowe. I'll contact him."

"Thank you." Mars took a step on the road and then stopped. "Be present for Clarissa. Protect her."

"Someone must. You aren't." On that note, Balfour shut the door.

Mars stood a moment, letting his friend's criticism sink in. Damn.

He made his way home. Dalton opened the door. "Is my wife here?" He handed his hat to the butler.

"Yes, my lord," was the dutiful reply, although Dalton didn't meet his eye. Could the servants already know about the duel? It was no secret that they all approved of Clarissa. Even Nelson had been boldly candid enough to let Mars know that she was a better wife than he deserved.

Mars took the steps two at a time. Wall sconces lit the hallway. A footman, Ellis, sat at his post at the far end of the hall in case the family needed him. On the other end of the hall, the door to the bedroom was slightly ajar. The room within was well lit. He heard someone moving around and knew it was his wife. He slowed his pace, his mind scrambling over what he was going to say to her.

Carefully, he leaned against the doorframe

so he could see inside. Clarissa was packing, her hair loose around her shoulders as if she'd removed the pins and then decided to act. She had her shabby little valise out on the bed and was putting her few possessions in them. She was planning to leave him? Tonight?

He pushed open the door. "Are you going to return to Belvoir now? This moment? Why not stay until morning?"

She faced him, unsurprised as if she'd known he was there.

"Does it matter?" She began taking off the ring he had given.

He moved into action. "No, Clarissa." He took her hand, preventing her from removing the ring. "Don't do this."

"I can't stay here."

"I went a bit wild when I saw him touch you." He could admit that. It was good he was protective, right?

"He didn't know my mother was pregnant when they parted. It broke him. It broke *me*." Her expression had softened but now turned angry. "What do you care? You came to London to challenge him and now you have. *Done.* Lord Marsden has his way again."

"Clarissa," he started without knowing what he wanted to say . . . because she was right.

"Clarissa, *what*?" she demanded. "Clarissa, how can you leave Dora? What of Dora, Clarissa? You can't be selfish."

That was what she was thinking? To leave Dora?

"I mean *nothing* to you," she said, answering herself.

"That is not true," he said, meaning the words. He caught her hands, held them, just as she'd held his earlier.

"Would you have married me if Dora wasn't involved?"

She made him sound shallow. "Clarissa—"

"*No*, because you didn't like me," she said, answering for him. "You said as much when you asked me to be her nurse. Oh, don't look so stricken. I'll stay with Dora at least until we learn if you are alive or not."

"And then?"

"Don't even mention the agreements you signed, Mars. Don't believe I am like all of those other people I met tonight who only think about money." She spit the words out, crossing her arms as if holding herself together.

"Clarissa, I'm challenging him because there must be justice. It is for my father," he tried to explain again, willing her to understand. "For your mother."

"There will *never* be justice, Mars. *Ever*. What happened to my mother, what happened to your father was tragic, but also was a result of decisions *they* made. My mother's heart was broken but there were people who could have helped her. The matrons were willing. Your father didn't have to challenge a man. And I will *not* be an excuse for you to *murder* someone. I am not the type of woman your mother is."

"If it is any consolation, she is not pleased with the duel either—"

"Then why do it? *Why?*"

"It is about *honor*, Clarissa. I can't expect you to understand—"

"Because I am *female*? I shouldn't worry my head over such things? You are a *fool*, Lawrence Eddington. A fool. And you should have married a silly-headed woman who would believe your excuses. I'm too intelligent to be her." She turned and started stuffing items into her valise as if she could not wait to escape him. "I'm a fighter, Mars."

She certainly wasn't going to listen to reason. She was like *all* the others, willing to let Dervil do as he pleased without penalty.

He turned on his heel, stormed to the library, and kicked open the door. The room was dark. He was tempted to stand there and let the darkness envelop him, except dutiful Ellis came running with a candle to light the desk lamp.

"Here you are, my lord. This is better for reading."

"Thank you, Ellis."

"You are welcome, my lord."

"And you are dismissed for the evening. We won't be needing you." Mars didn't worry about what the servants might overhear. They were loyal to him. Then again, the look Dalton had given him this evening might suggest otherwise.

"Yes, my lord." Ellis bowed out. A few seconds later, Mars heard him open the door to the servants' stairs. Their quarters were located two floors above.

Mars sat heavily in the chair at the desk. He didn't like arguing with Clarissa.

He didn't like having her so angry with him.

And, he *didn't* expect her to be his wife because of Dora. Well, it started off that way. He was honest enough to admit that . . . but he'd come to like having her by his side. He slept better when she was in his bed. Usually after a few romps in bed, he'd tire of his mistresses. But this was different. He couldn't imagine himself ever tiring of Clarissa.

Mars opened the secretary drawer and pulled out paper. There was ink in the well. He took out a wooden pen and put a steel nib in it. Balfour had advised him to put his affairs in order. Most of them were. He'd seen to that with Lowton. Clarissa might despise him but she'd be a rich woman if Dervil killed him. And there were a few things he needed to tell her about his lawyers and the estate.

If he ended up in exile, she must know to trust his staff. They would guide her on what was best for Belvoir just as they had guided him.

He had lots of advice to give. However, when he put pen to paper, what he wrote was, *Clarissa, I am sorry.*

The statement startled him, and yet it was true. He was sorry that he was leaving her—

A sound at the door interrupted him. Ellis had put out the candles in the hall. All was darkness. The door was pushed further open and Clarissa was there.

Her expression was pinched, as if she had

been crying and the air around her was heavy with sadness.

He didn't want to leave her.

Tears stung the back of his eyes. He wouldn't cry. He never cried, not even when his father had died. Tears were weakness. Maybe he did have some of his mother in him. However, he'd chosen his course. The die had been cast.

Still, she was a vision of everything he wanted in his life.

She walked to him, her steps measured. He shifted to face her. She stopped.

"Please, Mars, don't meet Dervil. *Please.*"

On those words, she reached to pull the lacing on the back of her dress. It fell into a graceful puddle at her feet. She was naked. The lamp-light gave her skin a golden glow. And then she reached down and kissed him.

Chapter Eighteen

I once thought I knew my own mind. I did not.
—*Book of Mars*

$\mathcal{B}$ooks claimed that a woman could seduce a man to her will. Stories from all the way back to antiquity lauded a woman's ability to change her lover's mind with her body. Or even for him to forget his actions.

Clarissa was desperate enough to try anything. She was no siren. She was a simple country girl who wanted the best for the man she loved.

And she did love him.

His lips parted beneath hers. She tried to relax. Her heart pounded so loud he must have heard it, he must suspect. He kissed her hungrily, as if he, too, yearned for there to be another way.

She wrapped her arms around his neck and met his kiss with a ferociousness of her own.

*She wanted him to live. To free himself of this quest
for vengeance. It would destroy them.*

Mars rose, lifting her to sit on the desk. He
began unbuttoning his breeches as his kisses
found her neck, her breasts.

And then he entered her, hard as if he needed
this connection. Except, instead of hard thrusts
he stopped, his body deep in her. He held her.
His lips brushed her ear.

"I never want to forget the feeling of you."

The words ripped through her heart.

She pressed her lips to his neck, tightening
deep muscles as if she would never let him go.
"Stay with me. Love me."

He began moving. There was an intensity
about him, a need. He didn't want this duel.
She knew it. He'd convinced himself this was
the only way and it was up to her to show him
that he was wrong.

Mars wasn't a killer. The cost of going
through with this action would be more than
he wanted to pay. More than she and Dora
could afford.

Except she was the one who was beginning to lose control. She was becoming the
one seduced. He kissed her neck, her chin, her
breasts.

She had to think, to keep her wits about her.

Cupping her hands around his strong jaw,
she lifted his head. His eyes were dark and
unfocused, his movements primal.

"Don't go tomorrow," she managed. "Please,
Mars, stay with me." She bound him to her,

legs around his hips. She would not let him escape, to leave. "Please—"

Abruptly, he pulled out of her.

The sudden movement shocked her. She wasn't ready to release. She tried to draw him back. His hands on the desk, he pushed away. Her legs broke their hold.

Free, he gave her his back. His breathing was heavy. Her mind was confused. Her body begged for the denied release.

Mars turned to her. He'd righted his clothing while she was spread across his desk, one hand holding the edge while her other palm braced for balance.

He was angry, the lines of his face harsh. "What are you doing?"

What *was* she doing? How to explain it?

Slowly, Clarissa gathered herself. She sat up, closing her legs. Her dress was on the floor. She would not apologize for her nudity . . . or for loving him.

"I don't want to lose you," she said.

He raked his hands through his hair and then shook his head before asking incredulously, "Do you think I can't defeat him? I've done *nothing but dream of this moment for a decade.*"

She'd never heard him sound so angry, and there was something else in his voice— disappointment. It was as if he was hurt that she didn't understand.

Clarissa tried to explain. "I think, no, I *fear* that you are about to do something that will haunt you every day of your life. Mars, there is *no* going back from this."

A muscle tightened in his jaw. "I know what is at stake, Clarissa. But you must understand, my life changed when he shot my father."

"And now you would do the same to Dora? To me? If you kill him, you'll be taking my father. I have no relationship to him, but still, it is wrong. It will hurt us, Mars. Can't you understand?"

He took a step back, then another. He faced the bookshelves, his hands going to his hips as if she had completely exasperated him.

She edged off the desk. The papers he'd been writing on fell to the floor. She picked up her dress and quickly tossed it over her head.

He made her feel ashamed—and she shouldn't. She loved him enough to fight for him. "I had so much hope for us."

His head lowered. She stared at his back, willing him to see reason.

"Mars—?"

He whirled around. "Clarissa, *I won't back down from this fight.*"

"There is *no* fight."

"*No one* cares what he does. He has been given a pass for countless crimes."

"I *care* for *you.*"

"Yes, by trying to bend me to your will, much as my mother would—"

"Now that is unfair."

"I must do this, Clarissa, and if you care for me, you'll support my decision."

"I can't."

"Because he is your *father*?" He practically spit out the word.

Clarissa stood straighter. "My father is Reverend Taylor. He was the man who guided me, who was there for me. He was the one who taught me that a sin like murder weighs on a man's soul."

"A duel is not murder, remember? It is an act of honor. That is what everyone said about my father's death."

"There is no honor in what you want to do. You've hounded the man, Mars."

"I must. That is what just men do—we right wrongs. You weren't there, Clarissa. You didn't hold your father in your arms as he choked on his own blood. Even Reverend Taylor would agree with me."

Clarissa looked down at herself, at the hastily donned garment, and felt shame. "I suppose I should be thankful that you didn't know about my parentage before we married. It wouldn't have happened, would it?" Her empathy was fading into disillusionment.

His response was to eye her coldly as if she had betrayed him. Well, maybe she had.

"You are so stubborn," she said. "And wrongheaded." There was a beat of silence and then she said, "I love you."

He reacted as if her words caused him physical pain. The air was heavy between them, and then he started for the door.

"Where are you going?" she asked.

He stopped, frowned, and then said, "To

prepare myself. I meet him in a matter of hours, Clarissa."

"If you go, Mars, there is nothing between us. I can't have this on my conscience."

"We will talk about this later—"

"*No.* I am asking you to choose me, Mars. If I'm not enough, then think of Dora. Please, I beg of you."

He shook his head as if to say she didn't understand, and then, he left.

She heard him charge down the stairs as if the hounds of hell were on his heels. And maybe they were. Revenge was obviously more important to him than anything she could offer . . . if she had ever mattered at all.

She sat at the desk, stunned by her defeat. She had lost him.

Of course, she'd lost many people in her life. However, losing someone who had come to mean more than she could have ever imagined was almost more than she could bear. "He doesn't want to do this," she whispered.

And yet he would.

One of the papers on the floor with his bold, slashing handwriting caught her eye. She read her name just as the front door downstairs was opened and closed.

Mars had left.

Clarissa picked up the papers, sorting through them to the one with his writing. Her anger and hurt built right behind her eyes making it hard for her to focus. She forced herself to be steady and read, *Clarissa, I am sorry.*

Sorry for what? Sorry because he wasn't

going to stay and be her husband? Sorry he had married her? Sorry he couldn't love her the way she loved him?

Or, sorry that his precious vendetta meant more than his daughter? So many reasons to be sorry.

Clarissa rose from the desk. Her initial impulse was to have a good cry, but she'd already done that.

Instead, she went to the bedroom. She barely slept. A part of her hoped Mars would change his mind and come back to her. She waited. She counted the minutes until half past six. The household was already stirring. She found Dalton and asked for the coach to be brought round. She was returning to Maidenshop.

MARS WAS the first to arrive at the appointed spot on Primrose Hill. He tied up his horse and waited. The hour was shortly before dawn. He stood with his case holding his dueling pistols under one arm.

After leaving Clarissa, he'd fetched his pistols from the chest in the study and gone to his club. There he'd checked the guns. They were perfectly balanced. A tribute to the gunsmith's art.

He'd not slept well. He could blame his restlessness on the duel, except that would be a lie.

No, he sensed that Clarissa might be right.

He'd pushed the thought away. He wished she saw his side. He didn't believe she would turn her back on him. That wasn't the sort of person she was. He also knew that regardless of what she said, he believed she would wait for him. When he returned, they would talk.

Mars had even spent a good portion of the night rehearsing what he was going to say. He would explain that there were some things a man must do. Yes, they were dangerous, but a *man* didn't dodge danger, not when his honor was at stake.

And this was all about honor. Hers as well as his.

Yes, the man might not have known that Clarissa's mother was with child. Mars hadn't known Deb was carrying his babe—but once he knew, he had done the right thing. Dora was important to him. His world had gone from a very small dark place to one with Dora and Clarissa.

Except what had really bothered Mars the most was seeing Dervil standing close to Clarissa. Mars had never experienced jealousy before. It had made him irrational.

As he stood in the morning dew, he began to wrestle with his own culpability. It was not comfortable.

A hired vehicle approached. Mars watched it coming, certain it wasn't Dervil. He was right. The vehicle stayed on the road and two men came out—Balfour and Thurlowe.

For the first time since Mars had issued his challenge, he felt relief. His friends were here. He walked through the wet grass to meet them.

Thurlowe appeared very grumpy. He carried his medical bag in one gloved hand. "You've pulled me out far too early from a warm bed."

"And a willing wife," Mars agreed. He held out his hand and Thurlowe took it. These two men were his brothers. He trusted them. "Thank you for coming," Mars said sincerely.

"I don't like the idea of this," Thurlowe admitted.

Mars would not argue the point.

"Are we meeting over there?" Balfour asked.

"Beside the oak where I was standing, I suppose," Mars said. The three of them walked to the appointed place, leaving the vehicle and driver to wait.

Balfour yawned and Mars had to swallow his. He should be excited. He'd dreamed of this moment.

Instead, his muscles felt lethargic.

"I can't imagine your wife approves of this," Thurlowe said.

Mars didn't answer. Instead, he said to Balfour, "Did you speak to Roberts?"

"I sent him a message. I didn't receive a response. We'll resolve the details this morning."

"Are you certain they will show?" Thurlowe said. "What time is it? It has to be the appointed time. Maybe a little after. I say, if he doesn't show in five minutes, we go to Mars's club and enjoy breakfast."

"Excellent idea," Balfour answered, "except here he comes."

Mars looked over his shoulder and then

faced the coach making its way toward them. The vehicle rolled to a stop at almost the same place the hack had.

Several men climbed out. In the murky light of early dawn, Mars saw Dervil, Roberts, and two others who perhaps had come to observe.

He forced himself to breathe deeply, to relax. Balfour had taken the pistols from him. They waited for the other party to approach.

Dervil appeared calm. Obviously he didn't have a wife pulling at his conscience. He stood off to the side while Roberts and Balfour checked each other's pistols and discussed details. Thurlowe stood a little distance away as if embracing his role of being a bystander until his services were needed.

Mars removed his hat and took off his jacket. The heaviness inside him seemed to be building. He was aware of every detail from the chill of the dew in the morning air to the bead of sweat on his brow. Oh, and the deep lines of disapproval on Balfour's face.

Balfour shook Roberts's hand and returned to Mars. He opened the pistol case. Roberts had chosen the weapon for Dervil, who was testing its weight and deciding if they would use Mars's weapons or what he'd brought. Dervil gave a nod, his acceptance of the gun.

"We are keeping it simple," Balfour said. "We will have you square off at ten paces. When Roberts gives the command to fire, you shoot."

And then it would be done.

For a moment, Mars remembered his father's

pale face. He remembered the count, watching the men fire, the smell of gunpowder.

"Very well." Then Mars said to Balfour, as if to lighten the mood, "Clarissa will be pleased that you are not happy with this."

"I'm certain she has no desire to be a widow before she's been married a month."

"Who is to say I will lose?" Mars was pleased his voice was steady, his tone light. It didn't reflect how he felt.

"Dervil has fought more than his share of duels. And this won't be easy, Mars. You saw your father killed in one—"

"Yes, murdered by *this* man."

"Aye . . . Dervil does have a request."

"Which is?"

"He would like for the two of you to talk. Mars, he doesn't want to fight. There is something about his being Clarissa's father? Do you know about this?"

"It is another reason I shall put a hole in him."

There was a beat of silence. "It doesn't have to be this way, my friend."

They were all turning on him.

Mars took the pistol. "No, I will not talk to Dervil. I have nothing to say to him. Where do I stand?"

With a heavy sound of exasperation, Balfour returned to Roberts. The two men paced off the field. Once satisfied, Balfour looked to Mars and motioned him over. Roberts did the same for Dervil.

The opponents took their places.

Roberts spoke. "I shall count to three *before* I shout 'fire.' Understood? Very well, hands at your sides."

Mars nodded. He straightened his shoulder, loosening some of the tension. The pistol weight felt good in his hand at his side.

"*One*," Roberts said in his booming voice, commanding the attention of all on the field.

Mars drew a breath, released it, and stretched his index finger.

High above them, a bird in a tree started singing to welcome the morning. And this could be his last morning and just like that, Mars thought of Clarissa. Of Clarissa laughing at something he'd said. Of Clarissa sweetly curling up next to his body. Of Clarissa so desperate for him to not duel she was willing to go to any lengths to stop him.

Of Clarissa saying she loved him—

"*Two*."

From the corner of his eye, Mars noticed movement. His first thought was that Clarissa had come. He had no reason to think she would, and he was surprised that he actually wanted her here.

But it had only been Thurlowe crossing his arms, his expression concerned.

"*Three*."

Mars steadied his breathing, his attention completely on Dervil.

"*Fire!*"

Mars lifted his arm, his hand on the trigger. He was a crack shot. He had Dervil in his sight. Except, something strange happened—he became not the man he was now, but the lad who had watched in horror as his father was shot. It was as if his mind leaped back in time.

Nor was it Dervil across from him. It *was* his father. Mars was struck by the image of the blood blooming on his father's shirt. The horror in his expression as he realized that not only had he been hit, his was a mortal wound.

Mars had forgotten that look, pushed it completely from his mind until this second.

And his last thought was—Clarissa had been right. He *hadn't* understood the full impact of this duel.

Unfortunately, Dervil did not hesitate.

Chapter Nineteen

*"There is no sense in marrying an intelligent woman
if one isn't going to listen to her."
Quote is from my wife.*

—*Book of Mars*

$\mathcal{A}$s if from a distance, Mars heard Dervil's shot. He felt it vibrate in the air all the way to his marrow.

In a flash, he pictured Clarissa smiling and holding Dora and he understood what a fool he'd been.

Then he released his breath and realized he was still standing.

Dervil had shot off to the side. He'd deloped, an admission that Mars had grounds to shoot him dead right where he stood.

Mars still had him in his sights. His gaze met Dervil's. His opponent was brave. His back was ramrod straight, waiting to take Mars's bullet.

And no one would blame him for killing Dervil. Or even wounding him.

But suddenly it didn't matter. He heard Clarissa's voice—*you are about to do something that will haunt you every day of your life.*

Just as his father's death had been a weight almost impossible to carry, so, too, would his next action be a burden . . . if he let it.

Mars lowered his pistol to the side and then pulled the trigger, the shot going harmlessly into the soft ground. *Honor served.*

For a long moment, it seemed as if everyone had quit breathing.

Thurlowe was the first to break the silence. "Thank God." And everyone seemed to relax in relief, except Mars and Dervil.

They didn't move an inch. Mars felt as if he had turned to clay. One step and he would crack.

He hadn't done it.

Years of waiting for the day when he could give Dervil the same treatment his father had received, and he'd failed.

Dervil was not so impaired. After several moments of silence, his shoulders slumped as if he had been steeling himself to take the bullet. He nodded, an acknowledgment that Mars was a worthy opponent.

Mars did not nod back.

Dervil turned and walked over to Roberts and the other man who had been holding his jacket and hat. He handed his pistol to Thurlowe and put on his clothing. The men laughed at something he said, and he and his compatriots walked off to the waiting coach.

No words had been spoken between the

duelists and Mars doubted if anything would ever be said between them again.

Balfour and Thurlowe approached Mars. "I'm glad you didn't shoot him," the doctor said.

"I wish I had," Mars answered. Then he might feel better. As it was, he'd been drained of all energy. "I have prepared myself for close to a decade and now—what? Did I lack the courage?"

"No, you came to your senses," Thurlowe answered in his forthright manner. "I can't tell you how relieved I am."

Mars could feel Balfour's scrutiny. He looked at the older man. "What?" Mars demanded.

Balfour raised his brow as if innocent. "Nothing. I, too, am relieved. Come, let us break our fast."

Mars shook his head and offered his pistol to Balfour to place in the dueling case. "No, I want to go home to Clarissa. She was worried. I need to tell her what happened." And he wanted to talk, to explain that she had saved him today. That, yes, she and Dora mattered. That maybe he loved her in return.

"Well, I for one will go to breakfast. Come along, Balfour." Thurlowe started for the hack.

Balfour smiled. "This was hard on him," he confided to Mars. "He had no desire to operate on you."

"And I am free to live my life as I wish," Mars agreed although there was little enthusiasm in his voice.

"Wait." Balfour took Mars's arm and turned

him to face him. "You handled yourself honorably. Your father would have been proud."

"Dervil escapes justice."

Thurlowe had stopped, hearing the exchange. "You pay him in kind and your life is ruined, just as it is beginning. Where is the justice in that? Besides, you have someone now who cares about you. Let us be honest, before our wives, we were all living very much on the surface of things. I didn't know how much I was missing until I had someone challenge me the way Gemma does. She is my closest confidante. I trust you two but Gemma brings a different depth to our discussions. Do you know, I would no more think of rejoining the Logical Men's Society than I would cutting off my right hand. Even the two of you can't match what Gemma means to me."

Balfour nodded. "I adore Kate. And our little Anne lights up when I enter the nursery and it is as if I've been knighted by the king himself. I agree with Thurlowe. I chased the wrong things for a long time. My life is richer with Kate." Then he lowered his voice to add, "And so is yours with Clarissa. She is a jewel, Mars. An intelligent woman is a gift to her husband. Yes, some women are annoying . . . but not the ones we married."

He was right. In fact, if anything, Mars was the selfish one. He pictured her as he'd left her. She'd done all in her power to deter him from what could have been an ill-fated action and she'd acted out of love. She'd also known that if he had shot Dervil, he would despise himself.

The bloodlust for revenge inside him had been changed by his love for his wife. She had been the one who was on his mind in those last minutes. The voice of reason inside of him, and he could no longer deny what was true—*he loved her.*

He still wasn't certain what love was, but he knew he must have Clarissa in his life. "I'm going home."

His friends smiled as if he had joined a new society. A society of logical gentlemen who admired and appreciated their wives.

He walked with them to where their coach waited, gave each a brotherly hug, thanking them for their support, and watched them leave before he untied Bruno's reins and set the horse for home.

The morning traffic had picked up. Usually it was an annoyance. Today, Mars was so pleased over the way matters had played out, he had a wellspring of patience.

Tonight, he would sleep well. He would admit his faults to his wife. Clarissa would like that. Then, he would make amends for what had happened last night. He'd show her how much he adored her. Tomorrow would be the vote. He would vote against Dervil . . . and they would head home. Dora needed them. He wanted his daughter to look at him as if he was the hero of her world.

He also wanted to be a hero to Clarissa. He trusted she would forgive him.

All was quiet in Grosvenor Square when he and Bruno reached the house. The front door opened. Dalton had been waiting for him. A footman came out to take Bruno to the stables.

Mars handed the horse over and went up the step, taking his hat off as he entered the house. He handed it to Dalton. He looked around, half expecting Clarissa to be waiting someplace for him—if for nothing more than to tell him how disappointed she was. He grinned. She was going to be so pleased she was right.

Except, she was not present. Her lovely face didn't poke around the corner of the reception room or the dining room.

He went upstairs, going straight for the bedroom. Nelson was in there, straightening out the wardrobe as if it was a painful task.

"Come now," he said to his valet, "it can't be that bad. You are the one who manages it."

Nelson didn't respond to Mars's teasing the way he usually did. No huffing and puffing. Instead, he appeared sad. "Yes, my lord." It was a perfunctory answer. The valet returned to his task.

Mars glanced around the room again . . . and that was when he noticed how empty it was. The area by the washing bowl didn't seem crowded. He stared at it and then realized why—Clarissa's hairbrush was not there. He wondered where it was, although now, he was starting to have an inkling, one he didn't like.

Mars left the bedroom. He walked down the hall to the library. If Clarissa was anywhere in this house, she would be here.

She wasn't. No one sat in the chair by the

latest novels. She wasn't poring over the bookshelves.

A letter had been placed in the middle of the desk, carefully folded and addressed to him.

He studied it a second, almost afraid to move forward. He forced himself to move, sitting in the chair and picking up the letter. He unfolded it.

Funny, he had not seen his wife's handwriting other than her signature. She had an almost mannish style in its lack of flourishes.

She was very direct in her commentary.

> *My lord, I thought I could make the best of our marriage of convenience. Unfortunately, I was wrong. I'm not good at pretending all is well when it isn't. I shall await your return at Belvoir where we can sort this out. I do believe the separation will do us good.*

There was no complimentary closing such as "sincerely yours." Certainly no, "your loving wife." No title after she wrote her name, *Clarissa*.

Damn, he could have written this letter.

Lowton always complained that Mars was too abrupt in his comments. The secretary would be horrified at this missive.

Mars was, too. Because she'd made her point clear.

She'd left him. She'd said last night she would.

A knock on the door startled him. Dalton was there. Mars covered the letter with his arm. Of course, the servants had known she'd left. If he hadn't been congratulating himself, he would have noticed the signs immediately. Instead, he'd been confident that his wife was tucked away here where he'd left her. He had expected that she would give him a pat on the back and then he would declare his love and all would be well.

Unfortunately, Clarissa wasn't that simple. She wasn't a fool either.

"You have a visitor, my lord."

Mars looked up at the door. He was not in the mood for visitors. He would have said so except Dalton came into the room without invitation and silently offered the card on the silver salver he carried. Mars lifted it. There was one word on it.

Dervil.

He flicked the card back onto the salver. "I am not at home—"

"I feared you would say that," Dervil's voice came from the doorway. He stepped forward, holding his hat in his hand. "Don't have a tiff with your butler. He told me to stay downstairs but I knew you would answer as you did. We need to talk."

"I have nothing to say."

"That may be true," Dervil said. "However, you are the one who left me alive."

"Obviously a mistake."

"Then let me rephrase. *I* must talk to you."

"I'm not interested."

In response, Dervil walked right in and took the chair closest to the desk. He looked to Dalton, "Please close the door and give us some privacy."

Dalton had the good sense to check with Mars, who was in a bloody killing mood right now. He had no idea what Dervil wished to say and he didn't care. Still, he nodded for Dalton to leave. Then, once the door was shut, he coldly asked, "What the bloody hell do you want?"

Dervil had the gall to smile. "For one thing, to thank you for not shooting me."

"The day is still young."

"I won't stand waiting like I did this morning."

"And what else?"

Dervil set his hat on a side table on top of the books that yesterday morning Clarissa had pulled off the shelves. She was a greedy reader. She wanted them all. He said, "I want to clear the air between us."

"You can't."

"Hear me out."

Mars shook his head. "You bastard, you shot my father under the same circumstances as this morning. I could have taken your life. I didn't. And do you know why? Because I'm a damn decent person. And you can credit my wife with any improvement I have made."

Any humor in Dervil's face vanished.

Instead, he appeared haunted. "You are right. I deserved for you to shoot me. It would be a blessing. I—"

He stopped, sat up, his elbows on the arms

of the chair, his hands dangling. And then he spoke. "I didn't mean to kill your father that morning."

"For not meaning to, you did a fine job."

"He moved."

Dervil acted as if that answered everything.

"You shouldn't have shot at him," Mars said. "You were sleeping with his wife."

"His unhappy wife. She told me he abused her, that he had a foul temper. I was actually more full of myself back then."

"I didn't know that was possible," Mars responded.

"I saw myself as her champion and I was infatuated with her."

"Tigers need more protection than my mother does. Father could lose his temper but he never raised a fist against her that I saw. And often, she was the instigator."

Yes, he remembered his parents' rows. His parents had not been happy together. And for the first time, Mars realized how much their unhappiness may have weighed upon him. Marriage had never seemed to be a pleasant state. It was full of distrust, anger over small issues, tension. Oh, yes, there had been so much animosity that even a lad, who only spent school holidays with his parents unless he was in trouble, had noticed.

This new awareness about the past teased him, begging the question, could he have been wrong about what he had believed?

He rarely spoke about his father's death.

He'd said more to Clarissa than even to Balfour or Thurlowe.

And now, he was curious. "What happened?" he asked Dervil, not knowing if the man would be telling him the truth. "And why did you delope this morning?"

"I deloped because you had grounds for grievance. You should protect your wife's honor." For a second, he reacted as if he'd felt a stab of pain. He rubbed his face before looking squarely in Mars's eye. "The greatest mistake I made was to allow Priscilla Comstock to slip away. I've spent a lifetime, two marriages, and a ridiculous number of lovers trying to recapture what she gave me. When Priscilla first disappeared, I searched for her, Marsden. You must believe me."

"I have no doubt you did." This was a side of Dervil Mars had never thought possible, or even believable.

Dervil shifted his weight. "I would be a different man if Priscilla was alive. She didn't take her life, *I* took it with my uncaring ways. And she gave me a daughter."

Mars refused to touch that statement. He had a feeling he knew what the man wanted, and Mars had no idea how much contact Clarissa would want with Dervil.

"We men are fools," Dervil said.

"Speak for yourself."

Dervil made a dismissive sound. "You have made me pay for years. You have blocked me from business associations I wanted, purchased land that I coveted. And if you don't particularly want me as a father-in-marriage, well, I'm not excited about you either."

"Why are you here?"

"Because I want matters settled between us. I want to approach my daughter, and I want to do it with your permission."

Mars could almost hear Clarissa's voice as he said, "That is out of my hands. My wife makes her own decisions." He looked down at the letter under his arm. He'd never said truer words, that was, if he still had a wife.

"I don't expect you to like me, Marsden. I don't like myself most times. I don't know how to approach your wife, but I'm going to try. I have really no one to show for my life except for her. And, yes, I am aware you will not vote for me and probably do your best to win the chair for Fenton. Power and politics have nothing to do with the reasons for my being here. I want an opportunity to redeem myself. Two wives and no children. I had come to believe I was doomed—and now, to learn I am a father. I don't expect you to understand. You are a young man, but this is a blessing. Even if she never speaks to me, she is a gift."

In that moment, Mars realized he wasn't looking at an enemy but at a lonely man. One whose decisions in life had brought him to where he was.

It was as if he was seeing a reflection of where he could be years from now. Yes, he had Dora . . . except he remembered something

Clarissa had said about how his position in the Lords should be more than just gamesmanship. The responsibilities were not about power. She would tell him, sounding like one of her father's indeterminate sermons, that one should do what was right.

"Why do you want the position of Chairman of Committees?" he asked Dervil.

"To keep it from going to your mother." Dervil laughed as if it should be obvious. "She derailed my life years ago. She treated me as if I was some nobody. I killed a man because of her. Do you believe you were the only one outraged? I was a pariah. However, I've worked hard to redeem what I could of my reputation. Or perhaps I want to be a part of history. To have my name recorded as a politician of prominence."

He wanted power. His mother wanted to be married to a powerful man.

No candidate seemed to be thinking about what was best for the country. A plan began forming in Mars's mind. One that Clarissa would approve. "My lord, thank you for calling." He rose and came around the desk, moving to the door, a signal the interview was over.

Dervil stood. He extended his hand. "Then, can we set our differences aside? I wish permission to speak to my daughter."

Mars did not touch the hand. "You will have to take that matter up with her. I was not jesting. I have known Clarissa all my life and she makes her own decisions."

Dervil's hand came down. "All your life? Did she have a good one? Was she well taken care of?" Instead of being offended by Mars's stiffness, he acted hungry for information.

Mars thought of the matrons, of the villagers. "My wife is well-respected." Far better than he was, although he was determined to change. He *had* to change. He wanted to be worthy of Clarissa's love. She didn't want a man who howled his frustration with the world. She deserved a husband who met her high standards.

And he may have already lost her.

"I am relieved to hear that she had people who cared for her," Dervil said. "I shall contact her. I shall write."

"You may do as you wish." Mars opened the door. "Dalton will see you out."

The butler had been waiting out in the hall. He stepped froward. "This way, my lord."

Dervil had no choice but to leave. Finally.

Mars returned to the desk. He pulled out pen and paper. In his slashing handwriting, he was equally direct to Clarissa. *Do not give up on us yet. M*

He sealed it and carried it downstairs to Dalton. "If there is a response, tell the rider I wish to receive it with all haste." He wouldn't put it past Clarissa to inform him he wasn't welcome under his own roof.

Mars hoped she didn't.

He then set to work on a plan that had been brewing in his mind as he'd listened to Dervil.

And he was motivated by more than just being the man Clarissa thought he should be.

No, he wanted to become the man *he* believed he should be.

AFTER A busy day and night, Mars made his way to the Thatched House Club located at number 80 St. James Street. Every politician and university man knew the place. It had a huge meeting room in a splendid location with good food and drink. What more could politicians ask for?

It was here the Tories were meeting for their vote today.

He rode. He did not plan to be long and wanted to head to Belvoir at his first chance. For a coin, a street lad was willing to walk the horse while Mars went inside.

Mars was just reaching the door when he heard his mother call his name. He turned and saw her leaning out the open door of a coach lined up in front. He approached her.

She sat back in the vehicle, inviting him in. He shook his head. He was a man on a mission this morning. "I feared you weren't going to make it," she said. "Thank you for not shooting Lord Dervil."

"Because you still have feelings for him?"

She gave a cackly laugh. "I gave up those long ago. No, I'm pleased because it wouldn't have gone well for us if you had killed him. It would have ruined our plans. I have worked hard to lay the groundwork for this vote. This is the first true threat to my husband's control and I won't stand for it."

"It is a pity you can't be inside with us."

His mother hummed her response. "It is a hinderance although I've learned to work around it. I have an informant. I will know everything that is going on."

"Then there should be no problems."

"I hope that this is only a beginning of your political career," she said. "Believe it or not, you are both an enigmatic figure and a well-liked one. Especially from those who remember your father." She paused. "They have always supported Fenton's position as chairman, until now. This is the first serious challenge . . . and to have it come from Dervil?" She shook her head as if the Almighty was playing a jest. "Fortunately, it is all arranged. You will have the final vote, just as *I* promised."

"Thank you." He started to climb out of the coach. She stopped him.

"I know you don't think well of me. However, I want you to know, I don't bear a grudge."

It was all he could do not to smile. "I appreciate the knowledge, my lady." He left to go inside the club knowing that very soon she would be so angry at him, she'd be happy to see him drawn and quartered.

And so it was that when the vote was taken, a *new* coalition had been formed—by Mars. He had in a day organized many of the younger members in the Lords who were not satisfied with Fenton's aging ways or Dervil's lack of anything. They had agreed with Mars that the Earl of Jessup, a young ambitious man whom Mars had known in school, would be better suited for Chairman of Committees.

Quite simply, both Fenton and Dervil lost.

Mars didn't cast the final vote because once members of Fenton and Dervil's factions saw what was taking place, they threw in their lots with the more progressive player. His vote was only one amongst many.

Of course, the new Tory coalition Mars had formed wouldn't let him escape after the vote. There were meetings to discuss "issues" and for some reason they wished his input.

Mars hated meetings.

And the only issue he was interested in was if he had a marriage or not.

Still, he had put this together and even though he didn't know the intricacies of all the problems and concerns involved, he knew how to gather people who did understand. He was actually rather good at it. Perhaps there was a bit of his mother in him after all. He knew Clarissa would be amused.

So it was that he couldn't start for Belvoir until late afternoon on Saturday. He wasn't about to wait another day. He missed his wife, and he wasn't fool enough to believe Clarissa would let him continue to take her for granted.

He also wanted to share with her about the vote.

The minute the last meeting adjourned, he set off on horseback and rode as far as he could. After several hours' sleep in an inn, he was on the road again before dawn.

He was going home.

Chapter Twenty

I have become that luckiest of all men,
one who loves his wife–devotedly, madly, deeply.
—*Book of Mars*

Clarissa was frustrated. She had wanted to take a pony cart to Sunday services at St. Martyr's. Gibson would not hear of it. Instead, he ordered up the coach.

"My lady, you are a countess. You should travel accordingly."

"I've been driving a pony cart around this parish for most of my life," she'd countered. "I can easily take Dora into the village for services."

"I'm sorry, my lady, a cart can tip or a wheel break. The earl would have my head if something happened to you."

Clarissa wasn't convinced Mars would be upset. Her temper had cooled since she'd left London, several days ago. She was now more resigned to the fact that he would never feel for her what she felt for him. And she could not and would not condone dueling.

At the same time, it could be only a matter of days, or even hours, when her husband would return. He'd not sent word save for his admonishment—*Do not give up on us yet.*

She shook her head. There had never been an "us."

What she did know because of the message was that Mars was alive, and that did make her glad.

Lord Dervil was alive as well. His lordship had sent her a letter stating he had asked her husband's permission to contact her, except Mars had told him to petition his wife directly.

At least her husband had that right.

His lordship requested permission to call upon Clarissa when he was next in Maidenshop. She had not replied. She didn't know how she felt about Lord Dervil.

Clarissa had turned to her friends the matrons for advice. They had met as a group yesterday afternoon. All of them, including the Dowager of Winderton. After being plied with sherry, Clarissa had confessed she didn't know what to do with her marriage. Mars didn't understand her. She didn't understand him. Perhaps it had all been a big mistake.

Except, instead of commiserating, she'd been given some stern admonishments about staying out of her husband's affairs.

"Do you think I agree with everything Mr.

Summerall preaches from the pulpit?" Mrs. Summerall said. "Of course not. However, I like my marriage, so I don't correct him."

"We are talking life and death," Clarissa had pointed out. "Lord Marsden wanted to kill a man. Certainly you can't agree with that."

"Pshaw!" Mrs. Warbler had answered. "In the military, dueling was the quickest way to resolve a problem. Men are so hotheaded that grudges could fester. My husband, the colonel, always said he preferred dueling rather than listening to them natter on about perceived insults and slights. Some men are very touchy."

That information hadn't even made sense to Clarissa. Shouldn't the king's troops be shooting the French instead of each other? No wonder the war had taken so long to settle.

And there were many women in the group who hadn't hesitated to let her know they thought she was being demanding. She was a countess now. Aristocrats shot at each other. It was what they did.

Consequently, Clarissa wasn't pleased with the world in general. Therefore Gibson's refusal to let her take the pony cart did not sit well. So much for being a countess.

The problem was, Clarissa felt she had need of spiritual guidance this shining Sunday morning. She didn't know what to do. She missed Mars. She felt as if a part of her had been hacked off and she felt off balance and more than a touch lost.

She'd turned to her friends yesterday hoping they would reassure her that not only had she been in the right, her husband would see it as well.

That had not been the case. These women who had been married for years and who had supported her for most of her life had turned on her. They'd made her feel as if perhaps she had been too rigid.

It also didn't help that for the past few nights, she'd found it torturous to sleep alone.

The one bright spot was Dora. She'd worried the baby would forget who she was, especially with Mrs. Rucker nursing her.

Instead, Dora had welcomed her with one of her brightest smiles and a squeal of delight. Since Clarissa had returned, she'd not let the baby out of her sight except for feedings. And the more she was around her, the more Clarissa feared she would not be able to make the right decisions when it came to Mars. She'd learned she wasn't one to go through the motions.

She was also too sensitive over the fact that Mars had married her for his daughter. Dora would grow quickly and then he would question his reasoning for taking a wife. They would grow apart and she didn't know if she could bear the sadness of a shell of a marriage.

So it was that on a lovely summer morning when the sky was deep, deep blue and the bees were busy, Clarissa rode in a coach to Sunday services. At the last moment, she decided to leave Dora behind with her nurse. A tooth was coming in and Dora was very out of sorts. She'd finally settled into a nap and Clarissa was loath to disturb her.

She also knew Reverend Summerall would not appreciate a fussy baby during one of his sermons.

Belvoir's matched team were faster than any pony cart could ever be. She arrived very early for the service. Mr. Summerall was fussing around, preparing for church, but no one else was there. Clarissa was rather happy to have a moment alone.

Hodner climbed down from the box, leaving the driver to hold the horses. He knocked on the coach door before opening it.

"We are here before everyone else, my lady. Do you wish to wait in the coach or would you like to walk a bit?"

"How well you already know me, Hodner," Clarissa said. "I would indeed prefer to walk a bit. You can drive the coach home. I won't be needing you until after the service and that will be close to one o'clock."

"I believe his lordship would wish us to wait."

She'd just had an argument with Gibson, she wasn't going to let Hodner defeat her. "If something comes up, I shall go to Mrs. Warbler's house to wait. There won't be a problem."

The expression on his face said he believed there would, and yet he was powerless to countermand her. He dutifully helped her alight from the coach. She straightened her straw bonnet that had tilted slightly when she'd gone through the door, and noticed the graveyard.

She'd meant to pay her respects to her mother's grave when she'd first returned but hadn't made the trip yet. Her mind had been too full of worries.

Clarissa walked to the oak. She knelt and pulled some of the ever-present grass threatening to overtake the stone before closing her eyes and saying a silent prayer. She told her mother that Lord Dervil was sorry. *I wish you were alive.* Because she could use a mother's advice right now. The matrons were good mentors although they had other purposes in mind when they offered their opinions. They worried about her security, not her heart.

"Please, Mother, give me a sign—"

And then she heard a step behind her. She waited, expecting whomever it was to move on. People often walked the graves before the service.

Then, as if she'd conjured him, she heard Mars say her name. "Rissa."

For a second, she feared she was imagining his voice. Slowly, she rose to her feet and turned around. Of course, he was standing there not more than five feet from her. Her senses had not lied.

He'd been traveling. His boots showed the dust of the road. He held his hat in his hand and his hair was windswept and careless. He smelled of fresh, wild air and horses. And he had never looked better . . . because he'd come to her.

But exactly what did that mean? There was an expression in his eye, a solemnity, that she'd not seen before.

He spoke. "Dervil is alive."

She nodded. "He sent me a letter. He told me you chose not to shoot him."

"I realized even before we started that you were right. I am not a duelist."

Clarissa could have collapsed in thankful relief.

"How is Dora?" he asked.

Of course, Dora. "She is growing chubby and will soon have a tooth. I know she will be happy to see you."

"And I her."

"What of the vote?" she asked. "Did you exact your revenge?"

"In an astounding way." He took a few steps toward her. "I did as you suggested and offered some leadership."

"Leadership?" He'd startled her. "I thought you didn't want to have anything to do with all of that?"

His smile was rueful, and charming. "When one has an intelligent wife, he should listen to her."

Clarissa cocked her head. "Possibly." She thought about what the women had told her yesterday and of her fears that he would not come back. "Sometimes, intelligent women can make matters a bit of a muddle."

"We all can," he said kindly and took another step toward her. "What I did was form my own coalition and encourage a good number of members to support a third candidate for Chairman. He's younger, more progressive, and will bring intelligence and energy to the position. It was not difficult to convince others to join me."

"Who is the new Chairman?"

"Lord Jessup. You will be hearing about him. Clever man. I have known him for years."

"Your mother must be furious."

"I assume so. We haven't spoken. Fenton appeared relieved. Well, I assume he will be relieved when he wakes up and someone tells him what happened."

"Now he can nap without pretending to be listening."

He laughed. "Too true." There was a beat of silence and then he said, "I don't like my mother. I don't like your father."

"I don't even know him," Clarissa answered. "When he wrote, he asked permission to call on me. I wanted to wait and talk to you."

"It is your decision, Clarissa. I have strong reasons not to trust him, however, I will support whatever you decide."

Clarissa was shocked. Was this even the same man? "I can't see inviting him into my life, Mars. He killed your father."

"He apologized."

"You are *defending* him? Is an apology enough?"

"No. Although, I am relieved I don't have his death on my conscience. You were right, once again."

Clarissa could not believe what she was hearing. "Mars—" she started, just as he said, "Rissa—"

They both stopped awkwardly, and she was thankful. She hadn't fully formed in her mind what she wanted to say without sounding as if she was listing grievances, grievances that were beginning not to matter . . .

Was this what the matrons had been trying to tell her yesterday?

Fortunately, she was saved from saying anything because he barged ahead. "I must speak first. If I don't, I may lose my nerve." Then he dove in almost ferociously, "I have been so *wrong* about everything. I thought I didn't need anyone, that I was better being alone. When you challenged me on the duel, when you told me I wasn't justified, I was angry. I said unforgivable things. They weren't words I meant." He made a frustrated sound and admitted, "I was also frustrated and confused. I mean, I married Dervil's daughter—"

"He has not been a father to me. He doesn't deserve the title."

"I'm thankful he doesn't. Because, if he had been, I wouldn't have married you. I am far too human. I've been lost in grief and wanting vengeance when I don't even know what that is. How does one measure the loss of a life?"

He stopped, drew a great shuddering breath as if gathering his courage, then said, "Clarissa, I'm sorry for my anger. I'm sorry you felt you had to leave. But I don't want you to leave *me*. I need you, Clarissa. And *love* is such a dangerous word. I thought my father was a fool for loving my mother to the point of giving up his own pride. Of course, the first time I held

Dora, I felt something strange move me. It was like I was being opened up, but only a crack." He took another step toward her. "What I feel for you is different. It's stronger. Bigger. Damn it all, I'm not a poet. I have no patience with fancy language."

"Keep going," she said, wiping a tear that had escaped with the back of her gloved hand. "You are doing a very good job."

He smiled at her then. No one's smile was better than Mars's. It was like the sun coming out from behind massive dark clouds. "You are always on my side."

"Not always."

He laughed and then said quietly, sincerely, and clearly, "I love you."

Clarissa could have fallen to her knees in front of him. *He loved her.* Her, the unlovable one. The village project. *Mars loved her.* Her tears started flowing freely now. Tears of joy and blessed relief.

She started to speak. He covered her lips with his leather-gloved fingertips. "No, let me say this because I don't know if I could ever do it again."

Clarissa dutifully quieted herself, so full of joy it was hard to contain.

"If you stay, I will do everything in my power to make you happy. Unfortunately, I'm a bit stubborn. I'll make mistakes."

"You managed to put together a coalition, my lord. I have great hopes for you."

"I have great hopes for myself. I'm a bit amazed that it all came together so well. I also learned you were right. There are some issues I should be paying attention to. Lowton is happily putting together weekly reports for me to study all the issues he believes I should know."

"That is a good thing."

"I suppose. It feels different. It feels responsible." He shook his head. "It is a big change."

"There are some things I don't ever want you to change, my lord. I like your stubbornness. It matches mine."

"Oh, no," he answered without missing a beat, "you are far more stubborn."

Clarissa swallowed a laugh. "Are you arguing with me?"

"I hope so. I want to argue with you every day for the rest of my life. Do you understand? Circumstances may have thrown us together, but I love you, Rissa. Even when you push me in directions I don't want to go. I need the push. I need *you*."

Her response was to throw her arms around him and to hug him tightly. He felt good and solid, a rock of stability. *Her* rock.

And he held her just as close—

A discreet clearing of a voice warned them they were not alone.

They looked up to see Mrs. Warbler and several of the matrons watching the scene. Reverend Summerall was lurking behind them. There were smiles on all their faces.

Mars didn't release his hold and neither did she. Instead, he said to Mrs. Warbler, "Don't get any ideas. You were lucky with us but we can't have you all matchmaking."

"Oh, we would never think of it, my lord," Mrs. Warbler promised, except there was a gleam in her eye. "Come, ladies. Let us give them their privacy."

Clarissa didn't care who saw them or knew they were in love. For the first time, she felt truly valued, and as Mars took her hand to follow the villagers into the church, she believed she was the most blessed woman alive.

As for her husband, well, he must love her because he attended the Sunday service. He sat beside her as Reverend Summerall gave his most rambling sermon ever.

In the middle of it, Mars laced his gloved fingers with hers. Clarissa looked down at their joined hands. There would be trials ahead. There always were . . . but she was no longer alone.

Epilogue

I've made my peace with the Matrons of Maidenshop.
We do it their way and all is happy.

–Book of Mars

Maidenshop
May 1816

It was the best Cotillion Dance in anyone's memory.

The world was finally at peace. Napoleon had been safely locked away, and soldiers and sailors were returning home. The mild winter had led to a good lambing season and a feeling of abundance abounded.

On this lovely May night, most had sheared their wool and the seeds had been sown for good crops. The time had come to celebrate.

Of course the Matrons of Maidenshop who decorated and made all major decisions for the Cotillions had everything in hand. The barn was filled with boughs of greenery and candlelight and everyone claimed the decorations had never appeared better. Even the musicians on the dais playing one lively reel after another sounded better than they had in previous years.

Or it could be, Mars surmised, everything seemed so fine because his brain wasn't fuddled with drink as it had been for every dance during the years before. He'd always believed he'd held himself together and made a good impression, but there had been one lady who had seen right through him, and today, she was the only one he wanted to please.

His countess. His Clarissa. Her name was the rhythm of his life. He couldn't imagine living without her.

As he'd suspected, his actions over the Chairman of the Committees had meant that he'd been pulled into politics. He didn't mind.

He and Clarissa were now considered guests of the first order on every important social list. He didn't mind that either. It rather made him proud.

For her part, Clarissa had turned out to be quite adept at managing different personalities. Her popularity amongst the *ton* was growing, making his duties easier. Apparently being a minister's daughter was excellent training for politics.

And women knew more than he'd ever imagined.

They took Dora with them to London now because of the length of time they had to stay. His little "precious button" was turning out to be a handful. She had a sense of determination and Mars gloried in it. His daughter was as headstrong as himself. She'd do well in life. After all, hadn't he been the same as a child?

Of course, the place he and Clarissa enjoyed most of all was Belvoir and Maidenshop. This was their home. They would no more think of missing the Cotillion than missing an audience with their monarch.

Tonight, Gemma and Thurlowe had hosted a lovely dinner for Mars, Clarissa, Kate, and Balfour. Gemma was at least six months gone with child and she glowed with happiness.

That wasn't Mars's observation. Clarissa had said as much when they left the house to walk to the dance, and watching his friend's wife move gracefully through the crowd in spite of her size, Mars agreed.

He almost always agreed with his wife. It was a blessing for a man to be married to an intelligent woman. An absolute gift.

However, now he, Balfour, and Thurlowe had an important announcement to make. He waited until the reel was over. Clarissa gave his hand a squeeze for luck, a habit she had started every time he was called upon to speak in front of a group. Her faith in him was unwavering. It gave him the courage to step to the forefront.

The musicians had already been prewarned to expect an announcement. At the sight of the three men moving forward, they brought the music to a halt.

Mars stepped up on the dais. His friends

flanked him. At one time, they'd been known as the Three Bucks, the most eligible bachelors in the parish. Smiling down at his wife, Mars marveled at how things had changed.

The crowd become quiet, expectant as they readied to hear what he had to say.

"We have just one announcement to make. As you know my great-grandfather started the Logical Men's Society several decades ago. I have been a proud member until I joined the ranks of the married. *Happily* joined the ranks of the married," he corrected to a murmur of laughter in the room.

"Now the Logical Men's Society, which prided itself on promoting fellowship amongst bachelors, has become more of a bowling club—"

A cheer went up from the Dawson brothers who were surrounded by the other single lads. They met several times a week at The Garland's back lawn to play. Gemma considered them The Garland's best customers.

"We have all changed, haven't we, lads," Mars said to the heads nodding agreement.

Well, not everyone was happy with the turn of events. Sir Lionel, who was here this evening in his red fez and jealously nursing a jug of something he had brought, was not content. He was a widower who had once spent his days drinking with his best friend Fullerton, another widower.

Now he stayed at home and drank alone because Fullerton had started calling on Mrs. Warbler and the matrons felt a promising match was in the making there. That Mars even knew this information and actually cared was of itself a small miracle.

Mars continued. "Suffice it to say that the Logical Men's Society is no more."

Another murmur went through the crowd. The matrons sitting in their one corner of the room exchanged triumphant looks. There had been a time when seeing such glances would have set Mars's back up. Instead, he could acknowledge the bachelors had lost—but look at what they'd gained. The Three Bucks were all happily married to women they cherished. Women they trusted. Women they loved.

"However, we don't want to lose the name," Mars said. "So, for the next portion of this announcement, I shall turn you over to Doctor Thurlowe who will be holding his fourth seminar on natural philosophy on the morrow as is tradition."

Thurlowe stepped forward. "We've never had a good name for our seminars. Nothing seemed to strike the right note. Also, as of last year, everyone, male or female, is invited. We do not refuse admittance because of one's gender. Learning should be universal." That was met with female applause with, of course, Reverend Summerall joining in. He was a strong proponent for the education of the female mind.

So was Mars. Especially since he and Clarissa would need something to keep Dora's active mind busy. Latin should do it. And French, of course, and possibly mathematics. Mars had always been strong in the study of mathematics.

Thurlowe continued. "That being said, we are going to increase the lecture series to at least four a year and possibly more. With Cambridge so close and Newmarket not far, we know there will be interest in attending, especially since our numbers have increased with each successive program.

"We have finally settled on a name for our lectures. We had thought of calling them the Logical Men's Society because we focus on matters of logic. My wife begged me to reconsider and we did. The new name of our lecture series will be the Logical Society. Our lectures are open to all."

The clapping was stronger now. Mars knew they would be pleased with the next phase. "Balfour."

He stepped forward. "The Garland will not be large enough to hold the numbers we expect to draw for the lectures to the village. So, with the Earl of Marsden's backing, we will build a meeting building on a piece of property not far from The Garland that he has donated. It is a nice piece of land. It overlooks the Three Thieves' rushing waters. I have created the designs and we will place them back by the punch bowl for all of you to have the chance to see."

As he spoke, Mars signaled for his men to carry in boards holding the designs. The villagers grew restless with their interest.

"Feel free to comment, if you wish," Balfour said. "This is not about us, but about the future of Maidenshop. We expect it to be an asset for all of our families."

Mars took over. "That is all we have to share. We thank you for listening."

Warm applause met their presentation even as a goodly number of people rushed to the back of the room to look at the drawings. Mrs. Warbler and the Dowager Duchess of Winderton led the way.

Mars turned to his friends. "Gentlemen, I believe we will be a success."

"I know we will be," Balfour answered.

"It doesn't matter," Thurlowe chimed in. "What we do is for the future, not of just our village but the country."

"Well, here is to a bright future," Mars said. Now would be the time for a toast except after the fight at the Cotillion two years earlier and the lacing of the punch bowl last year with strong spirits, the matrons had deemed it necessary to ban anything but a weak and rather watery concoction.

That was all right. They had toasted their success over dinner.

Meanwhile the musicians were anxious to return to their playing. The men walked off the dais and parted company to search out their wives. Mars found Clarissa waiting for him by the door.

"Well done, my lord," she said, her smile one of pride.

He felt himself flush. Clarissa was always lavish in her praise.

"Will you dance, my lady?"

"I have a better idea," she said, and took his hand. She led him out the door and into the night.

"We are leaving?" he asked.

"No," she said, a secret smile on her face.

"Is this a surprise?" He always enjoyed Clarissa's surprises.

She didn't answer at first. She led him toward the horses and the coaches. "Do you remember what we were doing at the last Cotillion?"

"Arguing?"

She laughed. "Yes, we were." She stopped at a coach set apart from the coaches in the line. *His* coach. It was dark here in the shadow of the hemlocks.

For a second, Mars could barely breathe as he remembered how miserable he'd been that night. "I escaped the dance to sit inside here and drink." He didn't even have a flask on his person this evening.

"And I escaped out here because I had learned my life was not going to go the way I had planned. You gave me good advice that night. Without you, I would be Mrs. Thurlowe."

"I like the advice I gave, although I can't imagine anything I said was very wise."

She smiled. "It wasn't, except you *were* honest." She moved to the coach door and opened it. "And I thought, perhaps we should reenact that night but with a different result?" There was a lift in her voice, a hint of desire. She stepped up to sit on the edge of the seat. The extra height put her on his level. She pulled on the knot of his neckcloth, pulling it loose so he could not mistake her meaning. "Well, my lord?"

"You are the most perfect wife in the world," he said.

"Then join me and show me all the ways in which I am perfect," she whispered, and he was happy to oblige.

Here's where it all began!
A peek at Cathy Maxwell's

His Secret Mistress

Book 1 of The Logical Man's
Guide to Dangerous Women

On sale now at your
favorite retailer!

Chapter One

He'd lost the damn commission.

For a good twelve months, Mr. Brandon Balfour had labored on a proposed design for a bridge crossing the River Thames in London. After repeated requests for elaborate and complicated changes, the Surveyor-General had assured Bran his was the best proposal submitted. He'd all but promised Bran swift approval, and then last night, the council had informed him that they were interested in a new contender. A Scotsman well-known to council members had expressed interest in the project.

And in less time than it took to down a brandy, Bran's hours of work and endless toadying to pompous asses who knew little about what made bridges work had come to naught. That bridge was to have been his signature, his mark on the world, the first important project of his small, struggling engineering firm.

Which meant that right now, the weight of the fowling piece felt damn good in Bran's hand. He was of a mind to shoot something this morning. Rooks were as good a choice as any other. In fact, he'd been so angry after the council meeting, he'd ridden through the night to join the hunt at Belvoir Castle. He'd known he was too bitter and frustrated for sleep. Or to cool his heels in London.

His friend the Earl of Marsden, the owner of Belvoir, walked beside him through tall grass toward a thicket of trees, the rooks' haven. It was shortly before dawn and the air had a hushed, expectant darkness.

Flanking them was Mr. Ned Thurlowe, the local physician and another valued friend. The three of them, tall, well-favored, and confident, were often referred to locally as "the Three Bucks" of the Logical Men's Society. Gentlemen usually envied them and women thought they should be married.

At six-foot-four, Mars was two inches taller than Bran. He was lean of frame with broad shoulders and blue eyes that could be warm and friendly or deadly chilling. His hair was the golden brown of winter wheat.

Thurlowe was the handsomest of their trio. He had wild, untamed looks with dark hair and slashing brows. It was claimed women feigned sickness just to have him place his concerned physician's hand on their brows and more than one had swooned from his touch.

"When I saw you in London last week," Mars said to Bran, his voice low so it would not carry in the predawn air and warn the birds of their approach, "you told me you didn't know when you would be returning to Maidenshop. Didn't you hope your bridge design would receive its final approval?"

A hard stone set in Bran's chest. "We had a meeting last night. I expected to be named the architect but then a new player was thrown into the game. A Scotsman who is a relative of Dervil's."

"Dervil? That bastard." Lord Dervil's estates bordered Belvoir. Years ago, in a dispute over property lines, Dervil had challenged Mars's father to a duel. The old earl had died of the wounds he'd received that day, and the feud between the two families had intensified. Mars claimed he couldn't wait to put a bullet into Dervil's black heart. "Did he block your plans after all the reviews you have been through?"

"He was at the meeting. He suggested an architect with more experience would be a better choice. Apparently his opinion was all that was needed for the Surveyor-General to table the matter."

Ned jumped in. "More experience? You've built bridges, canals, and roads in India. What have you not built? You have letters of recommendation from the Company, don't you?"

He referred to the East India Company, which Bran had left three years ago.

"My introductions and references have been presented," Bran answered. "Dervil suggested my work on foreign soil could not meet English standards." Dervil wasn't the first to do so. Establishing himself in England had been a challenge.

"Dervil is a fool then," Ned replied stoutly. "And what is this talk about connections? What does that have to do with engineering?" Ned was a man of science. He was the bastard son of a noted peer, and as such, like Bran, had to rely on his intellect to make his way in the world. They had both been successful, although many wondered why a talented doctor like Thurlowe would prefer to rusticate in Maidenshop instead of try his hand in London.

"Obviously, competence and intelligence isn't enough in the world of politics and power," Bran answered.

"The Duke of Winderton is your nephew and your ward," Thurlowe said. "You returned to guide him after his father died. That is a connection and a damn honorable one."

"A connection to property Dervil covets," Mars pointed out. "And property he would have convinced your sister to sell if you hadn't returned from India and stopped her. So, this is his revenge, eh? I assumed he would show his hand sooner or later. He prides himself on extracting a price, damn his soul."

"Apparently, it is." Bran tightened his hold

on the gun. "I spent a *year* meeting their every demand . . ." He let his voice trail off with his frustration.

"Did you say the meeting was last night? And you are here?" Ned asked. "Did you sleep?"

"I was too angry to sleep. Besides, late yesterday, my sister started sending urgent messages for me to return at once. Something about Winderton." Bran was the duke's guardian until he reached one and twenty in a few months. In truth, Winderton had been too coddled by his mother to take over such responsibilities. If Bran had been the author of the will, Winderton would need to wait until he was at least thirty, but the matter was not his to decide. "Do either of you have an idea what she could be in high dudgeon over this time?"

"I saw your young duke drinking with friends at The Garland the other night," Mars reported. "He was blissfully in his cups and appeared happy."

"I passed him yesterday in the village," Thurlowe offered. "He was barreling down the road without a sideward glance on some mission of his own making. You know how he is."

Self-important? Bran wanted to suggest. He didn't. It would be disloyal. Still, how could someone who was only twenty think his opinion mattered to anyone in the world? "Lucy cries wolf every time he doesn't do what she thinks he should. So, I've come to sort that out." *And himself. He needed to sort himself out. If he didn't receive that commission, then what future was there for him?*

His friends nodded, quieting as they reached their destination, a group of three huge plane trees off to themselves. Here was the rooks' roosting place. The birds would wake with the dawn.

Trailing behind the Three Bucks were the oldest members of the Logical Men's Society— Mr. Fullerton and Sir Lionel Johnson. They rode in makeshift sedan chairs carried by Sir Lionel's servants and were more interested in drinking port than shooting birds. Fullerton had been the estate manager for Mars's grandfather back in the day. Sir Lionel had once been the king's ambassador to Italy and he'd been dining out on the honor ever since. Rounding out the hunting party were Mars's gamekeeper, Evans, and numerous servants carrying more guns, powder, and, of course, the port.

A number of lads from the village, warned to silence, brought up the rear. They would race to collect the kill. Mars had offered a penny for every rook stuffed in their bags.

The goal of a rook hunt was to catch the fledglings as they woke. The young birds had the tender meat and there was no sense hunting birds if you couldn't eat them. The low mist drifting across the ground helped to conceal the men's stealthy advance upon the trees.

As the sun began to rise, the nests high in the trees' branches stirred. Against the dawning sky, the birds perched on limbs as if needing to shake themselves awake in the manner of grumpy old men in the morning.

Without a word, the Three Bucks raised their guns. Mr. Fullerton raised his as well, while still sitting in his chair. It was unloaded. Evans was not so silly as to give the drink-addled Fullerton a loaded weapon.

Sir Lionel raised a glass of port. *"Here's to the hunt,"* he shouted.

The clicks and wheezes of the birds went silent as now *they* listened.

It was of no mind. The Bucks had expected Sir Lionel to do something loud and silly. They fired, knowing that they had best not miss their opportunity. Rooks were clever creatures. The old ones would be gone in a flash. But the fledglings, well, they were like Winderton, not so wise.

After each shot, the gun was handed to a groom who offered a freshly reloaded one. The village lads began zigzagging under the trees, stuffing dead birds in their sacks. The hunters' aim was true and a good number were killed.

And then it was done. The birds were gone. They were either flown or bagged.

Mars laughed his satisfaction. He lowered his gun. "Excellent shooting! I'm glad to be rid of those pests." He looked to the boys. "C'mon, lads, all of you, join us at The Garland for breakfast. Andy promises to have a good one for us. We will count the birds there."

That was met with cheers.

"To The Garland," Sir Lionel now shouted, leaning sideways in his chair. "Pick up the pace, lads. We can't keep Andy waiting." His footmen set off at a trot and, of course, Fullerton had to give chase. Both men appeared ready to be bounced out of his chair at any moment. Still the footmen did not stop and led the way to breakfast.

"Evans, you and the others are to come as well," Mars ordered. "If I know Andy, there will be food for a hundred."

"Thank you, my lord." Evans waved a hurrying hand to his men. "Move this along. We must take everything to the house before we can break our fast." He didn't have to speak twice.

Bran's horse, Orion, a huge blood bay gelding, and mounts for Ned and Mars were brought to them by a groom. Orion was not pleased to find himself groomed, fed, and saddled again. Not after a night of riding.

He snorted his disapproval but Bran climbed into the saddle anyway. "You'll rest in a minute," he told the disgruntled animal. The answer was a shake of the head as if to deny the bit that was already there.

The friends rode at a walk to The Garland. The anger that had driven Bran was giving way to a cooler head. He'd needed to be out of the city and in country air.

"What are you going to do with all those birds?" he asked Mars.

"Andy will bake several huge pies," Ned answered. "You know the Cotillion Dance is tonight?"

Bran inwardly groaned. "I'd forgotten." The

Cotillion Dance was the biggest event in Maidenshop's active social season. The patroness of the acclaimed Almack's could not rival how the Matrons of Maidenshop organized this dance. Because of the village's close proximity to Cambridge, London, and New Market Road, the countryside was a favorite of the titled, upper gentry and even the rising middle class. Everyone attended the dance.

"Ned worries that the membership to the Logical Men's Society is not what it should be," Mars explained.

"It isn't," Ned groused. "It is truly just the three of us and those blighters." He nodded to where Fullerton and Sir Lionel had disappeared up the road. "The young ones like Winderton are not interested. We need to recruit more gentlemen into the Society or we will disappear completely."

"Especially since you will soon marry," Mars reminded Thurlowe.

The physician looked at him with a blank stare and then said, "Yes, to Miss Taylor." He frowned as if annoyed with himself for forgetting he was promised. Bran didn't blame him. Ned's offer for Miss Clarissa Taylor was not a conventional one.

As a baby, she had been abandoned on the late Reverend Taylor's doorstep. The reverend and his wife had raised her as their own, although the whole village had been caught up in the mystery of the child. They all acted as if she was a part of them.

The Taylors died when Miss Taylor was two

and twenty. Squire Nelson and his family took her in, but the Matrons of Maidenshop had decided that was not enough. She needed to be married, and one of the Three Bucks should be the groom. They'd stormed into The Garland, interrupting a night of merriment with their demands.

Mars had refused. He and Miss Taylor could not abide each other.

Bran was not about to marry anyone. At six and thirty, he'd been a bachelor too long to succumb to the parson's noose, especially out of pity. Over the years, Bran had formed quiet, unfettered liaisons with the occasional widow—although for the past year he'd done nothing but focus on that damned bridge commission.

In the end, it was Thurlowe who had broken down and sacrificed himself. He'd claimed to feel sorry for Miss Taylor since she had no family and few prospects. That was two years ago. Ned called on her every Saturday for fifteen minutes and made no move toward marriage.

Anyone who thought the good doctor was ready for marriage, or enthusiastic for it, was a fool. However, the matrons seemed mollified and Miss Taylor appeared at peace with the current situation.

Bran did not understand why the matrons didn't push for an actual wedding, but it wasn't his worry.

Meanwhile, Mars seemed to enjoy chiding their friend on his "someday" upcoming nuptials.

"To interest new members in the Society," Mars went on to explain, "Ned has arranged for a scientific lecture on matters of interest to men for tomorrow to take advantage of those gentlemen who will be staying over after the dance."

"A lecture?" Bran asked with some interest.

"Yes, every gentleman, married or not, is invited," Ned said with enthusiasm. "Mr. Clyde Remy will discuss the late James Hutton's theory concerning uniformitarianism as an explanation for the formation of rocks and mountains. I think that should draw them in."

Uniformitarianism? Bran withheld his opinion, although his gaze met Mars's amused one and he knew they both did not share Thurlowe's confidence. Bran had a deep interest in geology but he didn't know if it was a popular topic to others.

"Andy and I decided rook pie can't hurt our chances of attracting members either," Mars said. "After all, I had rooks to spare. Blasted nuisances."

They rode through Maidenshop now. The dawning sun highlighted the thatched roofs of charming whitewashed cottages and rose gardens filling with fragrant blooms. When Bran had first arrived here three years ago from India, he had thought he'd never seen a lovelier village—or a more English one.

Mrs. Warbler, a widow and one of the busiest of the matrons, owned the largest home in the village. It was built of yellow stone and set at such an angle she could sit in her morning room and see everything going on—and everyone going in and out of The Garland.

In the distance was the lichen-covered stone roof of St. Martyr's, a twelfth-century church the villagers had the good sense to leave alone. Like many churches of that era, it had been built by a nobleman, supposedly a Winderton ancestor, and the property included a long, high-ceilinged stone outbuilding that had once served as a barn. The Cotillion was held there every year.

Down the road a ways was the smithy. Another two miles would take them to New Market Road and the Post House, where a good number of those attending the Cotillion without local relatives or friends would find accommodations for the night. It was a major stop for travelers and could be busy day and night.

The Garland sat at the edge of the village on the banks of a racing stream known as the Three Thieves. There was a story behind that name, but no one knew it to tell it. Upstream, the Three Thieves bordered Marsden land and had good fishing, especially in the spring.

The Garland itself was built like three small cottages hooked together. Mars claimed that inside, it resembled a fox's den with low-ceilinged rooms and walls darkened by age. Save for the time the matrons had stormed it to demand a husband for Miss Taylor, it was definitely a male sanctuary. The Garland was the hub of the Logical Men's Society, and everyone in the county knew it.

The scent of roasting beef and fresh bread

greeted the group as they walked through the door. Andy must have been up for hours. He liked to cook on a spit out back and the smoke from it rose above the thatched roofs. Bran was surprised at how hungry he was. He'd been too anxious yesterday to eat much.

The sedan chairs were out front, a footman left to guard them as if they were in London and not the safe haven of Maidenshop. Boys carrying their bags were shoving their way inside, big smiles on their faces. The men dismounted and tied up their horses to the post. Orion grumbled his thoughts. Bran ignored him and went inside. He had to duck to go under the door.

"Come in, come in," Andy called in his soft burr. The old Scotsman stood in the doorway of what he called his taproom where he kept his keg. He was about as wide as he was tall with white whiskers and a shaved pate. "Why, look at all of these birds. I'll make you a pie that will sing itself with these," he promised Ned. "Sit yourselves wherever you like. I'll bring the food out."

A huge table had been set out in the middle of the room. Metal plates were stacked on one end along with knives and forks. Bran made himself useful handing them out. The air rang with the sounds of booted heels and chairs scraping the wood floor as they were pulled out.

Andy had left to bring in the meat on the spit. In the taproom, Ned started pouring tankards of ale and had the lads distributing them. Mars had tucked into the tray of at least seven loaves of cooling bread. One didn't stand on ceremony in The Garland. Once Evans and the Belvoir servants arrived, they began to eat and the room went quiet save for the sounds of hungry men enjoying themselves.

Food helped restore Bran's spirits. And, yes, he realized, being here with his friends was better than moping in London.

Soon, everyone in London connected with engineering and architecture would learn that he hadn't been awarded the commission. At least, not yet. They would wonder why and he and his small firm would be like the rook fledglings this morning—a target for gossip and speculation. His reputation was too new and he didn't know what the damage would be.

Mars began entertaining a group of lads with a story out of his youth when he'd been swimming and Ned had stolen his clothes as a jest. "Just as Mrs. Warbler and her daughters were out for an afternoon stroll."

"Did they see you, my lord?" the youngest boy asked.

"*All* of me," Mars said dramatically and the boys fell off the benches laughing. Even the servants had a giggle.

Bran caught himself smiling, until he noticed the blue-and-white of Winderton livery at the door. Damn, it wasn't even half past eight.

He stood and walked over to greet Randall, Lucy's butler and most trusted servant. "My sister has found me? Or were you just lucky?"

Randall had once served with their colonel father in the Guard and was around Lucy's age, which was twelve years older than Bran.

"Just lucky, sir. Will you come with me, sir?"

Bran ran a hand over the rough whiskers of his jaw. "I need to shave."

"She is frantic, sir." A not uncommon situation where his sister was concerned and yet there was a hint of desperation in Randall's tone.

"Very well." Bran waved to his friends. He noted that Fullerton and Sir Lionel were now back at their favorite table in the corner. The potted knight appeared to be sleeping, his head on his chest. Fullerton did not seem to mind since he was animatedly talking to himself.

Outside, Orion stamped his displeasure as Bran mounted. "A few minutes more, my friend." Randall had his own horse and the two rode off. Bran did not ask questions. Randall was extremely discreet when it came to Winderton affairs. Bran had learned how close-lipped back when he'd first arrived from India.

The Winderton ancestral seat, Smythson, was a forty-five-minute ride from The Garland. It could have been faster except Bran refused to push his horse more.

Smythson was a redbrick manse surrounded by gardens that had at one time been designed by no less a personage than Capability Brown. Lucy wasn't much for gardens or management, and her husband's death hadn't made her rise to the situation. When Bran had first arrived as the duke's guardian, the estate had been on the brink of ruin. The lawns had been ill kempt, the stables were a shambles, and his nephew's schooling tuition had not been paid in years. He was amazed they took him back term after term.

Bran had corrected the problems, using his money to do so because at the time Winderton didn't have any. The old duke had been an exceedingly unwise gambler. Bran had learned there was no investment too ridiculous for his brother-in-law to throw money at, no horse too much of a long shot not to wager upon.

Of course, Lucy had not wished for anyone to know the state of her affairs. What Bran had done for the estate and for his nephew was their secret, and, yes, when his nephew acted immature and entitled, Bran wished he was at liberty to tell him a few hard facts. His sister had always stopped him . . . but someday, he needed to sit the duke down and explain.

As it was, Bran had successfully turned the estate around. It was profitable again and meeting its obligations. The gardens were well-groomed and the stables organized. The money generated by the estate was going into a fund that was earning Winderton 3 percent, Bran's gift to his ward. However, Winderton was fast approaching his majority; the time would come for him to take over, ready or not for the responsibility.

A groom waited to take Orion and the other horse. After dismounting, Randall led Bran inside and up the front stairs to the Dowager Duchess of Winderton's private quarters.

Lucy was still in her black dressing gown and lace cap and standing in the center of the room when Bran presented himself. She was a handsome woman for her age with gray streaks beginning in her dark hair. Her figure was plumper than when she was married. She blamed her eating as well as everything else on the need for comfort in her loneliness. Bran thought the extra stone or so of weight suited her. Both brother and sister had the Balfour "silver" eyes.

She launched into him. "I sent my message demanding your immediate presence late yesterday morning. You should have been here last night."

"I was required to attend a meeting about the bridge—"

"The bridge. *The bridge*," she mocked. "I'm so tired of this bridge, especially when I need you here. Christopher needs you here."

"I saw Christopher in London a few weeks ago. He was fine."

"He is *not* fine now." She began furious pacing, her arms gesturing wildly. "You must talk sense into him because he is not listening to me. And *don't* tell me you hurried to Smythson because I know you went shooting with your fellows this morning. The Logical Men's Society! An excuse for men to behave like boys, if you ask me." Lucy was an important member of the Matrons of Maidenshop. "That you would choose them over your sister—" She made an exasperated sound before chiding, "And don't deny you wouldn't, because you did so today."

Bran couldn't take her charging around him a second longer. He caught her, a hand on each arm, and guided her to the wing chair in front of the cold hearth. Sitting her, he knelt on one knee and said calmly, "The hunt was before dawn. I assumed you were asleep."

"I haven't been able to sleep since Christopher said what he did. It was horrid, Brandon. *Horrid.*" Huge tears welled in her eyes and rolled down her cheeks, reddening her nose. Lucy had never been a pretty crier.

Bran pulled his handkerchief from a pocket and offered it to her. "Lucy, I am here now." He kept his voice low and controlled. "What has His Grace done to set you in such a tizzy?"

Lucy lowered the handkerchief and visibly struggled to regain control of herself. "He says . . . he is going to marry an *actress.*"

For a second, Bran didn't think he'd heard her correctly.

At his silence, she elaborated, "He has met an *actress* and he vows that she is the woman he has been searching for. The one he must have. He claims his heart is set afire for her."

Bran rose, not trusting himself to speak immediately. He pulled a straight-backed chair over to his sister's and sat. "An actress," he repeated.

Lucy nodded her head enthusiastically, causing the black ribbons in her cap to bounce. "You have been sending messengers and

tracking me down while I was trying to prepare for the most important meeting of my life
because Christopher is taken with an actress?"

"Not just 'taken.' He wants to make her *his
duchess.*"

She sounded so sincere.

And suddenly all Bran could do was laugh.
A good, hearty, well-isn't-this-life laugh. Her
offended stare brought him to his senses.
"Lucy, he is almost one and twenty. Of course
he wants an actress. We all do at one time or
the other."

She shook her head. "Not a mere *flirtation.*
He informed me he plans on *marrying* this
woman."

"He won't."

"He said he will."

"Lucy, he's twenty. He says a good number
of things he won't carry out."

"You should have seen him, Brandon. It was
as if he'd grown into a man as he was telling
me all of this."

Bran gave an indifferent shrug. "He still
has plenty of manly growing to do. An actress
might help him with that."

Her brows snapped together. "I don't want
her near my son."

"Says every mother since the beginning of
time."

"Stop patronizing me." Lucy twisted the
kerchief tight in her hands. "I know my son.
He is smitten and he'll do something foolish if
we don't chase this woman away. Worse, she is
older than he is."

His nephew was sounding wiser and wiser as this conversation progressed. Bran feigned a frown to hide his grin. "Fine, I will talk to him."

"He won't listen." She spoke to Bran as if he was a child. "This woman has bewitched him."

"When did he meet her? In London, the duke said nothing to me about any woman."

"Yesterday."

The word stopped him.

"Yesterday?" Bran shook his head. Mars and Thurlowe were not going to believe this story. "Lucy, he met her yesterday and he was bewitched on the spot? And you believe him? You have better common sense than that."

"You should hear him. He's not himself." Indignant color rose in her cheeks.

"And how did he meet this actress yesterday?" Bran tried to hide his skepticism. He was not successful.

"He came upon a troupe of actors on the road. Their wagon had broken down and he offered to help. He saw her and fell in love. He said it was that quick." She snapped her fingers for emphasis. "He told me there isn't anything he won't do for her."

Until he beds her, Bran thought, but wisely refrained from voicing this observation. In truth, he was a bit relieved his nephew was not so wrapped around his mother's finger. In fact, in London, Bran had suggested His Grace come for the Season. There were responsibilities to the title that the duke must understand and he wasn't going to learn them doing his mother's bidding in Maidenshop.

Bran patted his sister's hand. "All right. I will talk to him."

"He won't listen. I've talked and talked. We must buy her off. Pay her to leave. That is the only way that we can keep him from her. Truly, Brandon, he acts possessed. He was *humming* before he left the house."

Bran wasn't about to waste good money on an actress. "You are taking this too seriously. It is the normal course of things for young men to do. A rite of passage even."

"Are you trying to make me feel better? You aren't."

"Very well," Bran said patiently. "I was once in love with an actress. Heart and soul and you can see I survived the adventure." Barely . . . but he didn't need to say that to Lucy. If it hadn't been for his actress, he wouldn't have taken a position with the East India Company. He had literally exiled himself to be away from her.

He also realized that he himself had been a bit naïve like Winderton. His actress *had* made a man of him. Certainly, she had set him on the course that had made him a very wealthy man. This one might do the same for his ward and nephew. "He will be all right, Your Grace. He will."

She bit her lower lip as if to stop it from trembling. "I thought Christopher was safe from that sort of woman here."

"And that is why you don't want to let him go?"

"His father died. He needs guidance."

"Thomas died almost four years ago," Bran corrected quietly. "It is no longer an excuse to keep him tied to you. Young men must learn their own lessons and they often do it through trial and error. If you don't let him go, then he'll do things like making an actress his duchess."

"Those types of women are crass."

"They serve a purpose."

Lucy put her hands over her ears and closed her eyes, acting like a child herself. "I don't want to hear it. I wish Thomas was alive. I wish nothing had changed."

"Nothing stays the same forever, Lucy." And yet how many times over the past three years as he'd struggled to establish himself as an architect and engineer had he wished he was back in India where no one questioned his talent, his intelligence, or his connections.

She reached out to place a hand on his arm. "Please, pay her off. Do I have the money?"

"Enough. If you spend it here, then someplace else will suffer."

"Do it."

"Very well."

His sister released her breath with a sigh. "Thank you."

"Where is this actress located and does she have a name, or shall I just question every actress in the troupe?"

"Kate Addison. Christopher set them up on Smythson property. He offered our land for their use. Can you believe it? They are camped close to the Cambridge Road."

His sister continued with directions and worries, but Bran had stopped listening. *Kate Addison?* Memories he'd thought safely tucked away and hemmed in by regrets flooded his mind.

Just like that, everything came roaring back.

How many Kate Addisons could there be in the world? Especially amongst actresses?

Perhaps he misheard?

Perhaps this was the culmination of all his frustrations over the past twenty-four hours? A universe preparing him to hear a name he'd prayed to be erased from his life—?

"Brandon, are you listening to me?"

"I . . . am," he lied. And then, because he had to know, he said, "How much older is she than Winderton?"

"Oh, lord, I don't know. I haven't asked many questions. All he had to do is say she was older and, well, what man wants a woman older than himself, I ask you? Last night, he suggested he would take her to Cotillion. Brandon, I don't know what I will do if he walks into the dance tonight and fobs off this ill-mannered person on our friends."

"Not to worry, Lucy, I will stop it." There was no patronizing indulgence in his voice now. If this actress was *the* Kate Addison, she would not gain a foothold into his family. That woman had upended his life—and he'd be damned if he let her do the same to Winderton.

All thoughts of shaving or an easy slumber in his bed vanished. "The Cambridge Road?"

"Yes. In fact, Christopher might be there. He left the house and has not returned—"

She spoke to the air. Bran was already out the door.

And don't forget

Her First Desire

Book 2 of The Logical Man's
Guide to Dangerous Women
is on sale now at your
favorite retailer!